WHAT
YOU
NEVER
KNEW

WHAT YOU NEVER KNEW

A Novel

JESSICA HAMILTON

CROOKED LANE

NEW YORK

Copyright © 2021 by Jessica Hamilton

All rights reserved.

Published in the United States by Crooked Lane Books, an imprint of The Quick Brown Fox & Company LLC.

Crooked Lane Books and its logo are trademarks of The Quick Brown Fox & Company LLC.

Library of Congress Catalog-in-Publication data available upon request.

ISBN (hardcover): 978-1-64385-696-4
ISBN (ebook): 978-1-64385-697-1

Cover design by Nicole Lecht.

Printed in the United States.

www.crookedlanebooks.com

Crooked Lane Books
34 West 27th St., 10th Floor
New York, NY 10001

First Edition: April 2021

10 9 8 7 6 5 4 3 2 1

For my sister Rebecca, and for Tyree, and
the memories we made there.

MAY

One hour before I died, I was sitting in a stuffy lawyer's office dealing with the probate details of my mother's will. It figures I was dealing with her mortality right before facing my own. Very little happened in my life that wasn't in some way connected to her. She'd passed away seven months earlier, which meant my time of freedom from her had been brief and fleeting.

Lung cancer. It was long and drawn out, with great suffering, and cause for constant, round-the-clock care. During the months of her illness I often thought she'd finally gotten what she'd wanted all along—our undivided attention, daily displays of love, and deep concern for her well-being. She couldn't have chosen a more suitable and satisfying exit from the world.

I'd gone to the lawyer's that day confused. My mother had insisted that all her assets be divided while she was alive. She'd signed the house over to me (I'd sold it promptly upon her death, splitting the proceeds with my younger sister, June). She'd gifted her savings, jewelry, and antiques to me and my sister and my nieces—more efficient than waiting for lawyers to do it, and it meant she was present for the proclamations of gratitude that came with it.

I'd thought all her affairs had been wrapped up nice and tidy while she was alive. How very naïve of me. I should have known that my mother would leave something messy for me to deal with. One last reminder of what I'd spent my life trying to forget.

The lawyer casually passed the envelope across his desk to me, as though it were light as a feather. "The only asset willed from your mother's estate," he explained.

I kept my hands in my lap. "What is it?"

He pushed the document half an inch closer to me, as though he didn't want it either. "Just a deed of some kind. Property your family has owned for years. An island, I believe it said. Somewhere in Vermont?"

"You mean Avril Island? On Lake Champlain?" I shook my head. "That can't be right. My mother sold that place years ago."

The lawyer gave the envelope one last push toward me. "Yes, that's the place."

Avril Island. The words boomed around the room, bouncing off the heavy wood paneling and crashing back against my skull, making my head throb. I took the envelope from the desk and placed it on my lap. I didn't need to look inside.

My father had bought Avril Island for my mother as a wedding present. Her very own island, complete with a five-bedroom cottage and acres of land. Where we spent every single summer until the summer I was fifteen years old. That year we left in a hurry, never went back, and a couple of years later my mother told me and June that she'd sold it.

Staring down at the envelope, I could feel the lawyer's watery blue eyes on me, see the arch of his white hairy eyebrows out of my peripheral vision as he waited for my response.

"I'm just a little bit confused," I managed to get out.

He nodded sympathetically. "If only the dead could talk, I always say. Would make my job easier." He chuckled to himself, unaware that he'd just handed me a grenade that could blow up my life.

I tucked the manila envelope into my purse, thanked him politely, as I'd been taught to do, and then left his office. The world narrowed into a slim, silent tunnel, only expanding again with the beep of my car door unlocking. Inside smelled of the banana I'd eaten on the way to the appointment and was hot and stuffy from the early spring sun beating through the windshield.

The leather upholstery was warm against the back of my thighs as I sat in the driver's seat staring straight ahead—a little vessel of the familiar, which slowly helped to bring me back to reality.

I had to work hard to hold back the violent rage that was building. My mother had said she'd taken care of it. She'd lied. She often lied. I really couldn't understand why she hadn't told me about Avril Island before she died. It was like some sick joke she'd waited to play on me—waited to unleash until she was gone and didn't have to deal with any of it herself. I'd spent years trying to escape that part of my life, and she'd dropped it right back into my lap.

The smell of rotten banana, combined with the heat of the car and my roller coaster of emotions, brought on a surge of nausea. I opened my door and swung my legs out, taking deep breaths of fresh air. I grabbed the banana peel, threw it onto the black pavement, and rolled my window down before shutting myself back in the car.

Funnily enough, there were no tears. Me, who cried at the drop of a dime—I felt only empty inside. It might have been my fight-or-flight impulse. I wanted to protect June from everything she didn't know about our parents, but mostly from what she didn't know about me. I'd never hated my mother more than in that moment.

I reached for my phone, glad when it went to message. If my sister had heard me, she'd have known there was something I was hiding, just out of sight, tucked sloppily somewhere around my rib cage. She'd have heard the flutter in my voice, felt the restraint of my vocal chords, and then demanded to know what was keeping the real me from her. June never accepted anything but all of me.

I'm going to be a bit late for dinner. The appointment went longer than I thought, and I have to do a few things before I can come by. Should be there by seven instead of six. Love you.

I hung up before she could hear the catch in my voice, before the fake lilt faltered and she heard the darkness underneath. It didn't dawn on me to cancel the dinner plans we'd made only the day before. We were going to discuss my meeting with the lawyer over wine and some takeout. A light, airy plan that we'd thought would include a bit of reminiscing—some jokes about the good and the bad. Some healthy sorrow for the loss of the woman who at times had made our lives hell but was our mother still. But that was before the final parting gift of Avril Island.

I took a deep breath to settle my nerves and turned the key in the ignition. Slowly I pulled out of my parking spot. The world was fractured and unsafe all of a sudden, and my every move had to be in accordance.

I drove only a block before the urge forced me to pull over. Taking the deed from the manila envelope, I tore it into many pieces, then hopped out of my car and scattered it into a trash bin at the end of somebody's driveway. A garbage truck would be by soon, and my last tie to Avril Island, and all the horrible things that had happened there, would be swallowed up by pounds of other people's trash and driven far away from me. The thought was the only thing that allowed me to put the car in drive and carry on.

Once I was on the highway, moving with the flow of traffic, my grip on the steering wheel began to loosen. I had a two-hour drive and one hour at home to figure out a plan before I'd see June. What would I tell her the appointment had been about? Could I lie right to her face? Could I tell her the truth?

A flock of birds, black ones—I think they were crows, so then it would have been a murder of crows; very fitting—rose up from a farmer's field to the left of me, offering a quick distraction from my heavy thoughts. They looked like ink blotches on the gray sky, only their wing tips standing out with any definition. They soared upward, weightless, and swirled like a circus of acrobats, grabbing my attention, pulling it away from the road.

It would have been fine if it weren't for the white van, which changed lanes too quickly—impatient with the slow driver in front of him and unaware that I was bird watching.

I looked away from those fluid black spots too late. There was a wall of white, my foot on the brake, metal eating metal, glass smashing. The air bag inflated like an angry balloon, punching me in the chest and snatching my breath away.

Then the spinning started. For a second I thought I had turned into one of those black birds—free and twirling through the sky—but it was my car bouncing off the guardrail and dancing across the four lanes of highway.

There was the sound of squealing tires, brakes trying desperately to work; then came a flash of blue, and everything went dark.

I was dead in an instant. I leaked out of my body and into the atmosphere just above the road. I watched as the paramedics pulled me from my car, which was crumpled in the front, curled in on itself. T-boned, I believe they call it, on the driver's side.

The driver of the white van stumbled along the side of the road, refusing to be stilled. He gestured wildly at my car, called out obscenities. The driver of the blue car sat trapped in her vehicle, alive but looking as though she might be dying on the inside.

I watched it all unfold like some bad TV drama. The black birds continued to circle above the farmer's field, unaffected by the man-made tragedy only a hundred or so feet away.

One of the three ambulances pulled away from the gory scene, my body inside. My only thought—*June's going to be so mad at me.*

JUNE

I fit the plastic cup back into the round indentation of the seat tray. The wine tastes like vinegar, and I can bear only three small sips. My book rests open on the edge of the tray, but only to keep the passenger beside me from making small talk.

I haven't been able to read since May died. Forty-three days. I've lived without my older sister for *forty-three days*. I wake up surprised by this every morning—it's like realizing you don't actually need oxygen to survive. We always said we'd die if the other one did. It wasn't so much a promise as scientific fact. We just didn't think one could survive without the other. And yet here I am, on a plane to a place I should be going to with my sister.

The flight attendant drops a bag of pretzels on my tray, then moves on, his plastic smile locked in place. Reflex has me pull the small plastic bag open and bite down on one of the salty twists of sawdust. The wine is the only thing I have to move the dry clump down my throat. I wince as it travels through me.

"The red is just as bad," the man in the seat beside me says. I give him a polite smile and set my gaze back on my book. I used to be a friendly person, happy to engage in airplane small talk. Now everyone annoys me—all inane intrusions into my grief.

Except my teenage daughters and maybe my ex-husband. Actually, no, my ex-husband annoys me too, maybe the most.

Before I got in the cab for the airport, I said to Leo, "Keep our girls safe."

He did his little *you're a total idiot* laugh and said, "Of course I will, June. They're my kids too."

You only have to lose something once to feel like every other important thing in the world is in constant jeopardy. He should have known that. He should have put his arms around me and said he'd take care of everything. Instead he followed it up with, "This trip is a good idea. It will snap you out of this thing you're going through. I think it's exactly what you need." He gave me a polite peck on the cheek, and I resisted the urge to punch him in the gut.

I'm not on this trip to snap myself out of anything. Nothing will ever snap me out of losing May. My sister was ripped from my life without warning, no old age, no long illness. One minute she was there and the next she wasn't, and I had no say in it.

The plane bumps up and then drops suddenly, and the seat belt sign dings. We're starting our descent. I shoot back the rest of the wine, endure the burn, knock my pretzels onto the floor, lock the tray into place, and put my seat-back in the upright position.

Avril Island. The name whispers through my mind, getting louder the closer I get. My nerves of nostalgia stand on end.

MAY

I was only two and a half when they brought June home from the hospital. I remembered it, though, all through my life—vivid and clear as though memory hadn't started to matter until the day she arrived.

My mother took great efforts to settle me on the couch. She propped throw cushions on either side of my legs. She put a hand against my stomach and pushed me as deep into the couch as I would go.

Then she placed the tightly wrapped pink bundle into my arms, and I was surprised at how heavy she felt.

"This is your baby sister. This is June," my mother said softly. She pointed to herself: "April." Then to me: "May." Then she pointed to the baby: "June." She paused to let the understanding sink in. "The three of us are the best months of the year." She chuckled, the warm, rich sound sending happiness surging through my belly.

I would come to understand much later the narcissism of our names. She was a month, and therefore the two of us must be as well—her month starting things off, our months following right behind.

I looked down at June and she looked up at me, her eyes bottomless pools of navy. We stared at each other, our gazes

9

unwavering while a bond made up of blood, brain waves, and particles, pulled out of the atmosphere from sisterhoods that had come before us, was tightly knit together.

My mother stayed uncharacteristically still, smiling down on both of us. Her scent of French perfume, sour milk, and skin that had sweated out a baby draped itself all over us. Her closeness and unsolicited love, combined with the emotions my new sister inspired, brought me to tears. They rolled down my cheeks and gathered in short, toddler sobs in my throat.

My mother misunderstood, thinking my crying was out of sadness for the new arrival, that I saw June as competition for her affection. She swept my sister out of my arms and against her chest like I was only moments away from chucking the bundle right onto the floor.

My mother didn't understand unconditional love. She didn't know what it looked like, smelled like, or felt like. That's why she could never really understand my relationship with June. She was in awe of it as much as she was suspicious of it, fluctuating between believing it was a coup against her and taking it as an example of her superior parenting. No matter her outlook, June and I stayed steadfast in our love for each other. We had to. It was the only way to survive our mother.

* * *

I don't know if all dead people are assigned to just one person. It makes sense, though, that I'm assigned to June. Basically, I was assigned to her the day she was born, and now that she's dead, she's the one I haunt.

Being dead isn't as bad as everyone imagines. It's lonely in some ways, but peaceful, and there's a contentment that comes with it that you've searched for all through life but never found. Perhaps because in so many ways we spend our lives running from death, so when it finally comes we have no choice but to accept it. Gone are the fear, the avoidance, and the desperation that living so often brings.

No more insecurities, guilt, shame, or regrets. There's just no point to them anymore. Full memories have disappeared for me as well, my entire life presenting like a fuzzy dream that happened in the course of one restless sleep. I know who the main players were and have some sense of myself but can't gather together the full details of actual events that made up my lifetime. The only clear memory I have is of the moment of my death, and I try my best to avoid reliving that one.

My time, which feels simultaneously endless and momentary, is split between the living realm and floating in a beautiful abyss of nothingness. A sea of total darkness, with small bursts of light throughout and no definition between me and the nothingness. I am as much a part of it as it is of me. I'm peaceful in this nothingness, but there's a sense of limbo. As though I'm in some kind of ethereal waiting room until the universe has decided I'm ready for the next stage.

At times, undetermined by me, I slip from the nothingness and into the living realm. There, just by thinking it, I'm able to move from one spot in the room to another, where I spread into things or hang in the air like dust particles. I am aimless and powerless, but there's this feeling that I'm there to do something and I just don't know what it is yet.

When I'm in the living realm, memories appear in my consciousness like scheduled commercial breaks—unbidden and determined by something outside me. As though it's all part of a greater plan, one that I have yet to be made aware of. This is death, knowing all and knowing nothing at once.

The first time I shifted from the nothingness to the living realm, I arrived in June's bedroom. She was rolled up in a mess of sheets on her bed—a sloppily constructed cocoon of sorrow. The blind was pulled down against the daylight, but a stubborn thin line of sun at the bottom broke its way into the warm, stuffy room.

I remembered that I'd seen her like that before. After her divorce. She'd left the family home, moved into a townhouse, put the bed together, and then she hadn't gotten out of it for almost two weeks.

I went to say her name but quickly learned there's no such thing as talking when you're dead, so the word came out like a thought. Still, she lifted the covers, revealing her messy short black hair. Her blue, puffy, bloodshot eyes darted around the room. I thought her name again, concentrating even harder this time.

She squinted. "May?"

June. I'm right here. Words so clear and loud to me did nothing to penetrate the silence of the room. She pulled the covers back up over her and moaned like a wounded animal.

I stayed in that room as long as I could, talking at June, begging her to get up. I called her names, apologized, soothed her, challenged her. I tried every tactic until I became depleted by the effort and started fading away from the space.

I didn't understand how June couldn't hear me. Alive, we could practically read each other's minds. Being dead doesn't mean you don't feel things. In fact, your feelings flow out all over the place until you feel like you're drowning in them. So why couldn't she pick up on them?

Frustration, desperation, sorrow—they crashed through the space I was occupying like tidal waves. The fading away brought some relief. It happened quickly, as it always does. Like a sleep brought on by strong drugs.

Before I evaporated from the room completely, June threw back the covers, sat up, and swung her legs over the side of the bed.

"Okay, May. I'm up."

JUNE

I would never tell anyone this, but I'm pretty sure my sister is haunting me. Sometimes I hear her voice and am sure I smell her. Every person has their own scent, and I know May's better than anybody's—even my own children's. Their smells change from one age to the next, each new stage introducing something foreign. May's is warm skin and cinnamon—always has been.

Haunting isn't the right word. I don't believe in ghosts. Plus, May would never haunt anybody; she'd watch over them, protect them. It's more likely, though, that it's just pure longing that conjures her voice and smell, the imprint of her on me so strong it has residual effects.

But one day a few weeks after she'd died, in the middle of the afternoon, I was sure I heard her tell me to get out of bed. Not so much heard it as felt it. May's always been bossy, in that older-sister way that makes you feel loved and repressed at the same time.

Imagined or not, it got me out of bed. I showered for the first time in days and ate something. When my girls came home from school, the relief on their fourteen-year-old faces almost made me cry. Twin girls should have understood better than anybody the devastation of losing a sister, but for some reason they just didn't grasp my debilitating sorrow.

13

I faked my way through the making of dinner, the helping with homework, the watching of a sitcom. Just enough to give them back some sense of normalcy. Then I sent them to bed, intentionally ignoring the devices they had subtly tucked away in the pockets of their hooded sweat shirts so they would comply.

Once the house was in darkness, I closed my bedroom door and released the dam of tears that had accumulated while I was playing at normal. The next morning I slept through their departure to school and slipped right back into the dysfunctional zone.

The next attempt to get me out of bed was made by my ex-husband. He walked into the bedroom, as though we still shared one, and pulled at the blinds. They snapped back up into their tubular homes, letting light charge into the space. He might as well have thrown a glass of cold water on me. He's never been one for gentle tactics. At one point, when I still considered myself a writer, he'd been my editor as well as my husband, but that fact had never protected me from his brutally harsh editing style or, for that matter, his equally harsh husbanding style.

"What the hell, Leo?" I said, grabbing at the sheets to pull them over my head.

"June. You need to get up." I felt his weight land on the end of the bed. He's always careful not to get too close if he doesn't have to. I think it's because he still has the urge to wrap his hands around my neck and squeeze until the breath leaves me.

"You can't tell me what to do anymore, Leo. Remember we're divorced?"

He sighed with impatience, and I assumed that the girls had put him up to it. "May would want you to get up. She wouldn't want you wasting away like this. Or neglecting the girls."

Using the two most precious things in the world to me was a low blow. I swung my leg out in a vicious kick, but the tangle of sheets trapped it before it connected with his body.

He reached out and patted my foot as though thanking it for not hurting him. "Also, I got the paperwork for May's will from Jim."

Jim is our lawyer—mine, Leo's, and May's. He'd also been a family friend when Leo and I still made a family—a touch incestuous, but we got a decent discount. He shouldn't have given those papers to Leo, but it wasn't the first time he hadn't stuck to proper lawyer protocol.

"He said you weren't answering your phone or returning his messages."

"I'm in mourning," I mumbled through my wall of sheet.

"June." I hate the way he says my name, as though he can barely bring himself to utter it. "It's been a month. You've got to get back to the living. The healing can only happen when you start moving forward. Putting one foot in front of the other."

"Thanks, Deepak Chopra. Now leave the papers on my dresser and please get out."

He stayed sitting at the end of the bed. I felt him shifting, most likely running his hands through his thick blond hair, admiring himself in the mirror across from the bed. He was a good-looking man, even in his forties, and he knew it. Always had.

"There's some pretty big reveal in this paperwork, June." He tapped what must have been the envelope against my leg.

I wondered what that was even supposed to mean—*big reveal*. I ignored him. He got bored easily, and I was sure I could wait him out. But my bladder did feel quite full. I couldn't remember the last time I'd gotten up to pee.

"Jim said it's going to take some time for probate but everything is outlined here." He rustled the papers like they were some bone and I was a dog who would come out of hiding for it. "May left you everything. The only stipulation is that you put her stocks into an account for the girls' education."

I pulled the sheet taut against my face to answer him—despite myself. "I already know all of that, Leo. I know about every bloody penny and investment May had. There's no big reveal there."

He gave a smug little chuckle, and I began to untangle my leg from the sheet so I could actually kick him.

"Sure, but did you know that your mother actually had a will and in it left something to May?"

I sucked a breath in and held it there like a hostage. I'd completely forgotten about the appointment May had had with our mother's lawyer. The one right before the accident. I'd never found out what it was about.

"Weird, though," Leo continued, "that she didn't leave it to you as well." Nothing about it felt weird, which in itself was weird, but that pretty much summed up my relationship with my mother. She was unpredictable, and in no way had she ever played fair between me and my sister.

"Just please leave the paperwork and go," I begged. I couldn't deal with the grief of May and being reminded of how inconsistent my mother could be, right up to the end.

I finally felt the bed shift as Leo stood, but I could see through the thin white sheet that he was still staring down at me. "Avril Island is on the list of May's assets. It was willed to her by your mother."

The mention of my family cottage made the sheets around me suddenly turn to the brownish-green water that had surrounded the island. I could smell its earthy scent; feel the cold of its depths, the warmth at its surface. Before drowning in the sensation, I pulled the sheet away from my face.

Leo couldn't help but smile; he'd finally gotten what he'd come for, the *big reveal*. "Your mother never sold Avril Island, June." He held up the envelope, which contained that shocking truth. "And now it's yours."

MAY

I don't know where we are. It looks like a cheap motel room, but I wasn't around for the arrival. June is curled up on the bed, still in her clothes and on top of the multicolored polyester comforter. The TV is on with no volume, bathing the room in a depressing blue light and keeping true solitude at bay.

I'm not sure why June would choose to stay in a place like this. There are burn holes in the carpet, a lacquered, stuffed fish mounted on the wall, and bed linens that can't be bleached. Money isn't a problem for June, so it must be for some other reason.

There's a half-empty bottle of whiskey on the desk, and from the deep, raspy snores coming out of June, I know she's the one who drank it. She's a drunk snorer.

I want so badly to wake her up, make fun of her for being such a cliché—cheap motel, bottle of whiskey, passed-out drunk. I'd make her laugh, forget everything that's hurting. That's what we did for each other, take the hurt away, but now I'm the reason she's hurting and it was never supposed to be like that.

There are some important-looking papers on the bedside table. All I have to do is focus on that part of the room and suddenly I'm there, beside the bed, looking at things from a whole new perspective. Not a bad party trick.

A copy of my will sits under a cloudy glass from the bathroom that still holds a sip or two of straight whiskey. I know I'm dead, but the sight of my own will is not easy to see.

It's evidence that the world is moving on. That everything I've accumulated in life will be legally scattered about, sold, donated, hopefully at least some things treasured. My only mark on the world will be a passed-on vase or dining room table. Makes all the careful collecting I did seem pointless. The large sums I spent to have items shipped home from my travels, the hours I spent choosing just the right dining chairs—all meaningless.

I shift my focus to June to get my mind off the will. Am I allowed to use those expressions when I'm really only atmosphere now? *Get my mind off, my heart skipped a beat, can't believe my eyes . . .* There should be an instruction manual for this kind of thing—being dead.

June is still lying motionless with drunken sleep. Her skin shines with a film of sweat. I can imagine the itch of the polyester comforter against the warm skin of her cheek, the uncomfortable cling of her jeans against her legs and her T-shirt against her sweaty back. I'd open a window if I could, or turn on the air conditioner, which would chug loudly in a place like this.

Even in this drunk, sweaty state, June is beautiful. She takes after our mother, tall and thin, straight black hair, her face round, her lips full. I took after our father, shorter, rounder, with wavy blond hair and brown eyes, pleasant to look at but in no way striking like my sister.

June's never really seemed to understand how truly beautiful she is. Maybe that's why I never resented it. If anything, I'm proud of her attractiveness—happy that I didn't carry the burden of my mother's good genes like she does. Blending in came more easily to me than standing out. I used to wish I could be invisible. Especially when I had a camera in my hands. Now that I am, all I want is to be seen and heard.

The memory of a night not long after June and Leo separated reveals itself. June was at my condo. She'd moved just around the corner from me, so we were always at each other's places. Hers when the girls were at home, mine when they weren't. It was right before our mother's cancer diagnosis and my move back home to take care of her.

We were drinking wine, as we often did. A bold red with hints of dark chocolate and cherries. I remember because I'd give almost anything to be able to drink that wine right now, in this afterlife or whatever the hell it is.

June had had a bit too much, as had become her habit after the separation. Her lips wore a crust of purple; her cheeks were flushed from the tannins. I was at the kitchen island making a plate of cheese and crackers as she orbited the room, sliding across the slippery wood floors in her gray wool socks.

She's always had a hard time sitting still and would do rounds of the living room looking at the photos on the walls as though she'd never seen them before.

"I can look at your work over and over and never get bored," she used to say, when I teased her about it. "I'm always finding something new, some subtlety that I somehow missed before. You're the best photographer I know."

"I'm the only photographer you know," I'd shoot back. "And I'm your sister, so you're biased." I wish now I'd just taken her compliment, believed her, been grateful for the encouragement that she was never short on giving. That night she stopped and stared at a photo I'd taken when I was only twelve—an up-close black-and-white of our mother. She scooped her long hair up and pulled it away from her face. "Think I could pull off a pixie cut like Mom?" she asked.

"Sure, why not?" I was only half listening, preoccupied with the stubborn vacuum-sealed plastic wrap on a block of Gouda.

She set her wineglass down and left the room. I heard the bathroom door close, so I didn't think anything of it. Only when nearly twenty minutes passed did I start to wonder. I called out her name and got some muffled response in reply.

"June?" I said, tapping on the bathroom door.

"Are you ready?" Before I could answer, she pulled the door open and stood face-to-face with me, her eyes wild, her long, thick black hair gone—chopped into a poor attempt at a pixie cut.

She laughed a deep belly laugh at the shock all over my face, as though she'd done it for that alone. "What do you think?"

"Honestly? You look a bit like a Dickens street urchin."

She glanced at herself in the mirror. "Oh my god. I totally do." She looked back at me with horror, and then we both started laughing—the hysterical kind, with tears and snorts, the best kind, the kind I shared most with my sister.

The next day she went to a proper hair stylist and emerged looking even more stunning than she had with long hair. That's June—impulsive, impervious to societal dictates, and oblivious to consequences. Sounds like a magical combination, but in truth, it meant she needed a lot of taking care of.

Impulsive—she makes lots of mistakes. Impervious—she can never understand why people are so bothered by those mistakes. Oblivious—she never, ever seems to learn from those mistakes. She's also generous and caring, and she loved me deeper than anyone else in my life ever did, and so I put up with the roller coaster that is my sister.

June rolls over onto her other side, licking her dry lips and letting out a weak cough. "What are we doing here, June?" I ask, knowing there will be no answer.

"Avril Island." June's words are mumbled sleep talk, but there's no denying what she said.

The vision of our family cottage is suddenly right there for me to see. A quick succession of memories flash by—swimming, running through the forest, jumping from high cliffs, board games, suntanning—a kaleidoscope of beautiful childhood summers. The brightness of those memories is suddenly eclipsed by a shadow of something. Another memory, I think, but it's buried deep down in the darkness of my consciousness. Resting there like an ancient sea creature waiting for something to summon it, biding its time until it can devour me whole.

JUNE

There's no gentle waking this morning. As soon as consciousness hits me, pretty much every sense protests. My head is
pounding with pain; my skin is prickling, itchy with heat;
there's a horrible sickly sweet taste in my mouth—buried under
my furry, sandpaper-dry tongue. The musty scent of whatever
I'm lying on tops it all off, and my stomach tightens with the
threat of vomit.

I carefully push myself up off the bed and shuffle into the
bathroom. There's no glass, so I cup my hands under the tap
and splash water into my mouth over and over again until
finally the sandpaper is gone along with most of the sweetness.

Next I peel off my clothes and step into a cool shower, washing away the sweat and rot from that comforter. The water
brings some lucidity to my cloudy brain.

I remember a dream I had last night. May was in the room.
She stood over the bed, laughing at me for drinking too much.
Then she asked, *Why are we here?* I told her *Avril Island*, and
she suddenly disintegrated right in front of me, like she was
made of sand and was being blown away.

I find some headache pills in my travel bag and then go sit
on the bed, wrapped in a towel, to wait for them to kick in. The

sight of the half-empty whiskey bottle on the desk sends a wave of sickness through my stomach and a resounding pounding through my head.

Whiskey—what was I thinking?

I was thinking that I wanted to be drunk, and it was all I could find when I arrived last night. My plane landed at eight PM. I had to get a bus north, and by the time I arrived at the small lakeside town, it was well past midnight. Only one motel had any vacancies, and the only things on offer behind the reception counter were bags of stale chips, bait, and whiskey. I bought two of those items and retreated to my sad room to consume too much of both before passing out.

The sad cliché of it all motivates me to get moving. I put on some fresh clothes, shove my dirty ones into my suitcase, and I'm packed. The headache pill has kicked in and a few handfuls of chips have settled my queasy stomach, but I need to move slowly so as not to disturb this delicately constructed state.

It's a futile effort. As soon as I step out into daylight and see my surroundings, the nausea and pounding are back, an awkward combination of hangover and nostalgia.

I haven't been back to this town since I was twelve, but not much has changed. The main road crosses in front of the motel, and beyond that is the lake, sunlight flashing across its surface, so clear you can see the sandy, shallow bottom. Locals spread across the public beach in front of it, and children in bathing suits hang off the old jungle gym equipment that still sits on a patch of lawn too close to the road.

Wheeling my suitcase down the sidewalk, I pass the bright-red ice cream stand, the Red Engine—same sign, same wooden structure, just a new coat of paint, ready for summer, which is only a week away. It's closed, resting itself for high season when the cottagers arrive.

The chip truck is still there as well, and it's open for business. Its metal frame is rusting around the edges where it sits on gray cinder blocks, grease stains decorating the pavement all around it. The scent of malt vinegar hits me along with memories of chips shared with my mother and sister.

Every time we made the trip into town, my mother allowed us to get our own cardboard boat of hot, greasy chips. My sister bathed hers in ketchup. I coated mine in vinegar and salt. My mother never got her own, preferring to pick at ours instead, fooling herself that the calories didn't count if they were stolen from her daughters. I consider stopping to buy some for old time's sake, but my sensitive stomach pushes me on.

The marina isn't far, right where it always was, but it's been updated—more gas pumps, more boats, a few more floating docks. I scan the area for Jim, the owner. His mop of white hair spilling out from under a red ball cap always made him easy to spot. It takes a second to dawn on me that it's a vain search, considering the man was in his late fifties, at least, the last time I saw him. He'd be dead by now for sure. The thought is lead inside me, which makes me wonder if I'm really ready for this.

A flash of red appears from a side door, and I spot Jim's ball cap. It's not the friendly old man wearing it, though. It's his son, their likeness unmistakable. I yank my suitcase off the sidewalk and down the gravel path toward him.

"Hello," I call out, and he turns, shielding his eyes with one hand against the sun. "I need to rent a boat." I pull my suitcase up onto the dock and stumble. He steps forward to help, but I manage to right myself before he makes contact.

"What kind of boat you looking for?" he asks.

I survey the boats in the water around me and on land. I hadn't really given it any thought. I shrug. "I guess I just need one to get me and my suitcase out to the island."

He nods. "What island would that be?" I'm taken aback by his blatant nosiness, and he must see it in my expression. He sighs. "So's I know what kind of boat you need. Is it far from here? Shallow water? That kinda thing."

I feel like a true "citidiot." My time away has erased all sense of cottage consciousness. "Right, sorry." The apology sloppily tumbles out. "I'm headed to Avril Island. Do you know it?"

His round, sun-damaged face contorts in surprise. "Do I know it?" He huffs. "You some reporter or something? Come to dig up that old mystery? You'll need permission, you know, to get on that island."

I shake my head and hold up a hand. "No, no. I'm June Fin—I mean Bennett. June Bennett. My family owns Avril Island." A quivering starts under my skin—dehydration, fatigue, hunger, fear that I'll have to convince him of my right to the place. I've believed it gone for so long that it no longer really feels like mine.

He pulls his hat off and gives me an apologetic smile. He has his own mop of hair, not yet white, but one day it will be. "Aw, so sorry, miss. It's been so long since a Bennett's been up this way."

"Oh no, please, it's not a problem," I gush. Relief that he believes me without proof, without asking for a driver's license or the deed, inspires actual affection for the man. "I understand the confusion. It has certainly been a long time. My family moved across the country, and we just never got back here to enjoy it again." I work quickly to make the whole situation seem light and innocent, just as my mother would have wanted me to.

Don't let the public know your business. They'll use it against you, she always used to say. I was never sure why we weren't also considered the public but was afraid to ask. I think what she really meant was don't let the poor people see that we have problems too, that money doesn't mean we don't get dirt under our fingernails just like them.

He holds out a hand for me to shake. "It's a real pleasure to meet you, Ms. Bennett. I'm Jim."

I haven't been Ms. Bennett for years, but it makes sense up here, so I'll go with it. "It's good to meet you too." I shake his hand. "Was the original owner, the other Jim, your father?"

He slides his cap back on. "Sure was. Jim Senior. I'm Jim Junior, but I dropped the Junior when my dad died five years ago. Since there wouldn't be no confusion anymore. And I'm in my fifties, for goodness' sake." He laughs at the thought, placing a hand on his round stomach.

"I'm sorry to hear that your dad has passed." It comes out like some superficial sentiment from a summer person, but the feeling behind it actually threatens to choke me with emotion. "He always gave me and my sister mints when we came into town. And he'd never call us by the right name. He'd say, 'How's it going, September and October?' or 'December and January?' " I force a laugh at the memory.

Jim nods. "Yeah, that sounds like Dad. He was sure fond of your family. Especially your mother. Said she was the friendliest of all the summer people."

I'm not surprised by this. My mother was skilled at charming people, especially the ones who had abilities that she relied on. She didn't come from money, she just married it, so she had a way with "blue-collar folk," as she called them.

"He was pretty upset when your father went missing," Jim continues.

"Went missing?" I huff. "That's a polite way of putting it. My mother always just referred to it as abandoning his family."

"Never heard that version," he says with an awkward laugh. "It was always said around here that he went missing. My dad actually helped with the search."

I use the long handle of my suitcase to steady myself against this boulder of information. I didn't know there was a search. It dawns on me that I actually don't know much about when my father left. My mother's explanation was that he'd run off. He was at the cottage one night, and then when I woke up the next morning he was gone, and my mother whisked me and May back home and we rarely spoke about it again.

"So how about that boat, Jim?" I move the conversation to safer ground, not able to admit that I know nothing about a search for my father or what might have actually happened back then.

"No need to rent a boat, Ms. Bennett," he says, seeming relieved at the topic change as well.

"June. Please."

"All right, June. No need for a rental. We've kept your mother's boat in storage, maintained it, taken it out each year for a spin around the lake. It's dated but should run just fine."

I'm momentarily speechless. Nothing has even changed here; our boat is still our boat, but my mother just walked away from it all and never came back. "Have you been paid for the storage and maintenance?" I ask.

Jim waves his hand as though I'm offering him the cash right then and there. "Your mother told Jim Senior that he was free to sell the boat and keep the proceeds for his trouble. So no fees to worry about."

"Then why didn't he? Sell it, I mean?"

"My dad said he wanted to keep it just in case any of you ever came back. He said he just didn't feel right selling it."

I look out across the lake, waiting for the emotion of Jim Senior's gesture to pass. I literally feel like a mosquito bite would set me to bawling right now. It's not a normal state for me and certainly not one I'm comfortable with, so I have to work hard to keep it at bay.

My eyes finally make their way back to Jim Junior's face. "Well, that's incredibly kind and generous of your dad." I shrug. "And I guess he was right, 'cause here I am now, needing a boat."

Jim claps his hands enthusiastically. "And so a boat you shall have, me lady." He takes the handle of my suitcase and starts toward the marina office. "We'll just put your items behind the desk. You go grab a coffee and one of Ms. Jelly's famous cinnamon buns, and we'll have your boat ready in no time."

He glances behind him to make sure I'm following. "And don't forget to buy some supplies if you haven't already. Especially water."

I silently thank god for Jim Junior and Jim Senior. I was ready to just climb on any old boat and drive out to the island with nothing but my clothes and a half-empty bottle of whiskey. I've never done Avril Island as an adult. Only as a child with a mother who took care of everything.

*   *   *

It might be the best coffee I've ever had, or maybe it's just because for the first time this morning I feel like I've got things under control. Sitting at a café table outside Ms. Jelly's bakery, writing a list of supplies while the boat is being readied—I'm the adult now, and I kind of like it.

And the cinnamon bun is even better than I remember. Or does it just feel that way because the taste is a direct line to my childhood? I can never go back, but I can sample food that transports me, makes my taste buds feel young again.

How different everything feels now as an adult—smaller, less shiny, less hopeful and full of possibility but all the more valuable. The screen door behind me sings each time it opens and closes with a customer. The sound didn't truly register with me as a child, but as I sit here now, reunited with this setting, it cements me back in a place I loved dearly but took for granted, as the young so often do.

Ms. Jelly's is on the main street, and everyone coming from the marina has to pass by it. That's what made it an important landmark in my summer landscape. Along with the Red Engine ice cream booth, which was down by the beach and just up from the marina. It was the boat traffic that May and I cared about back then—boats that brought the other summer kids, whom we met at tennis lessons and sailing.

There were rotating crushes on the boys and superficial friendships with the girls. Age didn't matter the same way it did during the year at school. We all hung out in one big group, slumming it at the beach with the locals, daring each other to jump off rocky cliffs, racing our parents' boats. On rainy days we crammed in together under the wooden shelter of the tennis club weaving gimp bracelets to exchange or making circles of sailing rope around one another's wrists and then burning the ends so they melted together.

At the end of summer we all exchanged mailing addresses with the promise of writing, wishing our summer friends could be our year-round friends, but once those cottages were closed and the leaves began to turn, so did our minds. Summer friends became just a memory, no letters were ever exchanged, but when we were all reunited in July it was as though no time had passed at all. That was the magic of the lake, the spell of summer, the fickleness of youth.

The last summer I spent at Avril Island, I was twelve. The exact age when crushes on boys actually start to mean something and those friendships with girls are crucial to your very existence.

I had a boyfriend. Matthew. He had blond hair and freckles, a killer serve, and his clothes always smelled like the lake air that dried them on his backyard clothesline. He wore Stan Smiths, cutoff cargo shorts, and a wrist full of rope bracelets that I painstakingly burned together just so that I could touch the soft, tanned skin of his arm over and over again. We held hands walking around this very town, sat pressed together on boat rides, and had one fleeting kiss at a sailing club dance.

My phone buzzes on the table in front of me, breaking the spell of memory. It's Beatrice, asking me where her Rollerblades are. I imagine her sister, Madeline, already wearing her own Rollerblades and helmet, sitting by the front door waiting patiently for Bea to locate hers. They were made in one womb but are from different planets.

I text back a few options and then signal off with a kissy emoji. I hate them—emojis—but it's their language, so I'll speak it.

That slight bit of contact opens up a well of longing for them. I wish they were here with me now, enjoying a cinnamon bun and listening to me reminisce about my summers. They wouldn't even have a point of reference for my experiences up here. The thought makes my heart ache.

Leo and I used to take them on vacation every year—some exotic places, lots of beach houses, a few cabins in the woods— but the locale was ever changing. They never grew summer roots that called them back every year to a second home the way May and I did.

A piercing hate for my mother pushes through my heart like an overgrown thorn. If she hadn't kept Avril Island a secret, I could have been bringing the girls here all along. They would have made their own memories, built right on top of my own so that together we'd have made a lake lineage. Instead this whole world will feel foreign to them. They were robbed, but fortunately they will never know the value of what could have been. Only I do.

The bitterness turns the coffee rancid with my next sip. I push away from the table, gather my purse, and leave the last bit of cinnamon bun along with a puddle of coffee in the mug.

* * *

A very basic grocery store has swallowed the general store that used to be here. There's a greater selection, but it comes at a high price. I wheel my shrunken shopping cart up and down the narrow aisles, choosing only the necessities. I have no idea what state the place will be in when I get there, so I get lots of canned soup and tuna.

Will I be able to get the water running? Will the refrigerator even work anymore? Will there be hydro? Each question that surfaces erodes my confidence and raises my level of anxiety. The stupidity of this mission slowly dawns on me. If May were here, it would be an adventure. On my own it's just naïve and lonely.

I turn down an aisle of wine. The sight cheers me just enough to keep me going. I envision sitting on the dock with a nice glass of red, watching the sunset. Who needs food and water and hydro when you've got wine and sunsets? If May were here, she'd scold me for my careless attitude. But she's not, which makes me load three bottles of red and three bottles of white into my cart.

When I arrive back at the marina, my mother's boat sits bobbing on the soft waves, the sun bouncing off its clean white bow. The turquoise leather interior has remained in perfect condition, no cracking, no staining or mold. I'm amazed at how well it's been preserved.

When I was eleven, my mother taught first May and then me how to use her boat—a gas-guzzling bathtub of a motor-boat, but it was safe and held all of our supplies when we made the trip over to the island. She often sent us into town on our own to pick up milk or bread, cigarettes for her, sometimes even a bottle of wine or two.

May usually drove. She was cautious, slowing right down when other boats approached or waves rolled across the usually calm lake. *You're safer with your older sister than me*, my mother used to say. It was both a compliment of my sister's abilities and an insult of her restraint. My mother would push the throttle to full speed, bouncing over waves, racing against all other boats in the vicinity. I never needed my mother to tell me I was safest with May. I'd known it deep in my bones from a very young age.

Parental supervision was lax when we came up to the lake. My father made the drive up from Boston only every other week to spend a three-day weekend, at the most, with us. My mother's attitude when he was away was *We're all responsible people; you do your thing and don't cause trouble, and I'll do mine.*

Jim Junior steps out of the office with my suitcase. "She's all ready for ya." He stares down at the boat as though he built it himself.

"It looks just like it did the last time I saw it. I mean, it's amazing. You've taken such good care of it."

The twisted reality of it all hits me for the umpteenth time this morning. Jim and his dad have spent all these years taking care of this boat for us as though it mattered. As though we might be back at any moment, and we had no idea at all. My mother had to die for us to finally learn the truth and find our way back here. *My* way back here, I mentally correct myself.

Jim helps me load my suitcase and the groceries into the boat and then gives me a quick tutorial on how to operate it. I haven't driven a boat for years. The few times we rented them on family vacations, Leo always took charge and I just let him.

Even when he flooded the engine or nicked the prop on the shallow bottom, I just sat back and let him believe he was the expert.

Jim holds out a card to me. "Here's my number, if you have any problems. I filled up the gas tank and just put it on your account like always." I nod and take the card, tucking it into my back pocket. "Take her easy at first till you get used to her throttle."

I step forward and give him a hug. His body tenses in surprise, but he's no more surprised than I am. I don't really do hugs, but words fail me right now. I could never explain to him how much all of this means to me.

* * *

The boat is fast, its engine purring. You'd never know it was a relic from 1975. *Like riding a bike* could be replaced with *like driving a boat*, I think to myself. As soon as I'm out in the open water, it all comes back to me. My confidence and assuredness is restored as I navigate the boat across the choppy surface of the lake. The wind whips away the sluggishness of my hangover; the bright sun burns through my insecurities and my grip on the steering wheel grounds me to this place.

A whole new flock of cottages have been built along the shoreline, some so monstrous in size that they look as though they simply swatted trees out of the way before plopping down to greedily claim the land. Seeing the progress that's happened in the time I've been away makes me wonder if the opposite has happened to Avril Island. Will the elements have eaten away at the wood? The ground shifted so much that it has unsettled the very structure? Will everything have fallen in on itself from loneliness and neglect?

There's a point that stretches out into the lake where our bay begins. It's thin to start but branches out like a hand—a hand belonging to a giant made from rocks, trees, and earth. The bay's gatekeeper, ready to grab any unwanted guests and toss their boat back across the lake. As a kid coming into the bay, I always hugged the shore, flying past those rocky fingertips. Daring that hand to reach out and get me. Triumphant when it did not.

That point comes into view. It seems more land than hand from my adult vantage point. I slip past it, no longer fearing that it could come alive and catch my boat in its giant fingers—the fears I have now are much greater.

There are several islands in our bay, all of them privately owned, except for the biggest, which houses Windset resort. It was built in the 1940s and went through several transformations by the time my family bought property up here. My mother used it as an escape, slipping off for a round of golf or tennis in the afternoon, dinner, drinks, and dancing in the evenings.

The odd time May and I were allowed to go over with her, we swam in the pool, had french fries and milk shakes in the clubhouse, or dove for golf balls off the shore. But mostly we experienced the resort from our own dock. At night the music from the dance hall spread itself out over the calm, dark lake. By the time it reached us, it was a stripped-down version of the song, mainly bass, but May and I still sat on the dock with our feet in the water, listening. Thrilled to witness after-hours adult life—even if only an echo of it.

Glancing in the direction of the resort, I expect to see boats along the dock, the navy-blue shirts of staff moving from one building to the next and the bright green of the manicured golf course. Instead I see empty, half-sunken docks, not a person in sight, yellow overgrown grass and dark-brown stains traveling up what were once pristine white buildings.

Slowing the boat down, I stare at the abandoned resort in shock. It's an unsettling sight. Windset was a point in my compass on this lake. I'm not sure how to orient myself in this landscape without it.

Now that I'm facing the inevitability of time, the ruthlessness of change and evolution, I wonder if it would have been better to stay away, to have held on to the time capsule of my twelve-year-old self and never know what died here.

It's a little late to be asking myself that question. I can already see Avril Island in the distance. It's one of the larger islands in the bay. The boat drifts toward it, as though the lake is guiding me there, using its gentle current to get me where I'm supposed to be. I brace myself for what's to come and push down on the throttle.

*   *   *

Slowing the boat to a stop so that it bobs gently on the waves, I study the island from the middle of the bay. Trees crowd the shore, obscuring what was once a direct view to the cottage. Skinny birches have become round and thick, their branches reaching out over the lake. In between are clusters of cedars, creating a wall of green. It's as though the vegetation has swallowed the man-made structure out of spite and taken back the island. The wide dock, which extends from the rocky shore and out into the water, is the only evidence, at first glance, that the place was ever inhabited. And even that has begun to look wild, with boards popping up, moss growing in places, one corner sinking lower than the other.

I slide the boat into gear and very slowly make my way across the bay. The closer I get to the dock, the more I lose the boating confidence I regained on the drive over. Docking was always the hardest part. I take my time, reversing twice until I've got just the right angle, silently cursing the pull of the water. There was almost always someone on the dock to catch me, to lessen the impact of boat against wood, to correct my mistakes. I flip the bumpers down and hope they'll compensate for my rusty docking skills.

When I finally make it up against the dock, there's a slight crunch. I start to panic but then relax. My mother isn't here to witness the mistake and punish me. Nobody is.

I climb out of the boat and hurriedly tie up the bow before the stern drifts too far from the dock to reach it. Only once both ends are secure do I stop and let it all sink in.

I'm standing on Avril Island. On a dock I thought I'd never see again. I slip my shoes off so that I can feel its rough surface under my bare feet. How many splinters did my mother tweeze out of my feet from this dock? How many times did I pull myself from the cool water and lie on its surface, soaking warmth from its sun-drenched wooden boards?

I listen to the water breaking over the rocky crib beneath me. *Return*. It's an action that's taken for granted. Only appreciated when you lose the place you want to return to most. My anger that the possibility of this return was kept from me is slowly draining away, whitewashed by my gratitude. I'm back, and suddenly that's all that matters.

I leave my bags in the boat. There's no point in taking them up to the cottage until I know what I'm dealing with. Slipping my shoes back on to make the trek up, I step from the dock onto land. It's hard not to feel as though the trees have grown up to protect the place from the rest of the world. Now here I am, about to cross the barrier of new growth—to wake her from a deep sleep.

There's a hush as soon as I step through the gate of trees. It's cooler too—the sun has to work hard to break through the thick, leafy canopy. In the absence of people tramping along the path, the ground beneath my feet has become soft and spongy with needles and moss. Each step I take sends up a scent of pine and damp earth.

Right off the dock is a small shed, used to hold paddles, life jackets, and inflatables. Most of the dark-green paint has peeled away, and the small building looks as though it's ready to buckle under the heavy moss-covered roof. The sight disheartens me. Has the whole place just given up, ready to let the land claim it?

The answer is no. Arriving in the large clearing, where the main cottage sits, I see that she is standing as proudly as she always has. The green paint has peeled in many places to reveal the raw wood underneath, and the white paint on the windows is now a light gray. There's a slight lean to the front verandah and patches of shingles peel up and away from the roof, but those are comparable to my own signs of aging—inevitable and forgivable.

My chest tightens with nostalgia, and I feel a bit lightheaded. Is it apprehension, excitement, my hangover? It's hard to tell. It kind of feels like a dream. The dreams I used to have as a child in the months after we closed the place when we were back in the city. I ran up this very path, barefoot, still wet from the lake, to burst into the cottage, leaving drops of lake all over the worn wooden floors.

Those dreams still came, now and again, even after my mother told us she'd sold Avril Island. Less and less frequently as I grew older, but they never disappeared entirely. This place couldn't be exorcised from my subconscious.

The wide set of verandah steps groans as I climb them, and I have to kick away a layer of brown leaves to find my footing, inadvertently flaking off big chips of white paint at the same time. The rusty hinges of the screen door scream as I pull it open. As I reach into my pocket and pull out the key I was given, my hand shakes slightly. Surprisingly, the key turns easily in the old lock, and the door swings open wide in welcome.

The smell hits me first, before my eyes even have time to adjust to the darkness. It's like a wallop to my chest, its impact penetrating the bone and tissue, snatching my breath away. The combination of pine, smoky fires, and mustiness acts as an olfactory time capsule, sending me right back to my youth.

I breathe deeply as the room comes into focus. All of the furniture is still there in the very same place we left it. The pine board walls still hold our framed family photos as well as my mother's amateur attempts at painting the surroundings.

As I walk slowly through the living room, taking in each detail, the floors snap and creak underfoot, settling into place under my weight as I go. I stop in front of the large stone fireplace. Its hearth is the size of two small children end to end, and its mantel is one long piece of red, grainy wood. Thick gray stones with flecks of sparkle are piled on top of each other to make up the solid structure.

It's the backbone of the cottage, its chimney running right up to the second floor and out onto the roof. Without it, I'm sure, the whole place would crumble. It's been thirty years since a fire burned in it, but the smoky scent is still strong. I think of all the fires we sat in front of on rainy days and late August nights when temperatures started to drop.

Moving away from the fireplace, I head into the kitchen. It's silent and still, but there's an unnerving sense that somebody has only just ducked out of sight. Like a child playing hide-and-seek, holding their breath, waiting to be discovered.

Nothing in the place has been disturbed. The building hasn't risen up in retaliation for our abandonment and shaken everything about, as I almost believed it would. No animals have invaded the place, turning it into their home once our human scent dissipated. The island has kept everything locked up safe and sound, exactly where it should be, waiting for one of us to make our way back.

I pull open the cutlery drawer and find the pile of mismatched forks, knives, and spoons lying on a bed of mouse droppings. Some of the pieces have become slightly tarnished, but otherwise they're available for use. The sight of the colorful Fiestaware dishes, still neatly stacked in the upper cabinets, brings back a lifetime of summer meals in one split second.

* * *

Leaving the kitchen, I wander into the dining room. French glass doors give me a direct view into the backyard. The large raised garden bed where my mother grew vegetables is now just a mound of dirt and grass that looks like the grave of a giant.

The round charcoal barbecue grill on the flagstone patio has tipped over, and moss has begun to climb across its metal back. The very same moss that creeps up the legs of the old picnic table—one side sinking so far into the ground that it's lopsided.

I turn away from the decay to study the well-worn surface of the long harvest table. It's big enough to seat twelve, but it was usually just May, my mother, and me who ate at it. My father was away most of the time, and when he was there he preferred barbecues on the back patio.

My sister and I were left to fend for ourselves when it came to breakfast and lunch. We ate those meals on the dock or the verandah. On the nights my mother went to the resort, she fed us at the kitchen table, plopping down grilled cheese sandwiches or hot dogs in front of us before disappearing up to her room to get ready. The nights my mother didn't go to the resort, she insisted on candlelit dinners after eight in the dining room.

She'd been an only child, raised in a suburb of Paris by two alcoholic parents. Her father was a kind drunk, sloppy and slow moving, but her mother was an abusive one. Alcohol made her angry, suspicious, and quick to strike out. My mother said she was happy to leave France behind. She spoke mostly English, only allowing bits of French to escape now and again. She even protested when my father used the French version of her name, Avril, instead of the English one, April, to name the island, which he bought for her as a wedding present.

She rejected almost everything about her French heritage except for the wine and their relaxed, late-night manner of dining. Those nights were always my favorite. We lingered long after dinner. I remember being full from food but hungry for my mother's attention. The red wine and slow smoking of cigarettes lulled her into a sedentary mood. Laughter at her jokes and requests for her stories were what kept her there. She rarely walked away from a rapt audience.

The back doors were thrown open, inviting soft breezes to play in the candlelight and attracting dusty moths to risk their lives in the flames. My mother allowed us small sips of her wine. I pretended to enjoy the bitter sting of it, which seemed to please her. May always gagged and swore she'd never drink when she grew up, which caused my mother to roll her eyes. She'd cast a knowing glance at me, as though we were more refined, more mature than May would ever be.

Some nights my mother would reach across the table and take my hand in hers, wrapping her long, cool fingers around my small, hot hand. I'd study the red polish on her nails, the flicker of the candles skittering across the shine of it. She'd rub the back of my hand with her thumb, and I'd stay as still as I could. Even when the friction felt raw against my skin, even then I wouldn't disturb her touch.

The memories of those dinners are loud, as though they're seated around the table, calling out to be noticed. As an adult, I suddenly see the wrong in them. The rejection of May because she didn't like the wine my mother so adored, the affection doled out like a prize, nothing unconditional about it. The entire evening a stage for my mother, the two of us her captive audience. I run my hand along the smooth edge of the table as I leave the room—wishing my adult eyes would stop tarnishing my childhood.

The stairs are tucked into a corner of the living room, a narrow passage with a slight slant to it, making you feel as though you're climbing through the bowels of a rocking ship instead of a cottage. The place was built well over a hundred years ago, before grand staircases started showing up everywhere.

You could sit on the bottom step and get a clear view into the living room without anyone being able to see you. May and I used it like a superhero power when we were kids, sneaking down to watch my parents late at night as they read books by the fire or, better yet, entertained friends from across the bay.

I duck into the stairway and grasp the thin metal railing. The slant seems more pronounced, but I may be imagining it. Each step has a dip that's been worn down in the middle from heavy traffic. Even through my shoes I can feel it cup my foot as I go.

Reaching the landing at the top of the stairs, I stop to gain my balance and wait for my eyes to adjust from the shadows to the light. Windows line the entire upper hallway, and sun from above the tree line pours in. This cottage is a contrast of shadows and bright light, forcing you to recalibrate as you move through it.

The hallway is stuffy and hot. Dead flies line the windowsills and the curtains hang limp, heavy with dust. Exerting enough effort to produce a thin film of sweat on my upper lip, I manage to get two of the windows open. Going down to the end of the hallway to the bathroom, I pry that window open as well to create a cross breeze, and almost instantly I can breathe easier.

A ring of green grows in the dry bowl of the toilet. The sink is in better shape, with only a thin line of orange from rusty pipes staining the white porcelain. I turn to inspect the white claw-foot tub, which looks gray with its covering of dust.

We never really used the tub. My mother believed the best start to the day was a swim, no matter how cold the lake was. She swam from spring to fall and chastised us if we didn't do the same. We even swam in thunderstorms as long as the lightning wasn't too close.

The doors to the bedrooms are all shut, creating the sense that there are people on the other side wanting privacy. Bypassing my room and May's, I go straight to my parents'. It's the largest one, at the front of the cottage, the only one with a view of the lake.

I have to push hard on the door to unstick it from the wooden doorframe and half stumble into the room when it finally gives way. Like the rest of the cottage, this room looks as though someone was here only hours ago. My mother's perfume bottles, face creams, and jewelry are still scattered across her dresser—the display made monochromatic by the thick layer of dust.

The bed is still made with white sheets and the blue-and-yellow flowered quilt my mother bought one year at the farmers' market. Veins of black mold crawl across its surface, right below a water stain on the ceiling where the roof must now leak. I think about stripping away the dirty, moldy sheets, but it's all so overwhelming—the dust, the mouse shit, the dirty bathroom. Where do I even begin?

Turning to leave, I come face-to-face with the open closet and my mother's dresses, which are still hanging there. I jump, feeling as though I've just seen her ghost. The door is open only a few inches, and at first glance there's the illusion that she's in there hiding, ready to step out into the light.

When my heart slows to its normal pace, I step forward and pull the door fully open. Taking one of her dresses in my hand, I pull it up to my face. Inhaling, I'm able to pull the faintest trace of her scent from the cotton fabric—French perfume, outdoors, and cigarette smoke. It's buried deep under the pervading mustiness but it's there, triggering a longing in me so deep it cuts through my gut.

It's not the mother who died recently that I'm mourning. It's the one from the summers of my childhood. Before my father left and we rushed away from this place, taking nothing with us. Before I grew up and realized how truly destructive she could be, and selfish. Before I lost that innocent, naïve belief that because she was a mother, she was good and safe.

The bathroom door suddenly slams shut at the end of the hallway, smashing through the silence and startling away the sobs that were rising to the surface. It was just a gust of wind through one of the open windows, but it still sets my heart racing. I drop the dress and rush out of the room. Down the stairs and out onto the verandah, where I take deep, gulping breaths of fresh air. Air not laced with the scent of my youth or things I've lost and can never get back.

Sorrow, fear, adrenaline rush through my veins and set a soft trembling into my whole body. I fold over, put my hands on my knees to steady myself.

"Fuck." The word roars out of me into the quiet of the surroundings. I brace myself for a scolding. I can't shake the feeling that a parent is just around the corner, ready to pounce on my infraction.

Just take a few deep breaths. I suddenly hear May's voice in my head. *Don't let it get to you.*

I breathe in and push myself back to a standing position. I consider returning to the mainland and staying another night in the motel. Taking it all in baby steps rather than one giant leap. Maybe it was crazy to think I could do this on my own. Maybe I should just put the place up for sale.

A wind moves through the trees, making the leaves whisper. It catches in the partially open screen door and pulls it forward, making the hinges creak as though the place is speaking to me. Begging me not to leave. Beckoning me back in again.

Go inside and take care of things. There's May's voice again. *Mom taught you what to do, so do it.* I swat at the air as though the voice is an actual thing outside of me, not just my fucked-up head playing tricks.

"What if I can't?" I say out loud.

You can is the response I hear back. I think I might actually be losing it, but imagining my sister's voice and encouraging words does helps. My heart is no longer racing, and I have a somewhat renewed sense of confidence.

I go back inside and head right to the kitchen. The big, beige fridge is unplugged, and the door is propped open with a piece of wood. Inside is empty except for mouse droppings and, yet again, black mold. I bend down and plug it into the wall, but nothing happens. I flick the kitchen light switch, and again nothing happens. The main power must be off.

Just for the hell of it, I go to the kitchen sink and give the tap a try, releasing an angry hiss of air. So before anything can happen, I have to get the power on and the water working. Nothing unexpected, but I still feel like a child sent in to do an adult's job. Being the youngest meant there was always someone ahead of me to take charge, to boss me around and make things happen.

Now I'm the only one left, and I can't help but feel like it shouldn't have been me. I was the fuck-up in the family, the scattered one who rarely saw anything through to the end, who always tried to get out of any responsibility. How on earth am I supposed to handle all of this?

I pull my phone from my pocket. I've already been here for an hour and gotten nothing accomplished. A photo of my daughters is my lock screen. I stare at their faces until I feel like an adult again—their mere existence a reminder that I've been in charge somewhere in my life, so why not here as well?

In the storage room at the very back of the cottage is the fuse panel. Our reserves are still lined up neatly on the wooden shelves—cans of food, matches, a few bottles of French wine, cleaning products. Pulling open the door to the fuse panel, I see that the main fuse block has been taken out. I find it sitting beside the metal box that contains spare fuses, fit it into place, and push hard, grateful for the first time that my mother made both me and May learn how everything in this cottage worked.

She was militant about it. "If you partake in the enjoyment of the place, you must also take on the responsibility of caring for it," she said time and time again, when we were made to wash the windows, scrub the floors, weed the garden, change blown fuses, prepare the place for winter. The caretaker, West, did most of the yard work and fixed things now and again, but she insisted on doing the majority of it herself. Like a protective mother whose baby was a cottage, she just couldn't stop fussing.

I pull the chord of the bare lightbulb hanging above me and almost cry out in joy when it fills with light. Back in the kitchen, I'm greeted with the gentle hum of the refrigerator.

Encouraged by my first success, I look for the key to the pump room. The next task—getting the water turned on. If I can manage that, I can pretty much manage anything.

MAY

We're back on Avril Island. The fact hit me as soon as I surfaced next to June and saw the familiar green boards of the cottage, the metal glider sitting rusted on the front verandah, the thick forest circling the expanse of lawn.

June was screaming at the trees. I could feel her loneliness, her despair and desperation. It flooded me like sewage water. I don't know if it was seeing June suffering or if there was more to it, but surfacing there on Avril Island made me uneasy, anxious. It was the first time I'd had those emotions since dying.

Instinctively I spoke some encouraging words to her, which of course came out as weighted silence. I willed her to be brave, which I'm pretty sure she felt, because she stopped screaming, shifted her shoulders back, and marched inside. I moved with her.

It was obvious from the state of the place that nobody had been there for a very long time. I couldn't remember why. I spread myself out into the pine walls and down into the floorboards. There was a stillness and an emptiness that can only be found in buildings that have been uninhabited for a long time. I was sure I felt sadness trapped there in the bones of the place. Wanting to escape it, I quickly pulled myself back together and out of the depths of the lonely old building.

June was down on her hands and knees to scrub the inside of the fridge. How long did she plan on staying? I wondered. Why had she come back all on her own?

Independent ventures weren't like June. I'd be lying to say I wasn't surprised that she'd come all this way alone, managed to drive a boat, to get the water running, to be in this much solitude. I was proud of her but at the same time confused and a bit concerned.

I spent the afternoon watching June clean and unpack food that she'd brought, drinking glasses of wine along the way. She stopped only once to eat some carrots and celery, a little something to absorb the alcohol but not nearly enough to nourish her. She'd turned from curves to angles since I'd died. Her bones were more pronounced than ever. Eventually she put on her swimsuit, opened a new bottle of wine, refilled her glass, and headed down the path to the lake.

The sun had set the sky orange and the breeze was gone, leaving the lake a sheet of dark glass. June dipped one toe in and cringed. The lake doesn't really warm up until mid-July, so it must be earlier than that. She dropped the towel and, before she could lose her nerve, pushed off the dock into a graceful dive, disappearing into the deep water.

June had always plunged right in, cannonballing as a young child, diving when she got good at that. I'd always waded in slowly from the shore, introducing each body party to the water until I was up to my neck and then finally acclimatized enough to drop under the surface. An accurate analogy of our personalities all through life, I now realize.

As she sat on the dock after her swim, her eyes locked on the evolution of sunset before her, tears slowly began to slide down her cheeks. She didn't wipe them away. I knew those tears were for me and I couldn't do a thing about it, which felt more painful than any death.

Fortunately, she didn't sit long with the grief. She drained what was left in her glass and got up to make her way back to the cottage. Inside she poured herself another glass, set it carefully down on the coffee table, and then flopped onto the couch with a tired groan.

* * *

Now her eyes slowly roll closed, and she turns onto her side and curls up into a ball, not even bothering to discard the damp towel. My mother would have been mortified to see her on the couch in her wet bathing suit. I can almost hear her: *June Bennett, you get off that couch right now and into dry clothes. Sacré bleu!* My mother always added a French curse at the end of a scolding. It was involuntary, she said.

June begins to snore softly. It's been almost a full day, and I'm still here. Maybe I'm getting stronger. Maybe soon I won't disappear at all. It's hard to say, and I still don't understand it at all.

I'm not really sure what to do with myself now that June is sleeping. As if I'm testing a new superpower, I start to slowly drift away from the couch, moving first into the kitchen. A mouse is chewing into the plastic of the bag of bread that sits out on the counter but stops suddenly with my arrival and quickly skitters through a thin crack in the wooden paneling of the wall. Was it a mere coincidence, or could it sense me?

Moonlight streams into the picture window that looks out onto the backyard. Passing through it, I feel a strange tug, as though I suddenly have some density to me, so I stop and linger there, enjoying the sensation of it. Thinking this must be how a child learning the world for the first time feels, not sure what anything really means, finding new sensations at every turn with no background information to apply.

When I leave the patch of moonlight, I feel light again, as though a strong wind could blow me apart. I have to mentally pull myself together before moving into the dining room. There's no moonlight here to play in or mice to scare, and it's got a shadowy, hollow feeling that I don't like, so I keep going.

Wanting to try going even farther afield, I will myself up the stairs.

It's dark up here, but I can still see everything clearly. The doors to our bedrooms are closed, but my parents' room sits open, and the gentle breeze moving through the hallway pushes me in that direction.

It's obvious from the state of the bedroom that we left in a hurry. There are still clothes in the closet and things scattered across the dresser top. Right on cue, the sight of the room brings on the memory of our departure that last summer.

We packed up only the clothing we could carry, filled garbage bags with the remaining food, which would be taken to the dump, and then loaded my mother's boat until it sunk low in the water.

Before the exodus, my mother sat me and June down at the kitchen table. Her hand shook slightly as she lit a cigarette, and her eyes glistened with what looked like unshed tears. She disappeared briefly behind the smoke from her first exhale, and when she reappeared, the tears were gone and all that was left was firm resolve.

She explained, quite matter-of-factly, that she and my father had gotten into a fight the night before, a big fight. She told us that he'd threatened to leave and then stormed off into the woods. She'd woken up early in the morning and looked everywhere for him, but he was nowhere on the island and his boat was gone.

"I think your father has left us, girls," she said, before stamping her cigarette out in the ashtray on the table.

June sat in stunned silence. Sour bile surged up from the depths of my stomach, and I rushed to the bathroom to avoid puking all over the kitchen floor. My mother followed me in, locking the door behind her and kneeling down on the floor beside me.

When I pulled my head from the toilet, I fell against her and began sobbing. I expected her to hold me, comfort the tears away, and then clean me up before we went back out to face June together. She did none of that.

She gripped my upper arms with her clawlike fingers and wrenched me off her body. "Pull it together, May Bennett," she hissed into my face, her eyes full of cold fury. "We do not fall apart." She gave me a little shake. "Do you understand me?" I nodded and sucked in the rest of my tears, focusing on the pain of her sharp nails digging into my bare flesh instead of the greater pain that lay inside me.

"You will go back out there and face your sister with strength. Then you will help me pack up and leave. Is that clear?"

"Yes," I whispered against her wall of hostility.

My compliance caused her expression to soften, and she finally pulled me into a hug. "That's my good girl. We'll get through this, I promise. Just follow my lead, and it will all be fine." I nodded my head against her shoulder. She gave me a pat on the back and then wriggled away, pushing herself up off the floor.

Grabbing a washcloth from the side of the tub, she tossed it at me. "Clean yourself up. You have vomit in your hair." One hand on the doorknob, she turned back. "And hurry. The sooner we get off the island, the better."

The memory is an uncomfortable one, with too many loose ends. Why did we rush away, and where did my father go? Why did we never come back? The questions poke at the memory buried deep down, and I can feel it stir. I bring the fading on myself, wanting to return to the safety of the nothingness.

JUNE

Something jolts me awake. I have the sense of someone else being in the cottage. Moving from my dream world into the real world, I'm not sure what's fact and what's fiction. There's total darkness all around me, and I have no idea where I am. It's the smell that grounds me. I'm at Avril Island.

"Hello?" I call into the darkness, feeling as though someone might just answer me back. Silence is my reply, so I decide the feeling of company must just be remnants of a dream. Feeling around, I discover I'm on the couch in the living room. Some details from the end of my day are fuzzy—too much wine and not enough food, a common combination for me these days.

As I rise into a sitting position, cold air brushes across my bare shoulders. I fell asleep in my wet bathing suit, wrapped in my damp towel. My bones have absorbed the dampness, and I'm stiff and chilled. The air in the cottage has gone cool with the disappearance of the sun.

I have no idea what time it is or how long I've been sleeping— only that my head aches and my stomach is hollow with hunger. I reach out and pat around on the coffee table until I find my phone. The light is weak but better than nothing.

Pushing myself up off the couch, I switch some lights on and go into the kitchen, pull a bottle of water from the fridge, and gulp it down. Standing there shivering, I cram a couple pieces of bread into my mouth to placate my stomach.

I need a hot bath. I haven't been back upstairs since this morning. Maybe it was seeing my mother's clothing hanging there, or the fact that somehow, after all this time, her smell still lingers—like she only just left the room.

I rub my eyes hard with the heel of my hands. "Get a grip, June," I say out loud, as if that will help. A cold draft swipes across my bare skin, and I care more about that hot bath than anything else. Grabbing my suitcase from beside the couch, I boldly ascend the crooked staircase.

Once up there, I turn on as many lights as I can to chase off the shadows. The breeze coming in the windows has blown away the stuffiness, and now it smells mostly fresh and green like it did when I was a kid. I wipe the tub out with my damp towel—not clean, exactly, but it will do. With more effort than I thought I had in me, I unstick the taps of the bathtub and get the water running, then watch it transform from a rusty brown to nearly clear.

As the tub fills, I wander down the hall and into my old room. The lightbulb buzzes to life, and I'm thrown back in time yet again. Wandering around the small space, I touch everything to make sure this mausoleum of my youth is real. The red-and-white quilt is still folded neatly on the end of my bed, the books I read every summer still lined up on my bookshelf.

A gallery of photos ripped from my *Teen Beat* magazines are still tacked to the wall above my bed. Wrinkles run up and down the pages and the ends are curling, but Johnny Depp, Rob Lowe, and River Phoenix still smile seductively out at me. Untouched by age.

* * *

My skin tingles with liberation as I peel the swimsuit off. Stepping into the warm, slightly murky water, I catch a glimpse of myself in the mirror. It shocks me. I've never been an adult in this mirror, only a child. The last time I was reflected naked in this mirror, I was studying my chest for signs of development, wishing for breasts. Now I'm looking at stretch marks across my belly from birthing twins and seeing the droop in the full breasts that I once thought would never come. I sink down into the bath to escape the comparison.

Lying up to my neck in the warm water, I notice the white paint peeling in places from the shiplap walls and cobwebs clustered in the corners. The only sound is the tapping of bugs against the screen of the bathroom window—drawn by the light, fighting to get to it.

There's a creak on the stairs and I sit up, pulling my knees to my chest and covering myself as best I can. Holding my breath, I listen, my head turned toward the sound. Only silence follows and I make myself relax, wondering if I'll ever stop feeling so jumpy here.

After my bath, dressed in my warmest sweat shirt and sweatpants, I put a load of laundry on, hoping I'll be able to get rid of the mustiness in the linens that have been sitting here in closets for almost thirty years.

With that done, I think about getting a glass of wine but choose water instead and take it back upstairs, leaving a reassuring trail of lights on behind me. I'm wide awake, as if it's one thirty PM and not one thirty AM. I want to call the girls, but even with the three-hour time difference, I know they'll be in bed. It's a school night, and their dad runs a tight ship without me around.

Maybe to punish myself, or maybe just to get it over with, I decide to venture into May's old room. The door has warped so much over time that I have to give it a good kick. It swings open dramatically, and a fist closes hard around my heart. Just like in my mother's room, May's scent is released from its cottage tomb—warm skin and cinnamon.

I try the light switch, but nothing happens. I try the lamp on the bedside table, and suddenly the room glows with warmth. It's how I remember this room best—cozy, with sloped ceilings, like some annex room in a children's novel.

As kids, we would have what my mother called our night swim before bed. She'd walk us down to the dock, a cocktail in one hand and a cigarette in the other. Darkness would be waiting patiently at the doorstep as the sun slowly sank low in the sky. My mother would stretch out on a recliner, her long legs crossed at the ankle, slowly alternating between sips from her drink and inhales from her cigarette, which would glow red in the purple light.

May and I would splash around in the lake, ducking underwater whenever a bat skimmed across the surface in pursuit of dinner. We knew it was time to get out when the red tip of our mother's cigarette died away and the sound of ice against the walls of her glass rang out.

She'd hurry us both up the path to the cottage, warning us each and every time not to trip on the rocks or tree roots. Inside the cottage we'd kiss her good-night and take ourselves upstairs to put on our pajamas, brush our damp hair tight against our skulls, and brush our teeth with sharply minted toothpaste.

Our mother would stay downstairs, puttering around, listening to her records and doing whatever she did into the night. That time of night was when our worlds split into two, leaving me and May as one island and my mother as her own. She never said it outright, but we knew we were not to come downstairs after the night swim.

We'd turn all the lights out except for the bedside lamp and climb into May's bed. My mother's music would drift up the stairs and under the door, a soft soundtrack to our hushed conversations. Our cheeks would still be pulsing with the power of the day's sun, our eardrums still pressurized as though we were underwater—until we yawned enough to pop the sensation away.

We'd talk until May became sleepy; she was always the first to give in, which meant I got sent to my room. May was serious about sleep and claimed I kicked too much and called out. Restless in life and in sleep, Leo used to say about me.

Even when my mother left us on our own to go across the bay to the resort, we followed the ritual of a night swim and climbing into May's bed. When we got older, it was to talk about boys we liked and girls we didn't. I'd stretch my tanned legs up the slant of the wall to admire my brightly painted toenails. Once or twice we smoked a cigarette we'd stolen from my mother's purse, blowing the smoke through the screen, where the breeze whisked it away.

In the stillness of the night, we were always able to hear our mother's approach. The sound of the boat carried across the calm water and through the open windows. It was a high hum as she sped across the bay, then became a low rumble when she slowed down near the dock and a soft put-putting before the engine cut out completely. I was always safely in my own bed by the time I heard the creak of the screen door.

May and I read sounds at the cottage the way blind people read braille—to understand what was happening and prepare for what was coming next. Screen doors opening and closing, music playing, ice clinking against glass, creaks on the stairs, the rumbling of arguments between my parents like thunder from deep within the sky—all of them were instructions on how to orbit my mother: stay away, come close, come close but not too close. Those sounds were our points of sail in a windstorm.

As in the other bedrooms, the sheets are still on the bed, tucked in tightly at the corners as though just waiting for their occupants to return. The place was closed properly in every other respect—water and electricity turned off, fridge cleaned out—but it's like we forgot about the bedrooms. I wonder if my mother was planning on returning. Was it the grief over my father's departure that kept her from ever coming back? And if that was the case, then why didn't she just sell the island? The futility of these questions, with everyone in my family gone, exhausts me.

The quilt at the end of May's bed is lavender and white. I unfold it, give it a good shake, and wrap it around me—ignoring the musty scent. Lying down on her bed, I stretch my legs up onto the slanted part of the ceiling above me like I used to. My muscles sting slightly with the pull of it, and I feel foolish. I slide them back down and curl up into a ball with my head on the pillow.

Holding my breath, I listen for something familiar, for some sound to ground me to this place, but the creaks and buzzes are foreign to me. Avril Island has changed with age just like I have. The loneliness of it thuds around my chest like a trapped rat. I miss my girls. I miss May. I miss my youth.

Tears begin to leak slowly from my eyes, and I don't stop them. I just lie there, letting the pillow soak them up. I'm too tired to get up, too tired to try to escape the sorrow. And I have nowhere to go. I'm on an island in the middle of a lake in the dead of night with nobody here to interrupt my grief.

The slow leak of tears turns into sobs pulled from the depths of my gut. The sobs turn to bellows. There's no one to hear me, no one to be frightened by my primal display of pain. I unleash the monster of it, and we dance together in one long, ugly dance until I am too tired to move and it finally lets me sleep.

*   *   *

Hot sun beating down on my face wakes me. It's streaming strong through the windows of May's room, which means it must be midday at least. It's stuffy and I'm sweating, even under the light quilt. My head throbs, and my eyes are swollen and feel as though bits of sand have scraped across their surface. That's what crying will do. I don't recommend it.

Throwing the covers back, I shuffle into the bathroom to splash cold water on my face. I change into a pair of shorts, a T-shirt, and my running shoes. Each task feels difficult. My body is so heavy with grief. My outpouring last night did nothing to exorcise it. Instead it feels stronger than ever, as though it's taken over all of my soul instead of just one corner of it.

Downstairs I find the old CorningWare coffee percolator and plug it in to make coffee. The room quickly fills with the rich scent of it, making me feel a little more human. May and I took turns putting the coffee on each morning. My mother wouldn't come down until she smelled it brewing.

I stand at the counter and can almost hear the delicate padding of her feet on the stairs behind me as she arrives for her first cup. As soon as she appeared, the energy of the room shifted, became weighted and charged at the same time. As her daughters, it was our job to read her expressions and mannerisms so that we knew how to proceed. Did she need extra attention that morning or space to be alone? Did she need the little white pills she kept in a case in her purse? Did she need compliments, affection, or silence?

Reading those signs was important; if we made even one misstep, we'd pay for it. Maybe just a harsh scolding, or a pile of chores heaped on us, or the silent treatment, or maybe, the very worst, a character assassination—being told what horrible daughters we were and why. Those moments were the ones that left scars, the internal kind, our personalities growing and developing around the bumpy scar tissue so that we were never really rid of them.

Some mornings she came down and nothing was needed. She was feeling good, ready for the day, her spirits high, and everything in me would relax. I built my love for her around those moments, convincing myself that it was the real version of my mother, not the other, unpredictable one who could turn my whole world black with the flick of her tongue.

* * *

After forcing a piece of toast and some coffee into myself, I feel slightly better. I move to the washing machine in a fog and slowly pull out the wet sheets and towels. I'm relieved and surprised to find that the clothesline has survived; it still runs from a hook on the house to a tall pine tree on the other side of the yard. With the speed and agility of an eighty-year-old, I hang each item on the line and pin it into place. The task soothes me with its methodical movement, the quiet of outside and the warm sun on my back. *Just keep busy*, I tell myself.

A wall of linens is created, blowing in the soft breeze, dissecting the yard down the middle. The task exhausts me, so I lie down on the grass, right underneath a white sheet that hangs only an inch or so above me. It moves gently back and forth, changing my view of the sky second by second.

The grass under my hands is still damp from the dew and gently soaks my back. I imagine sinking down into the dirt below, so deep I can no longer see the sky; so deep my breath is buried. I imagine the worms feasting on my skin and bones, ingesting the grief that's in every piece of me. Those sad worms then become food for the birds. The birds ingest my grief in turn, then fly it out into the world and spread a plague of sorrow.

Tears bite at the back of my throat. I sit up before they can become full-blown. *Move,* some part of my brain screams. Pushing myself up off the ground, I swat the white sheet away and start running—across the lawn, around to the front of the cottage, until I find the faintest trace of the path that once led all the way around the island.

I run as fast as I can, slowing only to navigate tree roots, fallen branches, rocks, and the odd small bush that has grown up over time. My atrophied muscles tighten and pop, the loose flesh around them shaking until a hot itch spreads across my skin. My lungs expand and pull in the fresh air, stinging with the effort. The pounding of my blood echoes the pounding of my feet on the soft earth.

I used to run five times a week; I even did a half marathon every year. There's been no running since May died. Mourning has become my full-time job; I'd forgotten that running is a cure. My body protests the sudden onslaught of movement but celebrates it at the same time.

I don't stop until I'm at the other side of the island. It's not a long distance, maybe only a mile, but in that short time I've cleared away the fog and outrun my self-pity. The sweat dripping from my forehead and trickling down the inside of my T-shirt is cleansing, as though emotion has been released through my pores.

Squatting down on the rocky shore, I splash some cool lake water onto my face, let the water lap up onto my running shoes, wait for my breath to slow. Every muscle in my body is singing, and a warm calm has arrived after the sudden explosion of endorphins.

I stand up, ready to run back, and notice that another, more discernible path runs away from the shore and right into the forest. It actually looks like it might have been used recently; the ground is well worn, and nothing grows across it. Following it into the trees, I expect to find remnants of a bonfire, discarded beer cans, maybe condoms. Evidence of young people who realized the island was deserted and made it their personal outdoor party spot.

The path ends in front of a tree about fifty feet in. Right away I notice a small cross made out of sticks, stuck in the ground at the base of a tree. It looks like a child made it, so maybe it was part of some game May and I played when we were younger. There are bound to be surprises, things forgotten after so many years.

Nonetheless, I give the cross a little kick, just hard enough to send it into a pile of leaves a few feet away. Religion's never really been my thing, but since May's car accident my indifference to it has developed into full-blown resentment.

It was the cards I got when people found out she'd died: distant family members who had never even known her telling me she was in God's hands now or that I should trust in God and his plan for May. It did nothing to console me, only made me angry.

I leave the clearing, happy to escape the creepy feeling it gives me, and run back at a much slower pace, stopping now and again to clear away branches and pull free some of the vegetation that's grown in on the path. If I work at it, I may be able to get the whole path back to its original form in a couple of days. I imagine running laps around the island, the water and the trees as my scenery. The thought ignites a tiny flame of pleasure. One simple run and it's changed my mood completely.

Simple tasks, movement, being in nature—that's what's going to save me, I tell myself. I was right to come here. I've created my own grief retreat, and I'll power my way through it until I can go home whole again. Or better yet, maybe fly the girls out here for part of their summer vacation. Leo's already booked them in at least two camps, basketball and tennis—he doesn't believe idle time is good for kids—but I'm sure I could convince him to let them come here for a week or two.

I start planning all the things we'll do together: sailing, days spent on the dock and evenings on the verandah talking, night swims, trips into town for greasy fries and cinnamon buns. The three of us will pick up right where May and I left off.

I return to the cottage feeling like a new person, the heaviness of my grief dissipated. The run combined with the prospect of bringing the girls here has done it. For the first time in a long time, I have something to look forward to.

With renewed energy, I decide to tackle cleaning the upstairs of the cottage. Moving up and down the hallway, clearing dead flies from windowsills, I relish the creak of the floorboards underfoot. Sweeping dust from the stairs, I breathe in the smell of warm wood in the cramped stairwell. As I go from room to room, I note the cool solidity of the metal doorknobs in my hand.

These things went unnoticed when I was young, but they defined this place to my senses. These are the characteristics that left their mark on me, as familiar as my mother's own voice once was, as my sister's sweet hot breath was when she leaned in to whisper a secret.

In my parents' room I pull the sheets and quilt off the bed and once again catch a whiff of my mother's scent beneath the smell of neglect and damp. I leave the bed stripped to air out the mattress and throw open a window to get some breeze flowing.

After removing a thick layer of dust from my mother's dresser—removing each perfume bottle, jar, lipstick tube, and hairbrush to wipe down the surface before carefully putting them all back exactly where they were—I move on to my father's side of the room.

The surface of his dresser is bare. Pulling open the top drawer, I'm surprised to find it still full of his socks and underwear. Seems strange that a man who took off in the night—abandoned his family, as my mother always told us—wouldn't take his socks and underwear. Especially since he left from here and apparently never went back to our family home in Boston.

I think of the search party for my father that Jim Junior mentioned at the marina. Was there more to his disappearance than my mother ever told us? The question fits right alongside the mystery of why she said she'd sold Avril Island when she hadn't. You don't grow up thinking your mother is a liar, so when you come to understand that she just may have been one, everything in your world becomes suspect. Which makes me wonder: are there even more lies that my mother told us about Avril Island and my father?

Balling up the dirty bedding and leaving my parents' bedroom, I decide to take a trip back to the marina. I'll ask Jim if he knows anything more about the search for my father. I'm going to need to know the secrets of Avril Island if she's truly going to be mine again.

*　*　*

I steer the boat into an empty slip at the marina. Jim is busy with another customer, so I tie up on my own and go stand by the office door. I'm nervous but not sure exactly why.

"Back for more supplies?" Jim asks, once he's finished with the other customer and comes over to greet me.

"No, not quite. I was actually wondering, Jim—do you have any information about when my father disappeared? About the search?"

Jim seems taken aback by the question. Takes his hat off and scratches at a bug bite on his forehead. "To be honest, Ms. Bennett, I don't remember much about that time. I was a rowdy teenager back then, not too fussed about adult problems, if you know what I mean."

My heart sinks. "That's okay, Jim. I have two teenagers myself and can completely understand. It's a strange request, I know," I continue, hoping my honesty might jog his memory. "But you see, my mother told me and my sister that my father left. There was never any mention of a search or that it could be anything more than a man taking off on his wife."

There's confusion and sympathy in Jim's eyes, which makes me realize how strange it was that my mother would rather have us think our father was an asshole who took off than remember him as a great man who had something bad happen to him.

I'm starting to wish I'd never come when his features suddenly brighten and he claps his hands together. "I think I might have the answer. My dad, he kept a scrapbook of all the newspaper clippings about events around town." He motions for me to follow him into the office.

Reaching high up on a bookshelf packed with binders, carboard boxes, and the odd book, Jim pulls down a brown, leather-bound photo album. "This would be it," he says, placing it on the counter in front of me. The sound of a boat approaching draws his attention to the window. "Take your time with it. I'll just go help this customer."

The pages of the book are covered with newspaper clippings, no bit of the paper underneath left visible. I flip past articles on cottages being broken into over the summer, on the drowning of a little boy at the beach, on a storm that caused thousands of dollars in damages. There are obituaries from people Jim Senior must have known and stories about business openings and closings, bar fights, and how the recession affected tourism and the locals.

Jim Senior's love for his community sits right here in this meticulous preservation of his town's current events. As touching as it is, I flip forward until I find articles from 1991, the year my father disappeared. There are two whole pages dedicated to the frigid temperatures and record-breaking snowfalls of that winter. Just when I feel my frustration rising, I turn the page and the words *Avril Island* jump right out at me. I've found what I'm looking for.

I skim the headlines: *Summer Resident Disappears Without a Trace; Where Is Simon Bennett? Avril Island Affair Gone Wrong; Local Man Connected to Simon Bennett's Disappearance; Search for Avril Island's Owner Continues.*

My mouth is suddenly very dry, and I'm finding it hard to focus on the words in front of me. How did all of this happen without me ever knowing? It feels as though I've stumbled into some alternate, more sinister version of my life.

The bell over the door jangles, startling me out of my shock, and Jim steps inside the office. "Find what you're looking for?" His cheerfulness makes a surreal contrast to what is going on inside me.

"I did, actually." I force lightness into my voice. "But I was wondering, Jim. Would you mind if I borrowed the scrapbook for the night? Just so I can take my time with it." I give the book a pat. "There's so much history in here; would hate to miss anything."

"Of course. Take it for as long as you'd like. My dad would be right tickled to know someone's appreciating his handiwork."

"Thank you so much, Jim. I promise to take good care of it."

"My absolute pleasure, Ms. Bennett," he says, as I follow him out of the office.

"Please call me June," I scold, once we're back out on the dock. "Every time you call me Ms. Bennett, I feel like my mother." He laughs and holds up both hands in apology.

"Did you say June Bennett?" I turn at the question and see a man bent over in the act of tying up his boat while at the same time staring right at me.

He stands up, and I can't help but notice how handsome he is—tall, slim, tanned, with dark hair and sharp blue eyes. I'm guessing he's somewhere around my age. I feel like I should know him, but I can't put my finger on why.

"Yes. I *am* June Bennett. Do I know you?" I ask, sounding aloof, but mostly because I'm totally intimidated by his good looks.

"June!" he says in response. "It's me, Ezra. Ezra Keen." He points at his chest, but the name doesn't fit this person in front of me.

Back in the day we had a caretaker for the island, West Keen. He often brought his son, Ezra, along to help. That boy is locked in my brain somewhere around adolescence. I've thought of him many times over the years, but always as the boy I knew—stripped T-shirt, dirty knees, a laugh that carried, and the softest lips I've ever known.

This man in his white T-shirt with his man muscles and arm hair, khaki shorts, and clean knees—how could this be my Ezra?

He takes a step forward. "June?" he says again.

I look down at his feet—they're bare. It's this detail that makes me believe his identity. Ezra never wore shoes anywhere, not even into town.

I look back at his face, study the laugh lines, the stubble on his face that has hints of gray in it. I look right into his eyes, and that's where I find the boy I knew. The blue is just as deep, the look just as expectant and open, as if he's waiting for me to catch up, just like he always did.

"My god." The words breathe right out of me. "Ezra."

As though my recognition finally brings permission, he leans in to give me a hug. I return it awkwardly, one hand still clutching the thick scrapbook. "I'm sorry. I didn't recognize you at first." I try to explain my rudeness away.

He shrugs. "It's fine. I mean." He shoves a hand through his thick, messy hair. "It's been almost thirty years."

"Well I'll be," Jim says, reminding me of his presence. "A real live reunion. You both knew each other back in the day, did you?"

Ezra nods, his eyes still trained on my face. "When I was a kid, I used to go with my dad when he was working over at Avril Island, and that's how June and I became friends." He gives his head a shake. "What are you doing back after all these years?"

I go to give him a stock answer, but something stops me. I want to tell Ezra the truth, but not here in the middle of the marina dock with Jim listening in. I owe Ezra more than that. He meant something to me a long time ago, and I feel it once again give a tug on my heart.

"It's a long story," I say instead. "You should come out to the island for a drink, and we'll catch up."

A wide smile spreads across his handsome face. "I'd really like that." I give Ezra my cell number, and he sends me a text right there to make sure we're connected.

"All right then," I say. "I'll be sure to contact you."

"Please do, June," he says, with a sincerity that can't be faked. "I'd really love to have a visit. It's been so long. Too long."

"I definitely will." I give a quick nod. "So until then." Turning in the direction of my boat, I call over my shoulder one last thank-you to Jim for the scrapbook. Then I untie my boat and slowly back out of the boat slip while trying to ignore the nervous fluttering running all through me, brought on by the sight of Ezra Keen.

*   *   *

Ezra and I have history. He was my first kiss, but before that he was my best summer friend. West brought him every time he came to the island to do work, which felt to me like every day. Ezra would help his dad unload his tools or whatever equipment he needed for the day, and then the two of us would go off to explore the island. We built forts together, caught frogs, started tiny bonfires and then drowned them with lake water, had underwater breath-holding contests, played endless games of Scrabble and Uno, put on silly plays on the verandah—essentially, we did all the things kids at cottages do.

May was fond of Ezra too, but she floated in and out of our time together as it suited her, spending most of her time taking photographs or looking for things to take photographs of or studying the photographs she'd already taken.

There was a special kind of intensity to my friendship with Ezra. When we were nine, we went into the woods and held a secret ceremony. Using Ezra's jackknife, we cut into the soft flesh of our palms and then grasped each other's hands to become blood siblings. We vowed to stay friends forever, never keep secrets from each other, and always tell the truth.

When I turned ten and started going to sailing and tennis lessons, things changed. It was a place where Ezra was not allowed to follow; I knew that even without asking. I made new friends, kids from other cottages. Ezra still came around, but he was fit in between my lessons and other friends.

The summer I was eleven, it became pretty obvious to both of us that our friendship would not survive class distinctions and getting older. Ironically, it was the summer of our first and last kiss. It was raining that day. West was there to fix a cupboard door that kept falling off its hinges. Ezra and I sat out on the verandah on the glider. We rocked back and forth, not saying anything, just staring out into the trees, listening to the hypnotic squeak of the glider's metal mechanism.

"Koda died," he finally said, out of the blue.

I braced my feet against the floor to stop the swinging and sat up so I could see him better. "What? Why didn't you tell me right away?" Koda was his dog, and Ezra had brought him to the island more than a few times.

Ezra shrugged, and I knew he was holding back tears. I leaned in and gave him a big hug. He gripped me right back. We stayed like that for a few seconds, and then he pulled free but kept one arm around me.

"It's the summer of losing things," he said, with the seriousness of a wise old man. I didn't know how to answer, so I leaned in and put my lips on his. It wasn't a proper kiss, just lips on lips, but I inhaled his breath and tasted whatever he'd had for lunch that day. I pushed into the fullness of his mouth, wanting more of it, thinking I'd never felt anything so soft in my life. Then I heard a click. I pulled out of the kiss and spotted May hiding among the trees, taking our picture.

I sprang up from my spot on the glider and chased after her, throwing pinecones at her back as she fled into the woods. Ezra sat laughing at us both, and as was always the way with him, I couldn't help but laugh too.

We never talked about the kiss. The following summer, my last summer up here, he didn't come out to the island with West anymore. I saw him in town once with a group of local kids. They were hanging out at the beach; I was with my sailing friends at the ice cream stand. He waved. I waved back. My friends asked me who he was. I said, "Nobody," and a sliver of guilt lodged itself in my heart that has been there ever since.

*   *   *

As soon as I get back to the island, I pour myself a glass of wine and sit down with Jim Senior's scrapbook at the kitchen table. The first couple of articles don't really say anything conclusive about my father's disappearance, just the date he was last seen, who he was, when the search happened. The one new bit of information for me is that apparently my mother called local police a few days after my father left to tell them she suspected that there could be foul play involved. At that point we were already back in Boston, coming to terms with the fact that my father had abandoned us, not aware at all that the police were out searching for my missing father. Which one was the lie?

I take a long sip of wine and push on. The next article is downright shocking. I read it three times through to make sure I really understand what I'm reading. It alludes to the possibility of infidelity between my mother and West, our caretaker, Ezra's father. No wonder my mother protected us from this kind of press. A photo of West being led into the police station for questioning accompanies the article. Apparently, he was a suspect. I push the scrapbook away, my head reeling.

It's obviously just small-town gossip. I would have known if my mother had been having an affair with West. He was here almost every day, and we were all close to him. I loved West like he was part of my family. A twist of nausea shoots through my stomach. I realize I haven't eaten anything since breakfast, and the wine is not sitting well on my empty stomach.

Throwing together some cheese and crackers, I stand at the counter, eating them robotically, my mind traveling over everything I just read. I had no idea West was implicated in my father's disappearance. Did Ezra know? I look at the time—only quarter to seven. Reasonable enough time to invite him for a drink. Might come across as a bit desperate, I think to myself, but to be honest, I am. Pulling out my phone, I take some time composing a text, trying my best to sound casual and a little indifferent.

He writes back right away, thanking me for the invite, saying he'd love to, he just has to finish making his mom some dinner and then he'll be come by. Reading it over, I can't help but smile at his honest enthusiasm at the invitation. Then I chide myself for playing my own game of nonchalance. Ezra doesn't play games, so neither should I.

After grabbing a few carrots to shove in my mouth while I wait, I sit back down at the table and read the last article on the page. It's titled *Where Is West Keen Now?* Apparently, he disappeared shortly after my father did. The article claims that West's absence more or less confirms his guilt in the case of my father's disappearance. With no body, however, there were no charges to be made.

I sit back, drink the rest of my wine, and stare straight ahead in a quiet stupor. Ezra's dad went missing as well? Did he ever come back? Does that mean he actually did have something to do with my father's disappearance?

The buzzing of my phone interrupts the unanswered questions. It's Ezra, saying he's on his way. An unexpected kaleidoscope of butterflies swarm my belly. "My god, June, get a grip," I say to myself out loud, then get up from the table to go brush my teeth and put on some makeup. Something I haven't done for ages.

With a glass of wine in hand for fortification, I make my way down to the dock to meet Ezra. He pulls his boat in with expert ease, hopping out to tie up before I even have the chance to help. He's changed into jeans but is still barefoot and achingly good-looking.

"Sorry if I put you on the spot with such short notice," I say, once he's done tying up.

"Not at all, June. I was really happy to get your text. I mean, it's already been thirty years—why wait any longer to catch up?"

"Have you been here this whole time, on Lake Champlain?" I ask, wanting to get right down to the interrogation but knowing I'll need to lead up to it.

He looks out over the lake, squinting his eyes against the sun that's only just beginning its descent. "Aside from a few vacations, I never left."

"Well, I can see why. It's beautiful up here." Everything that comes out of my mouth sounds so fake and self-conscious.

He turns to look at me again. "It is, but that's not why I stayed." I can tell by the heaviness in his eyes that there's a lot of history behind his statement.

I gesture toward the cottage. "Shall we go up for a drink?"

He holds up his empty hands. "I didn't bring anything. I thought about grabbing a bottle of wine, but I wasn't sure you drank, and even if you did, I was worried it might look a bit presumptuous showing up with an entire bottle of wine, as though I was planning on outstaying my welcome. I'm sorry."

The pleading look of apology in his eyes makes me laugh. I put a hand on his arm. "It's fine—my god, Ezra—totally fine. No need to overthink." He puts his hand over my mine, and it's warm and rough and sends a jolt of feeling into the rest of my body. I slide my hand out from under his and take a step back, afraid of what he's stirring in me.

"Okay then," he says, not seeming to notice my withdrawal. "No more overthinking, I promise."

Walking up the path to the cottage, Ezra mentions May's car accident, says how sorry he is that she passed away, how he remembers how close we were and how hard it must have been for me to lose her.

His words cause explosions of red light behind my eyes. I haven't had to deal with other people's condolences and empty-sounding words for a while, and it blindsides me. I thank him and quicken my pace. I don't ask how he heard about it but quickly change the subject before the grief catches up with me and I have to tell him to leave so I can be alone with it.

"White or red?" I ask, once we're inside.

"Do you have any beer?"

"Aw, nope. Sorry. I only have limited supplies."

"Which include both red and white wine?" he asks, with a playful smile.

I pretend to be abashed. "It's called prioritizing." He laughs that laugh that carries, and there's the hint of what we used to be like together.

"I'll have white, please," he says, pulling out a chair to sit at the table.

I go to the cupboard to get down another glass and pour us both some wine. When I turn, I catch him watching me. Not in that creepy, objectifying, you-can-practically-see-into-their-dirty-mind kind of way; more of a study, as though he's trying to teach himself this new adult version of me.

He looks away as soon as I catch his eye and notices the scrapbook still sitting on the table. "What's this?" he asks.

Placing a glass of wine in front of him, I sit down at the table. "I actually wanted to talk to you about some things, Ezra. Some things I read in that scrapbook."

MAY

June is sitting at the kitchen table with a man I don't recognize. They both have glasses of wine, and June is showing him some newspaper clippings in a scrapbook. There's a new kind of intensity about June. She wants something from this man; I can feel it.

I zoom in, and the man looks away from June and into the space where I am. Like he senses me there. His eyes, they tell me who he is. Ezra—West's son. Memories of him suddenly flood me. He, June, and I spent a lot of time together on this island. We used to play hide-and-seek, have diving contests, and play epic games of Monopoly. I can't for the life of me remember the last time I saw him.

"So let me understand this," Ezra says to June. "You had no idea about the search for your father, about his disappearance?"

She gives an exaggerated shrug. "My mother told us they had an argument and then he ran off in the middle of the night. All her life she maintained that our father abandoned us."

A bitter-sounding chuckle escapes Ezra. "Funny, those are the same words my mom uses about my dad—'abandoned us.' "

"So West disappeared as well?"

Ezra gives his head a shake. "He disappeared ten days after your own dad disappeared." This bit of news surprises me. I actually remember how much West loved Ezra and this lake, and I can't imagine any reason that would make him leave either of them.

"And he hasn't been back since?" June asks, and Ezra shakes his head. "Like, you haven't even heard from him?"

"Nope. No sign of him in thirty years."

"My god, Ezra. I'm so sorry. I had no idea at all about any of this." She taps the scrapbook with one finger. "This is the first I'm hearing about any of the things that went on back then, and I feel like my whole world is turning upside down."

I move in to have a look at the open scrapbook and see that it's a collection of articles about my father disappearing. I try to remember the time around them, to call forth some memories, but strangely, nothing comes up.

"So," June says, leaning in even closer to Ezra, "just let me get this timeline right. My father disappeared"—she air-quotes the last three words—"there was a search, and your father was called in for questioning about it, since he was our caretaker and here all the time. Then he went missing just over a week after my father did?" Ezra gives a slow nod, and there's hesitancy in his expression. June notices it too. "What aren't you telling me?"

He takes a sip of his wine. "Well, you know it was more than just the fact that he was the caretaker here?" June shakes her head, sincere confusion in her eyes. "You don't know?" Ezra's words make the space I hang in buzz. "About the affair?" He pauses to study her reaction. She stares back at him blankly. "Between my dad and your mom. It went on for years, apparently."

June glances over at the scrapbook and doesn't say anything for several seconds. "I saw something about an affair mentioned in an article, but I just assumed it was small-town gossip."

"It wasn't just gossip, June." His words are blunt, and there's a trace of anger behind them. It's obvious that he's still hurting from all of it.

"I had no idea," she says, before mechanically lifting her glass and draining every last bit of her wine.

A memory breaks free from the depths and slowly rises to the surface. I questioned my mother about the affair only once. I was thirteen, that age when the mind is naturally drawn to things like love, attraction, and the illicit. When gray areas appear where once everything was black and white. When parents become fallible.

I asked her if she was in love with West. She acted affronted, told me I should be careful of what I accused people of. She said that after everything she'd done for me and my sister, it was just cruel to think so low of her. Something was thrown in there about all the sacrifices she'd made for us girls before she dropped the dishcloth in the sink and retreated to her room.

I followed her, apologizing profusely, as we'd learned to do, but she shut the door in my face. An hour or so later she came out, looking wounded but stoic. She made us a dinner of eggs on toast and somehow managed to get herself dressed and over to the resort for the evening. We didn't speak about it again.

My suspicions hadn't come from catching them in the act or anything like that. I'd caught moments of something that, when added up, were hard to dispute. I was the one who roamed the island with a camera round my neck, sitting for hours on a rock hidden by trees so that I could get the perfect shot of a bird or the sunlight—or my mother and her lover. And I'd kept it from June. Believing I was protecting her from something. That she didn't need to know that side of my mother.

Maybe it was a mistake to do that. In the end, I haven't protected her from anything. And finding this truth out for the second time feels just as bad as it did the first time.

*　*　*

Ezra visibly winces. "I'm sorry," he says. "I thought the affair was common knowledge." June gives a quick shake of her head. Ezra goes to say something, then stops, thinks about it, and says, "You never even suspected?"

She stares into her empty wineglass, pondering the question. "I guess now that I think about it, I'm not totally shocked." She looks up at him with a tight smile on her face. "I actually feel a bit stupid that it never dawned on me." She rolls her eyes at herself. "My mother said we couldn't tell my father how often West was coming here to do work. She said it was because my father didn't want to pay a lot of money. That she needed his help more than my father realized, which in itself should have set off alarm bells. I just never thought of them that way. Of my . . ." She trails off.

She gets up from the table, emptying what remains of the white wine into her glass, opening a whole new bottle and then bringing it back to the table with her. "Now, is this just rumor you're going on, or did you actually witness something?"

"Both, I guess. There was one time that made me think there might be something going on." He wipes the condensation off his wineglass, trying his hardest not to meet June's eyes.

"What happened exactly?" she pushes.

"Are you sure you want to get into this now?"

"No," June answers. "But that doesn't mean you shouldn't tell me."

Ezra looks like he wishes the ground would open up and swallow him, but he takes a deep breath and launches into the explanation June is demanding. "You know how your mother was up here on her own in the fall when you guys went back to school?"

June nods. "She always said she needed time and solitude to close the place up properly," she explains.

"Well, one of those times I came out with my dad to cut the grass and put the dock furniture away," Ezra continues. "My father hadn't wanted to bring me, but my mother insisted. They actually got in a fight about it. Probably because she suspected what was going on and thought me being here would mean nothing happened," he explains. "We got here, and my dad said he had to do some work inside and told me to cut the grass. When I was done, I came into the kitchen to get a glass of water. I was standing at the counter drinking it when they came down the stairs. They were both laughing, and—" He stops and studies June's face.

"And what?" June asks impatiently.

"My dad was doing up his pants."

"How old were you? And what did they say?" June asks, sounding almost frantic.

"I was around eleven, I think. And they didn't say anything, just tried to act natural, and I went back outside."

June nods her head slowly as she mulls his story over. I wonder if she's going to try to find holes in it as well. "Did your mother know?" She finally asks.

Ezra shrugs. "She denied it was true when it came out in the papers. Said it was just malicious small-town rumors, but I overheard arguments between her and my father, and it was pretty clear that she knew and had known for some time."

June gets up suddenly from the table and walks right through me. I absorb the confusion and anger that's running through her veins. I also smell her, so strongly, as though I'm right up against her skin—forest and sweet sweat. I want to hold her there, but it's a fleeting sensation and she's across the room, leaving me empty again. She finds some open space to pace back and forth in while she processes all of it.

"I'm sorry, June. This must come as a real shock to you," Ezra apologizes again.

June lifts a hand to bat away his words; she was never very good with other people's sympathy. She stops pacing and leans on the counter, rubbing a hand across her forehead. I notice the fresh tan on her long fingers.

"To be honest," she says, "the fact that they were having an affair does make it all seem more suspicious—my father disappearing without a trace and then your father disappearing once accused of something."

Ezra sits up straighter in his chair, and I see him visibly tense up. "It does, but my dad didn't have anything to do with your dad's disappearance." He gestures toward June dismissively. "And now, hearing the version your mom told you makes me think she called the police to stir up trouble to get back at my dad. That she knew all along that your dad just took off."

"Then why did your dad run?" June says, her words instantly pitting them against each other.

Ezra picks up his glass and gulps down the rest of his wine, then stands up. "I think I should go. I'm not rehashing this bullshit again thirty years later just because you're late to the party. My dad is innocent and always has been."

June steps forward and puts a hand on his arm to keep him there. "I'm sorry, Ezra. Don't go. Please. I'm just trying to understand what really happened. It all feels so crazy to me."

Ezra's expression softens, and he sinks back down into his chair. "I can only imagine what it would be like to be learning all of this years later." He sighs. "I'm sorry I snapped. I just spent so long feeling like I had to defend my dad, it's my default setting."

June grabs the bottle of wine and refills Ezra's glass and her own, then sits back down at the table. "Here's the version I was told by my mother: my dad took off because he was a weak-willed coward, and she sold Avril Island because we needed the extra money with him gone. That's literally all I knew about the time in our history."

"She told you that she sold this place?" Ezra asks in disbelief.

June nods and drinks greedily from her glass. "Why do you think West left, if he wasn't actually, you know"—she pauses, taking time with her words—"guilty of anything?"

Ezra shrugs. "I don't know. All that I do know for sure is that my mom kind of lost it when my dad disappeared. Became a bit unhinged from reality. Some days she's quite lucid, but other days it's hard to tell she's even in there or understands what she's talking about."

June spreads her fingers forward on the table as though she wants to take Ezra's hand, but she doesn't. "I can't believe I didn't know any of this. That you were here going through some entirely separate reality but one directly connected to me."

"Why do you think your mom said she sold the place when she didn't?" Ezra asks. "I heard that there were offers over the years, but she always turned them down."

June scrunches her face in confusion. "I don't know. I even asked her if we could come back to get our things. I wanted to say good-bye to this place. Mostly I just wanted to see it one more time. Memorize every tree, every rock, every . . ." She trails off, picks at a knot in the wooden table with great focus. She's trying not to cry. I know the signs well. She clears her throat. "Whenever I asked, she'd say maybe. Then one day I asked and she told me it was too late. That she'd sold it to another family."

"Maybe because the place reminded her of your dad?" Ezra offers.

June laughs. "This place was all my mother. She ruled it, and he got to visit on weekends. And now I know how well that suited her." She throws her hands up. "She was sleeping with your father." June suddenly looks angry. She stops talking and stares into her wineglass as though she might find comfort there.

"Maybe I should go," Ezra says, after a few seconds of silence. "I've dropped a lot in your lap here. You probably need time to think things over."

June gives her head a shake as though to clear it. "My god. I feel horrible. All we've done is talk about my dad's disappearance. I haven't learned anything new about you." She takes a quick sip of wine and forces a smile. "Are you married? Common law? Divorced? Kids?" she asks.

He shakes his head. "None of the above."

June puts on a fake grimace. "So, you're a single, forty-one-year-old virgin still living at home?"

I'm appalled at June's rudeness, but I know she's just attempting to use humor to lighten the mood. To get herself back on solid footing.

He's a good sport, though, and laughs it off. "Everything but the virgin part is unfortunately true."

"Well, I'm a forty-year-old divorcée who just found out that her mother had an affair and lied to her most of her life who's staying all alone on an island and is almost drunk and it's not even nine thirty."

Ezra holds up his glass. "Here's to our forties." June clinks him, and they both drink. "What about May? Was she married with kids?" he asks, after putting his glass down on the table.

June takes a deep breath. "No, neither." I'm grateful she doesn't expound. I'm not ready to hear her version of my life with all its failures. A natural silence inserts itself between them. They both seem lost in thought.

I can feel June's emotions flatlining as she works to disconnect herself from everything she's just learned. It's something she's always been good at, which meant I had to cry for both of us.

Ezra pushes away from the table. "Well, I think I've done enough damage here for the time being. Maybe we can have a less intense catch-up the next time." He stands, and June doesn't try to stop him. "Thanks for the wine," he says. "I promise to reciprocate, now that I know you like to get drunk."

June laughs her real laugh and nods. "Sounds like a plan, my friend." I can feel the warmth she has for him. She doesn't give it away very easily, and even after all this time, he still has it.

"So I can come by and see you again?" he asks.

"Of course," June answers without any hesitation. "I'd really like that."

He's on his way to the door when June calls out, "Hey, Ezra." He turns back. "I was curious. Do you know who's been checking on the place all this time? The grass has obviously been cut over the years. And I mean, someone must have been taking care of it to some degree."

"Me," Ezra answers, point-blank. "It was just something I started doing awhile back. Seemed like the right thing."

June nods. "Well, thank you for that. I'd tell you to send the bill to my mother, but she's dead." Another one of June's inappropriate jokes to break the tension.

Ezra chuckles, but his eyes are full of sympathy. He gives a little wave as he pushes his way through the screen door.

I want to hang on, to be alone with June, but I can feel the fading start, as though the breeze from the open door is blowing my loosely knit particles apart. June puts her head down on the table, resting it on her folded arms. I push in to see if she's crying, but it's no use. My time is up.

JUNE

After Ezra leaves, I sit on the couch and stare into space, my mind swimming through memories of our time at Avril Island, trying to capture evidence of this affair my mother had.

I know infidelity well. It's making excuses to have the place to yourself. It's finding reasons for frequent escape. It's lies and always trying to stay one step ahead of everybody. It's being distracted by thoughts of your lover. It's stolen moments and then returning home sick with guilt.

I think of all the times my mother sent us into town to buy only one or two items, but they were "of utmost importance." Of the many nights she stole away in the boat. The way her mood changed when my father arrived for the weekend—her laughter didn't come as quickly and she was tense and short-tempered, quarreling easily with him if he asked too many questions.

It's sad to say, but it's not hard to place my mother in the role of adulterer. Her longing for something more was palpable. *I wanted so much more than this*—at times she'd come right out and say it.

West, on the other hand, is a stretch. He was such a kind and gentle man, more comfortable working outside in nature than indoors. Growing up, I thought he was the perfect dad to

Ezra. Quick to forgive, always reaching for his boy to pull him close or ruffle his dark hair. A man easy to love but not easy to corrupt, I would have thought.

Then again, it would have been my mother doing the corrupting. Beautiful, charming, smart, and calculated, she could have corrupted an entire monastery of monks if she'd put her mind to it. Even as a child I noticed the lingering looks men gave her. The extra attention they paid her, repaid with a hand on the chest, a wink, a slow smile, laughter. I didn't think there was anything illicit about it at the time. I grew up thinking it was simply the way men and women interacted—that the whole point of men was to pay you attention. Without it, you didn't really exist.

My phone rings, breaking the trance I'm in. It's the girls. I shake off the feeling that I'm adrift on an island full of lies and secrets and put on a brave and cheery front when I answer the phone.

They've just gotten home from school. Bea is grumpy because she got an A minus on a test. Madeline is grumpy because she's fourteen. I wonder why they even bothered to call. Neither one is enthused about my plan for them to come stay with me for part of their summer vacation, and I have to answer a dozen or so questions about the availability of Wi-Fi, other kids their age in the area, duration of stay, how bad the bugs are, is it boring, what you do when it rains, whether they can bring a friend or not.

Somehow I resist the urge to scream into the phone that I just found out my mother was an adulterer and lied to me most of my life and so I don't give a fuck about Wi-Fi. Instead I patiently answer their questions, appalled at how spoiled they suddenly seem to me, and get off the phone as soon as I can, professing how much I miss them. Even from across the country they're able to suck the life right out of me.

I don't know if I'm really that well suited to motherhood, even after all these years. I didn't even think about having kids when I was younger. May was the one who played with dolls, the one who always said, *When I'm a mom, I'm going to . . .*

It was Leo who planted the seed in my head. He'd been the editor of my novel back when I was twenty-three. I was one of those rare cases in publishing—an overnight success. Leo, being familiar with the business and three years older than me, helped me navigate the unexpected fame, the book tours, the lectures, the awards and parties.

It was an intense, passionate relationship. I mistook his understanding of my writing as understanding of me and naïvely thought I'd met my soul mate. We eloped. I was only twenty-four. He talked about babies, about having a family. I got caught up in the idea, and before I knew it I was the mother of twin girls, my writing career had come to a complete halt, and I was spending my days being a wife and mother. I never resented the girls for it, though; I resented myself for giving up too easily.

*   *   *

Once I'm off the phone, the silence of the cottage pulses all around me as though it's holding its breath, hoping I won't notice the secrets spread throughout. Hoping I won't open its cupboards and drawers to go searching.

I push up off the couch, easily shedding the bad-mother feeling that the phone call gave me, and head upstairs to go looking for proof of my mother's affair.

I go through every drawer in my parents' room but don't find anything of significance. What I do find is a photo of my mother that May took. It's in the drawer of the bedside table that my father used. A candid shot, reminding me of how May used to sneak around this island, stealing moments from all of us with her camera. *It's more dramatic when you don't know it's being taken*, she'd say, in an attempt to justify the unapproved shots. We all found it extremely annoying, but I realize now that some of her photos might hold the clues I'm looking for.

May used to keep all of her cottage photos in an old suitcase in her room. It's not out in the open, so I go to her closet. A handful of dresses and a terry cloth robe still hang there. I can't resist the urge to bring the robe to my face and breathe in its scents—mothballs and suntan lotion.

A vision of May walking down the path to the lake in front of me, wearing that robe over her bathing suit, instantly comes to mind. The morning sun is high and the lake is like glass, and we are wasting no time getting there. We will spend the day in and out of the water and stretched out in the sun on lounge chairs and leave the dock only when the sun is fading. I let the robe go, the pain of the memory slicing through me too deep to let me linger there.

Pushing the clothing to either side, I don't find the suitcase, so I go to the next logical place: under the bed. Crouching down on the floor, I lift the quilt, and sitting there, tucked just out of plain view, is the suitcase. I'm surprised she didn't take it with her. She was always so particular about her photos.

I lay the suitcase on the coffee table in the living room but decide it would be better opened with a glass of wine. On my way to the kitchen to get one, I notice my parents' old record player and record collection. My mother loved music of all kinds, from Miles Davis to Patsy Cline and the Beatles to Frank Sinatra and Van Morrison.

I'm not sure it will still work, due to lack of use and years of damp, but I choose a Dave Brubeck album anyway, carefully place it on the turntable, and pull the arm back. It clicks into motion, and when I set the needle down, music fills the room. I feel the whole cottage sigh with pleasure. How long has she waited to hear music again?

Sick of the white wine I was drinking earlier, I grab one of the bottles of red from the storage room, throw some more crackers and cheese slices on a plate for my dinner, and head back to the living room.

The sun has set and there's a slight chill to the room, so before sitting down with the suitcase, I make a fire. Logs are still stacked against the side of the fireplace, kindling in the metal bin on the other side along with some old newspapers. It brings me back to the many times my mother sent me in here after dinner to build a fire on a cool or rainy evening. We'd all sit around it with jazz playing in the background, just like it is now. It was my mother's glass of wine on the table, though, not mine, and she'd be sitting in a chair reading while my sister and I played cards or a board game.

I was so safe and content back then, in my oblivion. Not knowing that behind the cover of her book, my mother's mind was most likely drifting to thoughts of West. I naïvely and egotistically thought that May and I were her main concern, that she didn't really have a life outside our family. As a child, you don't imagine that your parents are capable of ever making decisions that aren't in your best interest. As an adult, you realize your parents were human just as you are, and their mistakes along the way suddenly become illuminated by the phosphorescence of your own.

* * *

My hands tremble slightly as I flip open the clasps on the suitcase. The blue silk lining holds a mess of loose photos. The first photo I see is of a girl from sailing club. I remember her well. She came for only one summer, the cousin of one of the cottagers.

Her name was Kennedy. She had red hair that she always wore in a long braid, a Milky Way of freckles across both cheeks, and a deep, husky voice. When she laughed, she sounded like a seventy-year-old woman who smoked a pack a day.

The picture was taken on the sailing club dock, and there are boats lined up in the background. May has captured Kennedy mid-laugh. The girl was May's first crush, and they shared one brief kiss behind the sailing club. May was so scared of getting caught that it was all she could manage.

In high school, May finally got up the courage to tell my mother that she thought she liked girls instead of boys. My mother told her it was a phase and to keep it in check so as not to shame the family. May never spoke to my mother again about being gay.

May had a handful of secret relationships, telling only me about them, but none of them lasted. She just never found a way to escape the sense that she was doing something wrong, that she was dishonoring the family. Love can't grow from that kind of toxic soil. Even I know that.

I put the photo of Kennedy aside with the plan to tack it up in May's room. She wasn't able to bring it out of hiding, so I'll do it for her.

The next photo I pull out is coincidentally of me and Ezra and that one kiss we had on the front verandah. I study the smooth, tanned skin of Ezra's cheek and the way his dark hair curls up off his sweaty forehead.

Bringing it closer, I notice how our lips fit together just so and how I'd brought my hand to rest on his thigh, whereas his hands are clenched, one resting on the glider, the other at his side. Both of us have our eyes closed. The photo captures a raw innocence that magnifies the passage of time. Never again will I have so many firsts ahead of me. The children in the photo feel like strangers. I set it aside as well, to show Ezra when he comes back for a visit.

Pulling the photos together into a thick pile, I go through them one by one. A lot of them are of nature—rocks, the lake, sunsets, sunrises, trees, flowers, birds, insects. There are also a ridiculous amount of pictures of me—diving, tanning on the dock, making faces, swinging my tennis racket around, doing cartwheels, hiding behind a handful of cards. My mother is also a favorite subject of May's, but I don't find anything suspicious looking.

I find another one of me and Ezra; this one has West in it as well. We're all holding up jackknives and a piece of wood. I actually remember that day. Ezra and I had helped West put rocks into the dock crib, and as a reward he'd given us a wood-carving lesson.

We'd sat out on the front steps of the cottage. West had taken my hands in his to show me how to carve the wood without cutting myself. The rough calluses of his wide palms scratched the tops of my small hands, still soft and wrinkled from swimming for rocks.

In the photo, Ezra and I proudly hold up our carvings. He'd done a dog, its head too big for its body. I'd made a pretty good sailboat, and West had carved a bird.

Frustrated that I've found images of only the Avril Island that I already remember, I toss the photos back into the suitcase. Not thinking I'll actually find anything, I stick my hand into the flat compartment on the roof of the case. My fingers brush paper, and I reach in farther to pull out a medium-sized manila envelope wedged deep at the very bottom. As I slide it out, my heart beats just a little bit faster.

Inside is a small stack of photos, obviously ones that May didn't want out in the open. I take a big sip of my wine and ask myself if I'm really ready for the proof I've gone looking for. In truth, it's a rhetorical question. Who is ever ready to have their mother fall from grace? So many of us have to work too hard to keep our parents on their pedestal as it is.

The first photo is of my mother and West, standing at the end of the dock, their backs to the camera. My mother is leaning into West, pointing at something out on the water. There's a definite sense of familiarity between them and the skin of their bare arms is touching, but it's no declaration of an affair.

Not on its own. The next few photos, though, are similar, my mother and West engaged in some activity or discussion, their bodies leaning toward each other, always some part of them touching—both unaware that they're being captured.

The photo I flip to next leaves no room for dispute. It's deep in the forest of the island. They must have sneaked off to steal a moment together, not knowing May was tracking them. My mother is in West's arms, her hands on either side of his face as they go in for a kiss.

May knew all along. The fact hits me like a ton of bricks. Why else would she have hidden these photos? And why would they have been taken in the first place if she hadn't been looking for proof of something?

I reach for my wine and stare into the fire. The secret she kept is like a hot poker being pressed into the open wound left by her death. If she were alive, I'd pick up the phone and demand to know why she didn't tell me. We weren't supposed to have secrets from each other. We were supposed to suffer through it all together, or at least I thought that was the rule. She had no right to protect me from this.

The record ends, and the needle bumps up and down. I don't get up. I sit in the silence, trying not to feel betrayed by my dead sister. I can almost hear her voice: *I was only trying to protect you. Why should we both suffer?*

That idea settles the hurt down enough for me to get up and flip the record. I pour the remainder of the wine into my glass, not caring that I've drunk it way too fast and feel light-headed. Then I sit back down with the photos.

It takes me a few seconds to recognize the person in the next one. She has long black hair, which is lifting in the wind, and smooth, tanned skin that looks as though the sun radiates right from it. She's kneeling in our garden and looking to her right, away from the camera, showing her profile. Her green eyes are narrowed into slits and her mouth is pursed. At first I think it's because of the bright sun, but when I follow her gaze, I see that she's looking directly at my mother and West, who are standing in the corner of the yard, talking. It's Ezra's mom, Willa.

She came to the island with West now and again, mostly to help with gardening because she was good at it. Did she know about the affair in this photo, or was it just a budding suspicion? She always intimidated me. A wild and free kind of woman, she went everywhere in bare feet just like her son, could make flowers grow from sand, and seemed to see right into my soul every time she looked at me.

I told my mother once that I thought Willa was the most beautiful woman I'd ever seen. In reply, my mother told me that Willa thought she could talk to trees. That she was barren and that's why she and West had adopted Ezra, which proved that looks could be deceiving. Then my mother got angry at me for some trivial thing and sent me to my room. I didn't know then that it was pure jealousy talking. That my praise of Willa was like poking a rattlesnake with a stick.

I stare at the photo of Willa staring at my mother and West. How could my mother carry on like that under all our noses? Did she think everyone was too stupid to realize? The betrayal is bad enough, but it's just insulting that she didn't think she would be found out. You always get found out.

I toss all the photos onto the coffee table, and they fan out into an accordion of visual secrets. I'm emotionally drained, and a slow-moving headache is traveling across the top of my skull. *I should probably drink some water,* I think to myself while sliding into a fetal position on the couch. I pull a cushion up under my head and close my eyes, wanting escape more than anything. Escape from my longing for the Avril Island days of my youth, no cares and concerns weighing on my innocent mind. Wanting to be once again unaware that my mother was spinning all of us into a cocoon of lies and betrayal.

* * *

The next day, despite a bit of a hangover and the heavy weight of the secrets I learned the day before, I go out to the shed in the back to look for some tools to help clear the path around the island. I want to do mindless and productive work that will make me feel like I'm taking Avril Island back for myself, regardless of its sordid past. I'm thinking it's best to just let the past stay in the past and keep moving forward.

The inside of the shed smells of gasoline and damp earth. The tools are neatly hanging from hooks along one wall above an empty workbench. An ancient lawnmower sits in the corner along with some red gas tanks. I didn't come in here much as a kid. There was no need, with West around taking care of things.

I pull a rusty pair of pruning shears off the wall. It takes some work to open and close the blades, but eventually the rust is rubbed from the hinges and I can get it going at a good pace.

I go the same way I ran yesterday, since I already started on that side. There's something cathartic in hacking away at the overgrowth, and I quickly get lost in it.

By the time I make it to the other side of the island, there's a line of blisters across my right hand. The skin is pink and raw. How stupid was I not to think to wear gloves for this kind of work? Chucking the pruning shears on the ground, I soak my hands in the cool lake water, but all that does is deepen the sting. I decide to call it a day. I'll do the other side of the island tomorrow, hopefully after finding a pair of gloves.

Before heading back, I decide to check in on the tree where the cross was to see if there's any more evidence of people trespassing. An icy chill slides down my spine as soon as I step into the clearing. The cross is back, stuck into the dirt at the bottom of the tree. Somebody obviously retrieved it from the bushes where I kicked it. I would have preferred beer cans and condoms, signs of kids just having a good time.

"Hello," I call out. The sense of not being alone on this island is here again and stronger than ever. My voice bounces back to me, and a bird laughs from a tree above me. I turn in every direction, looking for clues of someone or something, but there's only forest in every direction.

I take my phone out and snap a photo of the cross before giving it a kick and sending it flying even farther this time. I take another photo of the tree without the cross, wanting a clear timeline of what's happened. Proof that I have indeed gotten rid of the cross. I'm sure it's just some young people messing with me, but there's been a lot of wine drinking on this island already, a lot of fuzzy moments, so documenting things seems like a good idea.

* * *

After bandaging up my blistered hands, I spend the better part of the afternoon cleaning lounge chairs that I found in the storage shed down by the lake. It takes a lot of scrubbing and I probably could have just gone out and bought some new ones, but it's important for me to keep busy.

By the time I'm finished, circles of sunburn pulse with heat on each exposed shoulder. The chairs are set up in a row just like they used to be, as though waiting for the rest of my family to come down and take their place.

I go for a quick swim and then sit back in one of the chairs to enjoy my handiwork and let the sun dry me. With my eyes closed, bright-orange flashes from the sun appear behind my lids.

I'm able to be still, drifting between the past and present, not allowing any one thing to stick with me other than the visceral sense of my surroundings then and now. It is a quiet, peaceful place, but only briefly. Heavy thoughts soon creep in, and I must get up and move once again. It's okay, though. I'm getting things done, building myself back up with each little accomplishment.

After May died, I spent weeks doing nothing. I wasn't sure I would ever feel the will to get out of bed and get back to life. I didn't know how to live without my sister. It was as if the moon had suddenly disappeared from the world and I was expected to create my own orbit cycle, control the tides, and know when it was night and when it was day. Being back here has given me new purpose and in a way has brought me back to May. I feel closer to her here, as though she's all around me.

*   *   *

Standing in front of the open fridge, I peer in at the limited collection of food I've curated. For the first time in a long time, I'm actually hungry. Hard work and a day outside are good for the appetite, my mother always used to say, even though I rarely saw her consume more than cocktails and cigarettes.

There's not much to put together for a nice dinner—just cold cuts, cheese, some raw vegetables, and a tub of dip. It looks like I planned for a picnic, not multiple nights at the cottage. I've just resigned myself to a tuna fish sandwich for dinner when I hear footsteps on the verandah.

"Hello? June?" Ezra calls through the screen door.

"Come in," I answer, leaving the kitchen to greet him.

As he steps into the cottage, I'm again shocked by his good looks. I'm not sure I'll ever get used to grown-up Ezra. He's wearing worn jeans with a brown leather belt and a blue T-shirt that glows against his tanned skin and deepens the color of his eyes. His dark hair is messy from the boat ride, and he clearly doesn't make shaving a priority, but on him it works—really well. I have to force my mind not to be illicit just looking at him.

He has a six-pack of beer in one hand and two grocery bags in the other. "I brought dinner." He holds everything up and smiles. It's that same open, up-for-anything smile that he had as a kid, and it makes me laugh. "Some steak, fresh bread, and salad."

"Sounds delicious, albeit quite presumptuous of you. Who says I haven't just finished a lovely meal myself?"

He moves right past me and into the kitchen. "Well, I saw inside that fridge of yours yesterday." I follow behind him and watch as he makes himself at home—putting away the beer and unpacking the food. "I also wanted to make up for dumping all that shit on you." He leans against the counter and looks at me, his eyes once again full of apology.

I wave a hand at him dismissively. "I asked you to come over, remember? I wanted to know more about the newspaper articles. And it's better I find out now than never."

He cocks his head to one side. "Are you sure about that?"

"Yes," I say, with a firmness I don't actually feel. "But more importantly, do you ever wear shoes?" I point at his feet, which are once again bare, hoping to change the conversation to lighter things.

He shrugs. "Why would I when I'm in and out of a boat constantly?"

"That's the Ezra logic I remember."

He glares at me but then laughs and goes to the fridge. "Would you like a beer, my dear?" He grabs two and holds one out to me. I take it, and we both twist our caps off. "These are from a local brewery," he says, taking a sip.

I do the same and am pleasantly surprised. "It's good."

"Yes, June Bennett, we do have things to offer up here. There are many reasons to stay for the summer."

"That's handy, because I wasn't planning on leaving anytime soon."

He reaches out and clinks his bottle against mine. "Good to hear." His words and the way he looks at me make my stomach twist with excitement. I take another sip of beer to wash it away, but it's pretty persistent.

"So how about that dinner?" I say, trying to direct my mind to utilitarian matters only. "Am I helping with this, or shall I sit and watch?"

He points to the kitchen table. "You sit there and keep me company." For once I'm happy to do as I'm told.

Ezra goes out back and manages to get the barbecue grill standing again. He finds charcoal in the storage room and in no time has it cleaned off and lit. While he waits for it to heat up, he starts on the salad. I sit there and drink beer and watch him. He seems to know the cottage well, which makes me wonder if he might know about other things on the rest of the island.

"Do you know anything about a clearing in the forest on the other side of the island?"

He stops cutting the red onion and gives me a confused look. "A clearing in the woods? Nope, can't recall it. I only ever pull up to the dock. Haven't been to that side since we were kids."

"It's no big deal," I say, even though the truth is that the cross creeps me out. "It's just that when I first found the clearing, I saw a cross stuck in the dirt in front of a tree. I chucked the cross into the woods, but when I went back there today, the cross had reappeared." I hear how ridiculous it sounds as soon as it's out of my mouth.

He frowns. "Weird."

"Whatever; just forget about it. I'm sure it's nothing," I say, worried he's going to think I'm some nutcase going on about crosses in the woods.

"Maybe just put up some 'no trespassing' signs?" he suggests.

"Good idea," I say, then quickly move the conversation on to new things.

*　*　*

We use the time to get caught up. I learn that he runs a cottage maintenance business just like his father did, Keen Cottage Maintenance. That he lives in the apartment above the boathouse of his childhood home so that he can take care of his mom without living in the same house. I learn that he's a university graduate but did it all online so that he could run his business and be there for Willa. That he had a husky named Salinger but had to give him away because his mom mistook the dog for a wolf one too many times, which caused her to have episodes.

I learn that he likes books more than TV and that he listens to podcasts about music while working and music in the car.

He drinks only craft beer and would one day like to open his own brewery or maybe a retreat for troubled youth on one of the islands up here.

By the time dinner is on the table, I feel as though no time at all has passed and we're right back where we left off. I open a bottle of red to go with the steak, and we settle in the dining room with the back doors open and only candles to see by. My mother would have been very proud—dinner with a handsome man by candlelight.

"You were pretty hungry?" Ezra says when we finish. I look at what remains and realize I've eaten an entire steak and half the loaf of bread.

"I haven't eaten that well in a long time. Thank you." I bow my head in gratitude, wonderfully full from the meal and perched on the right side of tipsy.

I clear the table and do the small collection of dirty dishes, and Ezra goes into the living room to put a record on. Already we have that nice rhythm back to our time together—natural and easy.

Several minutes pass before the heavy drumming of the first song on the Beatles' *White Album* reaches me in the kitchen. I finish up the dishes, dry my hands, and grab my glass of wine before heading into the living room.

Ezra is sitting at the coffee table. "Did May take these?" He holds up one of May's photos. I unintentionally left them out on the coffee table.

I nod. "I found them last night."

He holds up the one of us kissing. "My first kiss," he says.

"Mine too."

"And if I remember correctly, it was you who initiated it."

I scoff loudly. "It was so not. You leaned in."

He shakes his head. "Nope. Totally you."

I go over and pull the photo from his hands. "Whatever. We kissed. End of story."

He goes back to the photos, picking up the one of his mother, and suddenly his smile fades and his face gets a fixed, serious quality to it. He's quiet while he takes in the details, examines the look she's sending his father and my mother. "A picture really does speak a thousand words," he finally says. Tossing the photo onto the pile, he gets up. "I think I need another drink."

While he's gone, I gather the photos up and slide them back into the envelope. It's obvious that Ezra is still very much affected by that time in our lives. No matter how long ago it was.

"Wanna smoke a joint?" he asks from the doorway.

I haven't smoked weed in about a million years, so I'm surprised to hear myself answer, "Sure."

It's dark out on the verandah except for a thin sliver of white moonlight. Lighting the joint, he inhales, then passes it to me.

"I read your book." The statement catches me off guard, and I cough out a puff of smoke. Not very smooth at all. He laughs and pats me on the back. "You okay there?"

I swat his hand away. "I'm fine." Taking another hit, I pass it back to him.

He holds the glowing joint in his hand. "I've actually read it multiple times." He puts it to his lips, his eyes squinting against the smoke.

The weed works fast and suddenly everything zooms into one tiny speck of existence, just me and Ezra. I'm light-headed and feel as though if I look out into the darkness, I'll get sucked up into the night sky and disappear forever.

He holds the joint out to me. "I thought it was great. Really well written. And profound. Like crazy profound."

"Thanks." I take the joint so that I have an excuse for my one-word answer.

"You haven't written another."

"Nope." I exhale the word along with the smoke.

"You don't like to talk about it."

"Nope." I pass the joint back to him.

He takes a long, slow inhale while studying me closely, then asks, "Why?"

I take my chances and look out into the darkness, now wishing I could get sucked away into oblivion. I can feel his eyes on me and know there's no way out of it. He'll keep asking me that question until he gets an answer. That's his way. He's not one to give up.

"I guess because I feel like a failure." My answer comes from some part of my brain that the weed has unlocked—the honest, vulnerable part. I would never have admitted that without some help. I'm not sure I've admitted that even to myself.

"A failure?" Ezra's voice sounds too loud all of a sudden. "Are you fucking kidding me?"

"What?" I was expecting a bit of sympathy, but he actually looks angry.

"You write a book in your twenties that's a huge success, you were called the voice of a generation, and you call yourself a failure?"

"Key words, Ezra. *A* book, and in my twenties. I haven't written another one since."

He swipes his hand through the air. "So that's it, then. Not writing another book cancels out the accomplishment of the first book?"

"Well, not exactly, but I mean, that success was in my twenties, and I'm forty now."

He throws the joint on the ground and stamps it out with his foot. "You don't think people are reading that book now? You don't think it's still having a profound effect on people?" I shrug, and he sighs loudly. "My god, June, what is wrong with you? Most people don't write even one book in their life, and if they do, it sits in a drawer and never sees the light of day. You should celebrate that one accomplishment for the rest of your life. As far as I'm concerned, you are failure-immune because of that book. You literally don't have to do another thing in your life."

He's even more handsome when trying to make a point—his cheeks flushed, his brows furrowed, his eyes intense lasers. I have this sudden flash of when we were kids and he was trying to persuade me that UFOs existed. He ended up convincing me—he always did—and we spent that summer looking for clues of alien existence.

"June. Are you listening to me?" He snaps me back to the present.

"Yes, Ezra. I'm listening. I get it. I'm failure-immune."

He frowns deeply. "You don't get it, do you?"

I reach out and put a hand on his arm. "I do. Really, I do, and thank you. I've never looked at it that way. And I'm glad you read it and liked it. The idea that even after we lost touch you were reading my book makes me feel really good. You were one of my best friends back then, Ezra, and it means so much to me that even after we went our separate ways, you were still connected to me in some way. That you still cared." I'm rambling a bit, but I don't seem to be able to stop. It's just all pouring out of me.

"Went our separate ways? I think you mean when you went to sailing club and got too cool for me and barely managed to say hi that day in town." His words stop my words short.

I wince. "Yeah, but let's just forget about that little blip in our friendship, shall we?"

"Deal," he says, holding out his hand. I shake it. He gives his empty beer bottle a shake. "Let's go inside so I can get another one of these."

I flip the record over, and we sit on the couch. He asks me about my girls. I enjoy describing them in detail, their likes, dislikes, quirks, accomplishments. I, of course, show him way too many pictures of them on my phone. He asks me about Leo, but the song change distracts him and I'm grateful I don't have to answer.

"My dad used to play this song on his guitar." He's absorbed in a memory for a few seconds and then holds out his hand to me. "Care to dance?"

At first I think he's joking, but he keeps his hand there until I take it, and then he pulls me up off the couch and into his arms. I can feel his body through his thin T-shirt. I put my hand on his neck, and he puts his on my lower back. The placement is calculated, on both our parts. I can move my hand up into his hair to further the intimacy, and he can move his down.

Strategies I know well. One slight move of the hand and you've gone from harmless and platonic to intimate and illicit. A game I thrive on. I let my breath catch and then sigh it out, and his grip on me tightens. Taking my hand out of his, I wrap both arms around his neck to deepen our embrace.

I'm steering this thing right in the direction I know I shouldn't. I promised myself I would be better; take things slower, care less about the conquest and more about the relationship. But this is Ezra and we already have a relationship, and it's been so very long since I've been touched or done any touching.

We're moving but not at all to the music. "This song is a bit awkward to dance to," I say.

He pulls back just slightly. "I agree. I think it was just a lame excuse to get close to you."

That's all I needed. I lean up just slightly—he's not that much taller than me—and put my lips on his. Unlike the first time, we know what we're doing. My hand finally makes its way into his thick hair. His hand makes his way down. The kiss is soft and gentle at first, but I grab the back of his neck, go in deeper. The weed buzzes through me, intensifying everything. Then he stops. Taking a step back, he laughs and shakes his head.

"What is it?" I ask.

"I'm just high and the tiniest bit drunk."

"Yeah. Me too. And?"

He sighs and rolls his hand forward before he can find his words. "I don't think we should do anything this way. I mean, if that's where things are headed. And it's so soon. I just—I don't know."

I give him a pat on the arm. "It's okay, Ezra. It's no big deal."

He gets a wounded look in his eyes. "It's a big deal to me, June. You're a big deal to me. Always have been."

"I didn't mean that you and I aren't a big deal. I just meant it's not a big deal if we don't do anything else."

He nods but looks a bit confused. "Maybe I should go. It's pretty late."

"Can you drive a boat like this?"

"I could drive blindfolded, I know this lake so well."

I take a step closer, put my hands on his chest. "You could also stay over. We won't be high all night." The words sound desperate, I know, but he's flipped that switch inside me and it's hard to turn it off if I don't get what I want.

He groans and moves away from me. "My god. Don't do that."

"What?"

"Look at me like that. And even if I thought it was a good idea"—he raises both eyebrows—"which I don't, I can't stay, not without telling my mom first. If she needed me in the night and I wasn't there, it would be bad."

His explanation deflates me. "You're certainly devoted to her," I say. It comes out sounding a bit resentful, so I try to soften it. "I mean, that's good. It's admirable."

He shrugs. "She's the only family I've got left."

"You've got me. Your blood sister." I take his hand and stroke the place where I cut into his palm a million years ago.

He smiles, a soft, warm, authentic smile that twists my insides up for reasons I can't quite name. "That's good to know."

"Have you ever looked for your birth parents?" I ask, thinking he might actually have more than just his mom in the world.

He's quick to shake his head. "No. I don't think my mom would be able to deal with that. According to my neighbor Judy, who's my mom's best friend, my mom had a really hard time with the fact that she couldn't have a child of her own. Adopting me was a huge deal for her, and she's super possessive, to this day. Doesn't even like me to mention that I'm adopted."

"Makes sense," I say, but deep down I'm thinking that his relationship with his mother sounds a tad suffocating.

* * *

I walk him down to the dock to say good-bye and thank him for bringing dinner. He says he'll be away for a couple of days—he has to pick up a boat for one of his customers—but when he gets back, he wants to see me again.

"Too bad we can't go for a nice dinner at Windset," I say, nodding in the direction of the closed-down resort. "Whatever happened, anyway?"

"Poor management, mostly, and some scandals with senior staff members, or something like that."

"It's really too bad. As a kid I used to watch my mother get herself all done up for her evenings over there. I'd always thought I'd do the same when I grew up." I sigh deeply, feeling sorry for myself. "Obviously, that was never meant to happen."

"I may be able to arrange that night out for you." There's a hint of mischief to his voice.

"What do you mean?"

"I mean, be ready and waiting on this dock at seven o'clock Wednesday, and you'll find out."

"I don't like surprises," I say flatly.

"Well, you should really get over that. Surprises are fun, and so am I." He gives me a quick peck on the cheek and then steps into his boat. "See you Wednesday." He starts the engine and reverses away from the dock without taking his eyes off me.

I stand there watching until the lights of his boat disappear into the darkness. He's left me with that new-relationship sensation; life suddenly feels shiny and hopeful. I certainly wasn't expecting this to happen when I came to Avril Island. Most of me wants to fall right into it, drown myself with the distraction of it all, but I can hear May's voice in my head: *it's not the right time*; *you barely know him and there's too much history*; *don't use him as a way to escape your problems and pain.*

They're all things she would say if she were here right now, and I hear them as if she were. I look up into the night sky—a dome of blue black, dusted with Milky Way and heavy with glowing white stars.

A loon calls out in the distance—beautiful but sad at the same time. The lonely cry reverberates from one creature to another, like a radio signal of aloneness. I can feel the heavy weight of my own loneliness start to settle over me, so I turn and leave the dock, letting my mind wander over each bit of the evening I just had with Ezra.

The cottage glows warm from the lights we left on, and the music finds its way outside, beckoning me back as I make my way up the path. When I was a child, I'd come outside to stand on the path and look up at the bright cottage. The shadowy form of my mother would pass by several windows as she moved from room to room. My father's shadow was a stationary silhouette as he sat in the living room, reading a book. My sister's would often appear in an upstairs window, searching for me out in the night.

Back then I looked up at the cottage with a gratitude so deep I would not have been able to verbalize it. It was a refuge I saw before me, my favorite place in the world. A place where my mother hummed through her days in happiness. Where my father sat still and actually found a way to relax. Where my sister and I were free to roam and fill our days with sun, lake, and forest. Little did I know that secrets were being collected by those shadowy figures, secrets that would rip our family apart, extinguish those glowing lights, and keep me away from this island for almost thirty years.

MAY

June made it to her bed tonight, which is a good sign. To be honest, I'm surprised Ezra isn't in there with her. It takes a strong man to refuse June.

I arrived when she was in the kitchen doing the dishes. I didn't have to see Ezra to know he was there. I could feel the wound-up sense of attraction in June, the calm, contented focus she always gets when a man is around. It's her brand of pheromones, and I know it well.

In the living room, Ezra was looking at some photos. I saw from the envelope that they were mine, the ones I'd kept hidden in the pocket of my suitcase. June must have taken it out from under the bed and gone through it. Can I be dead and still view this as a violation of my privacy? Does my life become everyone else's property now that I'm gone?

Even dead, I was mad at June. It's one thing to go through my things; it's another to put it all out on display like some coffee-table book. It was an age-old battle with June—me wanting to keep some part of myself to myself, her taking personal offense when she wasn't invited into everything in my life.

I can only imagine what she thought when she found those photos, the hurt and confusion she's probably carrying around with her. For me, as I watched her, there was relief in the fact that I wouldn't actually have to deal with it or answer her questions, but also desperate guilt. I would never get a chance to explain myself and make her feel better.

Although, seeing her with Ezra, it didn't look like much was bothering her. Even when he asked her about her book, she took it in stride. That used to be a taboo subject. After the girls arrived on the scene, June just stopped writing. It was as though she couldn't be both, mother and writer, and since she had no choice about the mother part, she had to let the writer part go.

I thought she'd given up too easily, but I would never have said that to her. I actually appreciated Ezra's fury at June's idea of being a failure. I could never have said it to her, so I'm glad he did.

Watching them dance earlier brought back a memory of my mother and West dancing to that very same song—"Blackbird" by the Beatles. I was around twelve. It was in the middle of the summer, when the heat held on through the day and night, refusing to budge even though the sun had disappeared. I couldn't sleep and went looking for my mother to fix it for me. A mistake I'd never make again.

Tiptoeing down the stairs, I heard music playing softly and the murmur of voices. I stayed within the cover of the staircase and peeked around so I could see the living room. The song "Blackbird" was playing, and my mother was in West's arms. They swayed back and forth and spoke in low voices, my mother looking up at him. While I was watching, West said something, and she threw her head back and laughed deeply, all of her white teeth on display. She was wearing a strapless sundress and he wore a tank top. In my child's mind they might just as well have been naked with all that skin almost touching, shiny with sweat from the heat.

That night the seed of understanding about my mother and West was planted deep in my gut. It would take time to bloom. I'd need more evidence than two adults dancing together. I'd been to a wedding before and knew that sometimes adults danced without it meaning anything other than mutual enjoyment of the song. I denied to myself, as children do, that my mother had been doing anything wrong.

Seeing June and Ezra dancing in the same place to the same song made their coming together suddenly feel ominous. Was it just the incestuous nature of it—like mother, like daughter; like father, like son?

Oddly, I felt relief when Ezra pulled away, stopping the kiss, and relaxed even more when he told her he should go. I knew June wouldn't let that happen easily. I could feel her surprise when he didn't give in and actually did leave. I could feel her loneliness and disappointment as she walked back up the path to the cottage and got herself to bed.

June has always been like a deflated balloon, looking to men to inflate her. To make her float high above the real world, her real problems, the real her. She uses up everything they have to give and then moves on to a new source of air.

She started doing it as soon as hormones kicked in and she saw boys as boys. June was the girl who climbed out of her bedroom window to meet boys after dark. The girl who got caught in the school chapel with a boy from another private school during a co-ed dance, both of them half-naked. They threatened to kick her out of the private school we both went to, but my mother spoke to the principal and it magically turned into a two-day suspension, off the record, rather than an expulsion.

Her explanation to me after I found out about her extramarital affairs was that once the girls went to school, she felt like an empty shell with no purpose, useless and inconsequential.

As though she might fade away over time and nobody would notice. That's where the men came in. They all noticed her, made her feel important, substantial, and as soon as they didn't, she moved on to another one who would.

While she was dancing with Ezra, something dawned on me: June is not so unlike my mother. She too seeks out and devours men's adoration like some necessary sustenance. My mother couldn't interact with a man without infusing it all with subtle—and sometimes not-so-subtle—sexuality, just as June does. Maybe it's just one of the side effects of being beautiful— the beauty is in the forefront of all you do, whether you want it to be or not. Or maybe it's learned behavior.

A wave of hatred for my mother suddenly rushes through me. I hate her for her infidelity and for keeping secrets that June is now being forced to face all on her own, secrets that I'm having to reconcile with even in death. It's possible, I guess, to love and hate your mother at the same time. It takes a lot out of you, though, and my fading comes on fast.

JUNE

I wake slowly. The sun shines white behind my closed eyelids, and I realize it's morning. I've slept right through the night. It must have been the weed and red wine. I'll have to remember that magical combination.

My mind travels directly to Ezra and our kiss. It felt explosive and gentle, familiar and new all at the same time. Mostly, though, it felt safe. Not a feeling I normally have when kissing men. Not even Leo. When I kissed him, I felt as though I were on the edge of a cliff and might fall over it and lose myself completely. And with the men of my affairs, each kiss felt dangerous. I was risking everything to do it; I knew it; I'd set it up that way.

I didn't have those affairs to be loved and cared for. I got that at home from Leo for the most part. I had those affairs to scare myself, to prove that I was still alive, not the ghost of some previous self. I used those men to define me outside my role as wife and mother.

I told them to pull my hair, to grab me, push me where they wanted me to be, to go harder, deeper. The more pain I felt, the more real I felt. I came home with bruises, sometimes even cuts. When Leo asked what happened, I brushed them off as trivial accidents, spills while out running or getting to the bathroom in the dark at night.

Each lie Leo swallowed felt like an accomplishment. I was winning at a game he didn't even know he was playing, outsmarting my intelligent husband. I know now that I wasn't outsmarting anyone. He wasn't stupid, he was trusting, and that thought still breaks my heart.

The secrets I kept from May still break my heart too. I was practically living a double life, and my sister didn't know anything about it. There were so many times I almost dumped it all at her feet but then stopped at the last moment. I didn't want to make her an accomplice.

*   *   *

Throwing on some clothes, I go downstairs and make coffee and an actual breakfast, two eggs and toast. It's as though Ezra's dinner opened the gates of hunger in me and I can finally eat.

It's not just a hunger for food that he's awoken. My mind continues to conjure the feel of his lips, the smell of him, what might have happened if he hadn't stopped the kiss. Wanting to get my mind off these ridiculous schoolgirl thoughts, I grab the scrapbook and make a plan to return it to Jim, but only after I take some photos of the articles so I have my own copies.

On the ride over to the marina, I notice the Swann cottage. My mother and father used to be friends with the owners, Suzanne and Walt Swann. It looks as though it's been maintained all these years, and the Swann name plaque is still nailed to the boathouse. I wonder if they might have some information about the disappearance of my father. Suzanne and my mother were quite close at some point. Hell, she might even know some of my mother's secrets.

Jim is busy at the marina with a lineup of customers wanting gas, so I just put the scrapbook on his desk, wave, and mouth a *thank you* before getting back in my boat.

Heading home, I slow down in front of the Swann cottage, looking for signs of life. Summer doesn't start officially for a few days, which means most cottagers aren't even up yet, but there's some furniture out on the dock, so somebody might be around. What harm could it do, just a friendly drop-by from an old neighbor?

I take my time tying up the boat, waiting to see if anyone has noticed my arrival. Standing at the edge of the lawn, I call out a hello just to give some warning, but when I get nothing in response, I make my way up to the cottage.

The only sound is the gentle toll of wind chimes, no dog barking protectively or people talking. The Swann cottage is not so different from mine, the same age and of similar style, but because it's been diligently maintained over the years, the place looks brand-new compared to Avril Island. *What a waste*, I think to myself, a surge of annoyance at my mother rising up yet again.

"Hello?" I call through the screen door, and then knock loudly. There's the sound of quick footsteps on the stairs, and a woman appears. She's roughly my age, short and stout with a head of wild, gray curls, wearing a loose sundress that looks like it came from Thailand or Malaysia. Not the person I was expecting to find.

"Are you my twelve thirty?" she asks. "I thought it was Ann, but maybe I mixed things up. I'll have to check my appointment book. Come in, come in." She holds the screen door open to me and waves me inside. A black cat appears to rub up against my leg. "Right this way," she orders, before turning on her heel and floating down the hall toward the back of the cottage, leaving the scent of lavender oil in her wake.

"Um, excuse me," I call out, but she's already disappeared. Feeling that she's left me no choice, I follow her down the hall and find her in a small sun-room spreading a sheet over a massage table. "Look," I say loudly to get her attention. "I'm not your twelve thirty." At this, she finally stops moving and looks directly at me. "I'm your neighbor. June Bennett from Avril Island."

Her eyes go wide; she drops the sheet and steps around the table to get closer. "Well I'll be," she says breathlessly. "The Bennetts have returned."

"Just me, actually. My mother, she's passed away. May, my sister, she . . . well, she's not here. It's just me," I say again, clumsy over the avoidance of my sister's death. "I'm sorry to just barge in like this, but I was looking for Suzanne Swann."

"You don't know who I am, do you?" Her eyes narrow, and I can tell it's a trick question.

"Are you related to Suzanne?"

"I'm Leslie. Her daughter?" She pauses, waiting for my recognition, but unfortunately the name doesn't ring any bells for me. She waves a hand dismissively, the silver bangles on her wrist jangling loudly. "We played a few times together when your family came over, but I guess I didn't make much of an impression."

"I'm sorry. It's been so long. I didn't even recognize Ezra Keen the other day, and he was at Avril Island every day when we were kids." I'm hoping she'll see that it's just me not being good with faces or names and that she won't take it personally, but I can already feel a slight edge to her that wasn't there when she thought I was her twelve thirty.

"Ah yes," she says, with an exaggerated nod of her head. "Your lot and the Keens were pretty tight back in the day." The comment sounds heavily loaded, but maybe I'm just paranoid.

"Is your mom still around?" I ask, attempting to return to the reason I'm here.

Leslie shakes her head. "No, she passed away years ago of a heart attack."

"I'm sorry to hear that." My words barely seem to penetrate her leathery, tanned skin. "What about your father?" I would have preferred Suzanne, but he'll do.

"We're estranged. I haven't seen him for years. Don't plan to, either." She lets the bold statement sink in. "He and my mother had an ugly divorce, and I can't ever forgive him for some of the things he did to her."

"I'm sorry to hear that too." I try to hide my disappointment within my condolences.

"Aw, it's just life. We got this place in the end, which was a victory."

"So you're up for the summer, then?" I ask, trying at some friendly conversation.

"I'm here through most of the year, not just summers. Moved up after my mom died. Just me and Solomon." She points at the black cat, who's now lying in a patch of sunlight on the rug. "I do Reiki treatments and tarot readings from May to January, then take off for a few months of travel. Get some beach time in, if you know what I mean."

It seems unimaginable to me, but I nod my head anyway and smile. "Well, I'm sorry to have barged in on you, and I know you have a twelve thirty, so I'll just leave you be." I turn toward the door.

"You're looking for answers," she says, stopping me in my tracks. "I'm a bit psychic," she explains. "Come sit down and have a cup of tea. I have some time before my client arrives." Again she disappears from the room, expecting me to just follow.

It wouldn't be hard to deduce that I came here for answers, since I was looking for her parents, but something about her is intriguing, which is what compels me to follow her into the kitchen.

I pause in the doorway, not sure where I'll fit in the chaotic clutter of the room. The sink is full of dirty dishes, the counter is packed with jars and the kitchen table with books, and every other free surface holds a plant. There are even plants hanging from the ceiling, creating an overwhelming rain forest vibe.

"Go on out to the screened-in porch," she instructs, while filling the kettle with water. "I'll bring the tea out there where it's not so busy."

Busy is an understatement, I think to myself as I leave the kitchen for the porch. I'm relieved to see that it's exactly how I remember it as a child—white wicker furniture with down cushions covered in chintz. There were more than a few afternoons where I sat with my mother on this porch while she and Mrs. Swann drank gin and tonics and gossiped about the other cottagers on the lake. I move a pile of newspapers to the floor and sink down into one of the chairs.

Leslie appears with a tray, her cat following close behind. "Hope you like chamomile," she says, setting it down on the table in front of me. I'd prefer a strong cup of coffee but keep that to myself.

"Chamomile is lovely, thank you." I take the steaming mug and sip tentatively, hating the floral taste of it. "You were right about me looking for answers, by the way."

"I usually am," she's quick to say.

"After arriving here, I realized that I don't know much about when my father disappeared. I didn't even know there was a search for him. My mother just said he'd left us."

"Your mother was quite the woman," Leslie says, before lifting her tea to her lips.

It's not said with admiration. There's bitterness behind it, so I can't help but ask, "What do you remember of my mother?"

She shrugs. "Not too much, really. Just that she was beautiful and always dressed so nicely. Most of what I know about her came secondhand from my mother."

"Your mother was my mother's closest friend on the lake."

"I wouldn't necessarily use the word *friend*." Her words startle me, and I take in more tea than I meant to, burning my tongue. "More like a keep-your-enemies-close type thing," she adds.

"I always thought they were good friends."

"It was my father's fault," Leslie explains. "As most things were. He was constantly flirting with your mother, a getting-caught-in-dark-corners-at-parties kind of thing. Your mother didn't do anything to discourage it, and that drove my mother mad."

Suzanne Swann was neither attractive nor unattractive; feeling that she was competing with my mother for her own husband's attention would have been horrible. "I'm sorry to hear that" is all I can think to say.

Leslie points a finger at me. "You look a lot like her. Your mom. Lucky I don't have a husband around for you to steal." She lets loose a loud, obnoxious laugh, and my stomach twists into knots. The comment is too close for comfort. "But seriously," she continues, once she's had her laugh. "That's not even the main reason for their final falling out."

"They had a falling out?" Again, information about my mother that I didn't know.

"They sure did." Leslie pauses, seeming to revel in the suspense she's building. Her cat jumps up onto her lap and she bends down to rub noses with it, prolonging my agony.

"About what?" It comes out too impatient. "I just had no idea," I say, trying to soften my words. "I thought they stayed friends for years." It's a bit of a lie. I actually never gave Suzanne Swann much thought after we stopped coming up here.

"It was a couple of things, actually," Leslie says, finally getting to the point. "First was when your mother asked my mother to lie to the police for her."

"What?" The word comes out on a breath of shock, and Leslie seems to like that.

"It was a week or so after your dad disappeared. Your mom was back up here, but she said she didn't want to stay alone at Avril Island, so my mother said she could stay here with her. Your mom went out one evening and was gone for hours, and when she got back, she refused to tell my mother what exactly she'd been doing all that time, just said she was taking care of some last-minute things at Avril island. The weird part was that she asked my mother to tell the police she was with her all evening, if they ever called."

"And did they?"

Leslie shakes her head. "No, and good thing they didn't, cause there's no way my mother would have lied to the police. She was an honest woman to a fault."

Unlike mine is the unsaid sentiment. "It's understandable that your mother was uncomfortable with being asked to lie and didn't want anything to do with my mother." I don't know why I care, but I want Leslie to know I'm not like my mother.

"It wasn't only that," she's quick to say. "Before your mother left that weekend, she asked my mother if she could borrow some money. Something about being unable to access your dad's bank accounts until she could prove he was really dead."

A gentle tremoring begins under my skin that I think might be shock, and my breath turns shallow.

"What did I say?" Leslie asks. "You look as white as a ghost."

"I didn't know that she thought my father could be dead," I'm able to explain through short breaths. "My mother always said that he just ran off. Never anything about him being dead."

She leans forward and pushes on the hand that holds my tea. "Drink some of that. It will help."

I force more of the chalky tea down and feel as though I might puke. "You're right, that does help," I lie. "So, did your mother end up lending my mother that money?"

"You sure you want me to go on?" she asks. I nod, and she dives right back in. "She wrote her a check for fifty thousand dollars. Your family had money, so she was sure she'd get it back. And she said she just wanted April to leave that weekend. She felt like she was already mixed up in something she didn't want to be."

""She wrote her a check for fifty thousand?" I repeat in disbelief.

"To be honest, I think my mom enjoyed having your mom indebted to her. At least at first." She pushes her cat to the floor and takes a long swig of tea. "April never paid her back." She lets this bit sink in. "My mother even went to your house in the city, but you'd left. Moved to Seattle, apparently?"

I suddenly feel so tired I can barely nod in response. "My mom said the change would do us good."

"But my resourceful mother did some digging and found out the name of your mother's lawyer. She sent an offer through him, saying she'd forgive the debt if your mom signed Avril Island over to her. Your mom flat-out refused, which seems pretty strange, since she never even came back to the place."

"Did my mother ever pay yours back?" I think I already know the answer, but I want to hear it from Leslie.

She shakes her head. "Nope. So my mother tried to sue her for the money, through the lawyer."

"And?"

"Your mom went right to my father, who was divorced from my mother by that point, and got him to write an affidavit saying the money was a gift. Since it came from their joint account while they were still married, there was nothing my mother could do about it."

The knots in my stomach tighten even further. "Wow" is all I can think to say.

"She ranted about your mother right up until the day she died. Said if your mother ever stepped foot on that island again, she'd burn the cottage down to the ground with her in it. My mother just never got over the betrayal from either of them."

"Of course she didn't. It's terrible what my mother did." I do my best to console while at the same time processing this new bit of information about my mother. "I'd like to pay you the money." The sentiment comes out of my mouth without a second thought. "I inherited some money when my mom died, so technically some of it belongs to your family."

Leslie holds up her hand. "Money is an evil thing, June, and it can't right the wrongs that have been done. My mother suffered because of what your mother did, and me getting that money now won't do a damn thing about that. So thank you, but no thank you."

"I can't say I agree, Leslie, but I respect how you feel. If you do happen to change your mind, the offer will be a standing one."

She gets up from her chair, and I get the sense that the visit is over. I feel as though my offer of money has insulted her, but I can't understand why.

"I won't be doing that, June, but I do appreciate the fact that you have enough honor to want to pay your mother's debts for her. Unfortunately, the time for that has come and gone."

I get up as well, placing my mug down on the table. "I understand. Thank you for the tea and the information. As you know, I was in the dark for most of it, but it was some truth that I needed to know."

"You're a brave one, June Bennett," she says, sounding almost like she means it. "Returning to Avril Island on your own. There are a lot of ghosts there, my dear." She leans forward and widens her eyes. "A lot of unhappy ghosts."

I give a light-hearted laugh, hoping to god she's speaking metaphorically. "Guess I should dust off the Ouija board, then."

She gives me a condescending smile and reaches out to pat my hand, her bracelets jangling loudly. "Just be careful, June. Stay aware and wary." It feels like a veiled threat, but what on earth could this woman do? "As for your sister," she unfortunately continues, "she's all around you. Open your heart and you'll feel her."

"I'm sorry?" The mention of May immediately gets my back up.

"I'm a medium as well," she explains. "I can communicate with spirits." Before I have the chance to tell her my thoughts on ghosts and her predictions about my sister, there's a knock at the door. "There's my twelve thirty," she says, then turns and exits the room in a flurry of billowing fabric and lavender.

"Welcome, Ann," she calls to the older woman waiting at the front door. "Ann is head librarian for the town library," she reports to me over one shoulder, as though it really matters. "I was just visiting with June Bennett here," she says once we reach the door. "But we're all done, and I'm ready for your session." The woman steps inside and nods politely at me as I pass by her.

"Thank you again, Leslie," I say on my way out.

"Come back anytime, June," she calls out loudly, even though I'm only a few feet away.

Before stepping off the front porch, I hear the older woman say, "That's not an Avril Island Bennett, is it?"

"It most certainly is," I hear Leslie reply.

I suddenly feel watched and scrutinized. Does everyone know about what happened years ago? Everyone but me?

*　　*　　*

After my visit to the Swann cottage, I spent most of the day trying to distract myself from what Leslie had told me. I cleared the rest of the path around the island, checking in on the tree in the clearing, relieved that the cross hadn't found its way back again. Now, washing my dinner dishes at the sink, a Van Morrison album playing in the background, I work at getting lost in the view of the garden outside the window. The tiger lilies and daisies have started to come up, and the ferns are bushy and a vibrant green. I never fully appreciated the landscape as a child. Returning to it as an adult, having thought it was lost forever, I'm grateful for every blade, bloom, and bit of earth.

With the dishes done, the evening stretches out in front of me empty. My mind inevitably travels back to everything I learned today. It didn't do much to answer any of my questions; in fact, it only seemed to create more. Is my father actually dead, or did my mother just try to make it look like he was dead to get his money faster after he left? And why would my mother ask Mrs. Swann to lie to the police for her? What was she doing that night after my father disappeared that needed to stay a secret? Most confusing, though, is why she didn't take Mrs. Swann's offer to buy Avril Island and settle her debt. She'd already told us it was sold by then, and she never came back here, so why hold on to it?

The number of questions piling up actually causes my head to throb. I resolve to venture into my parents' room in search of some clues. If May had a stash of secrets in her room, maybe my mother did too and I just didn't look hard enough the first time. I grab my glass and the bottle of wine, which is already half-empty, turn the music up loud enough that I can hear it in the bedroom, and head upstairs.

I start with my mother's dresser first. The top drawer still contains undergarments, and after close inspection, I realize that's all it holds. For the first time I actually notice the finery of my mother's lingerie. The other drawers hold nightgowns, T-shirts, and shorts but nothing of great interest.

Checking the nightstand on the side of the bed where my mother slept, I find an old sewing kit, a novel in French, an empty tin of butterscotch candies, and a lighter. I take the novel out and hold it in my hands, imagining her lying in bed with it late into the night, her mind soaking up the words of her native tongue—a reprieve from always speaking and thinking in English, which she said was a clumsy, unattractive language, though she insisted on using it more than her own.

I put the novel back and get down on the floor to look under the bed. There's nothing there but giant dust balls and unidentifiable bits of things. I get up, making a mental note to vacuum under the bed, and move to the closet.

Pulling all her dresses out, I lay them on the bed. When they're lined up on display, I realize that every single one of them would still be considered fashionable today. My mother was never one for trends; she liked classic looks and often said she preferred the 1950s to the 1980s, which were, in her opinion, *garish*.

I pull my tank top off and slide my shorts down so that I'm just in my bra and underwear. Choosing my favorite dress, a white one with red flowers and capped sleeves, I lower it so I can step into it, then slide it up my body. It smells of damp and mustiness, and I have to contort my body to get it zipped up. It's a little tight around the chest but otherwise fits perfectly. The bodice is tailored and the skirt is full, so when I turn, fabric swishes around my thighs.

I remember zipping this up on my mother more than once. She wore it to the bigger events, not just dinners but parties and fund raisers. She had lipstick that was the same color as the red flowers, a purse and high-heeled sandals to match.

The sight of it brings back memories of when I'd watch her getting ready for a night out. She'd lazily thumb through the dresses hanging in her closet, a silk robe draped over her but left open against the heat. When she found the right one, she'd drop the robe to the floor, not caring that I sat watching her every move, studying the economy of curves and the flat plains of her body, the warm brown of her tanned skin. I was proud of my mother's beauty and I think she knew it, as she never shied away from putting it on display for me.

After choosing the right dress, my mother would carefully apply her makeup—wiping eye shadow across her eyelids, outlining her full lips with a deep-red pencil and then filling them in with an even deeper shade of red lipstick. Her final step was dabbing perfume behind her ears and on her wrists. She'd then drink the last of whatever cocktail she'd fixed for herself, touch up her lipstick, and lean down to give me a hug good-bye.

Bonne nuit, mon amour, she'd whisper in my ear, overwhelming me with the heat of her body, the scent of perfume and alcohol, before disappearing from the room. She was always in a good mood on those nights—happy to escape.

I'd stay sitting on her bed, listening to the echo of her heels on the wood floors and her careful descent down the crooked staircase. The screen door would slam, and I could hear her as she made her way down the path to the lake, humming a song to herself. Most nights she'd drive herself across the bay and I'd hear the boat start up and then roar away from the dock until it was just a faint whirring. Other nights friends from the lake would swing by to pick her up—their laughter and talking bouncing from the water up to the cottage until their sounds became faint murmurings as they sped away from the dock.

About this time May would appear in the doorway. We'd often put my mother's makeup on, covering ourselves with so much color that we were unrecognizable, then head down to the lake to wash it off with a swim. Other nights we'd play a board game or pick a VHS tape from the shelf and watch a movie that we'd seen at least three or four times before.

We'd eat peanut butter straight from the jar and make bowls of popcorn drowned in butter—neither one a great offense, but they felt liberating all the same as a child. When we got older, we graduated to the odd sip from one of the bottles in the liquor cabinet and the smoking of no more than one cigarette between us. May liked to rebel, just like any other teenager, but she gave even rebellion a set of rules.

*　*　*

Going back into the closet, I pull out some shoe boxes, throwing them open until I find the pair I'm looking for. Stepping into them, I move to the full-length mirror on the wall to survey myself. The sight is somewhat startling. With my tanned skin and short hair, I could be my mother back in the day. All I'm missing are the red lips and hazel eyes. When did I turn into her? I wonder. And the affair? She runs deep in my blood, even in her death. The thought doesn't warm me like it might some daughters. It prickles through me. I step away from the mirror, pull the shoes off, and carefully unzip the dress and toss it onto the pile of other dresses on the bed before putting my own clothes back on.

Going back to the closet one more time, I reach up and feel around on the top shelf. My fingers brush up against something. Straining to reach higher, I can feel that it's a small wooden box tucked in the very back corner. Inside are some rings and necklaces, nothing of great value, most of it green with tarnish. Underneath everything is a delicate handkerchief folded into a neat square.

I pull at one corner and a ring slips out, a gold wedding band. Picking it up, I see an inscription carved on the inside, the date of my parents' wedding. It was inscribed on both of their rings. My mother's ring is sitting at home in my own jewelry box, so that would mean this one is my father's.

I slide it onto my finger. It's too big, and the weight of it feels strange on fingers that have been bare for at least two years now. Turning it in circles, I wonder, did he give it back to my mother before he left? Shove it into her hand before storming out? Or was it taken from him? Why did she leave it locked up here on Avril Island? Why didn't she sell it the way she did all his other valuables?

The record downstairs ends, and the cottage is suddenly very quiet, making the unanswered questions once again echo too loudly through my head. I pull the ring from my finger, tuck it back into the handkerchief and return it to the jewelry box, and then place it in the closet where I found it.

It could have just been sentimentality that made my mother keep it. The explanation feels weak and hollow. My mother was not a sentimental person. In any case, the ring doesn't explain anything, and I'm left feeling even more confused and in the dark then when I started looking through the room.

I begin gathering the shoe boxes up to put back in the closet, but a creak on the stairs freezes me midmotion. "Hello?" I call out. Leslie Swann's warning about the place having many ghosts runs through my head, but I quickly tell myself to get a grip. It's an old cottage with lots of sounds, nothing else.

I finish putting the shoes back and am scooping up the pile of dresses when I hear another creak. Turning off the light in my parents' room and shutting the door, I head straight for the stairs. Looking down into the dark, I can't see anything. I flick on the light and there's nothing there, but as I move downstairs, I can't shake the lingering feeling that I only just missed someone.

After throwing the dresses in a laundry basket in the bathroom, I pour the dregs of the wine bottle into my glass and take it with me as I do a quick round of the cottage—opening each closet, peering out windows into the night, then locking each door.

The inspection makes me feel better. Again I tell myself it's just an old cottage with creaks and drafts, all of it magnified because I'm here on my own. Putting my empty glass in the sink, I turn off all the lights and head up to my bedroom.

*   *   *

Something wakes me from a deep, wine-fogged sleep. Was it another creak, louder this time? Was it real or in my dream? I have that distinct feeling, yet again, that I'm not alone. Rolling out of bed, I go to the door. Grasping the handle, I turn and pull, but it won't open. Twisting it from one side to the other, I can't get it to budge. My head is still foggy with sleep and I can't figure out if I'm doing it right. I give the door one more tug, and still it won't open.

Shuffling back to my bed, I'm just too confused and groggy to know what's real and what's not. Too afraid to actually find out. I pull the covers over my head and fight to find sleep again.

In the morning I forget about the locked door and get up to go use the bathroom. As soon as I turn the handle, I remember. The door still won't open. So it wasn't just half sleep and a lot of wine that rendered me useless. The door is actually locked, and it would have been done from the other side with a key.

I give it a kick, but it's a futile action. Panic starts to rise up in me. My phone is dead, with no charger in here, and nobody is due to come to the island until Ezra arrives back tomorrow night. My bladder feels as though it might explode, and my throat constricts with dryness. I can't be locked in here.

Turning to see if there's a cup or something to pee in, I see the open window and the roof just beyond and remember the fire escape. It's on the other side of the cottage, but I can crawl across the roof and drop down onto it.

I give the door one more try, just to be sure, then throw on some pants and a sweat shirt. Opening my bedroom window wide, I unhook the screen and pull it free from the frame. There's just enough space to squeeze through. Out on the roof, I stay low and crawl across the rough black shingles, which are already hot from the morning sun.

I used to sneak up here when I was a kid. I loved being able to look out on the lake and see the tops of islands. As an adult, all I can think about is not falling or peeing my pants.

I make it to the other side of the roof where the fire escape is. It's a narrow metal staircase that runs down the side of the cottage. You can access it from a door in the upstairs hallway.

My father put it in when he bought the cottage, since the entire structure is made of wood.

I shift onto my bum and shimmy along the roof until I'm able to drop down onto the first step. The fire escape door is miraculously unlocked. I never thought to check it when I first arrived or anytime after, just assuming it was locked as it always had been—lucky for me, it isn't.

Back inside the upstairs hallway of the cottage, I go straight to my bedroom door. The main skeleton key for all the doors is sitting in the lock. I turn it and the door swings open, the hinges creaking as though laughing at me.

Walking back to the bathroom to finally relieve my bladder, I try to remember if the key was in the lock when I got here. If it was, maybe when I shut the door before bed last night, it twisted in the keyhole and locked. It's a weak explanation, I know, but it's the only one I can come up with, so I'll take it. And maybe go easy on the wine, I tell myself.

*   *   *

Taking my morning coffee out to the verandah, I plop down on the glider. It's another stunning day. The sun is out; the lake is calm and as clear as glass, light bouncing off it in ethereal rays. I plant my bare feet on the smooth wooden floorboards and gently rock myself back and forth. The squeak of the rusty metal is hypnotic, lulling me into a dreamlike trance as I stare out at the peaceful landscape.

The locked door rises into my consciousness without me calling for it, but this time it feels like a memory, not something that happened only last night. I can see my hand on the doorknob, but it's a young hand; can feel the panic and confusion of being locked in my room and retreating back to my bed. It happened before.

We left Avril Island for good the morning after my door was mysteriously locked, which meant the unexplained occurrence got swallowed up by that and the events leading up to it. By the time we were leaving Avril Island, I'd forgotten all about the locked door.

A couple of days before we left Avril Island, I'd seen my mother and West out on the front lawn arguing. I'd never seen them argue before, so I watched with fascination from the kitchen window.

It ended when he chucked the hammer he was holding onto the ground and stormed off. When my mother came inside, I asked her if West had just quit, but she didn't answer. She swept past me and went straight to her room. When she still hadn't come down by dinner, May went upstairs to check on her.

"She didn't say much," May explained. "It's just one of her episodes. I'll make us hot dogs for dinner and take her one later." We didn't give it much more thought. We ate dinner together, went for a swim, and then put ourselves to bed, and still my mother had not emerged from her room or eaten the food we'd left on her bedside table.

My childhood was peppered with "episodes." May and I were included in a lot of them, mostly when we were guilty of some crime that had hurt my mother so much that she had to take to her bed. My father always gave us the same lecture: *How can you treat your mother this way when she does so much for you? You need to do better. You need to be better daughters.* The crime itself was never really revealed; we just knew we were the offenders and had to make up for it. So, we apologized with big, blanket apologies that covered every possible offense. We praised her, doted on her, and eventually she came round again and was back to her normal self.

The other episodes were about my father. There would be yelling. Sometimes we heard things being thrown, shattering against the wall like porcelain fireworks. Sometimes there was the packing of bags and threats of leaving, always by my mother.

The fights never made it past the fortress of our home. My father always found a way to placate her, talk her down. It took hours, but by the next day or even later that day, they both acted as though nothing had happened. We were all supposed to forget the horrible things that were said, the destruction that had occurred, and carry on like a happy family.

This particular time my mother got herself out of bed the day after her "episode." She still seemed frail, which wasn't unusual, but she also seemed nervous, which was. She said she had to go into town for a few hours but wanted us to stay on the island. I didn't put too much stock in it. I was just relieved that she was leaving for a little while and we'd be out of reach of whatever it was she was going through in that moment.

My mother came back around dinnertime. She seemed better, less fragile, but still distracted. We went about our normal evening routine. My mother drank wine and read a book. May took photos of the sunset while I played solitaire and made gimp bracelets for my friends at the sailing club. We had our night swim and retreated to May's room to talk.

Lying in May's bed, I started to relax and trust in the normal that seemed to be settling over the cottage. My mother had put on a record and I could hear her moving around downstairs. Her episode appeared to be over; it had been short-lived and neither May nor I had been a casualty of it, which was a rare and wonderful thing.

When we heard the hum of an engine approaching the dock, May was the first to leap out of bed and run to the window in my parents' room that had a view of the lake.

"It's Dad," she said, when she got back to her room.

"But it's Wednesday. He never comes on Wednesday." She ignored my annoyingly obvious declaration and sunk down beside me on the bed. The simple change in family routine was like an alarm suddenly going off, ringing through the summer night to alert us to the fact that things were not right.

We sat in silence, breathing as quietly as possible, waiting for sounds from downstairs to give us some indication as to what was happening. We heard the sound of the front screen door slamming shut and then the low, deep rumble of our father's voice and the high-pitched surprise of my mother's. There was a screeching sound as the needle on the record player skidded across the record, and then the music stopped. Raised voices followed, and my sense of normal quickly slipped away.

Up in May's room, we couldn't hear anything but the tone of our parents' voices. We sat in silence, listening, for a little while, but then May told me to go back to my room. She said she was going to sneak down and listen at the bottom of the stairs. I told her to come back as soon as she knew what was going on and tell me. She promised she would. Looking back now, I realize it was the only promise to me that my sister didn't keep.

My room was dark and lonely compared to the warm glow of May's room. My sheets felt cool and too crisp when I slid into bed, and I immediately regretted letting May leave me on my own to go downstairs. I lay in bed, straining to make out any word at all from the steady hum of voices below me. They all suddenly seemed so far away, as though I'd been left behind and nobody had realized. I lay there waiting for one of them to remember me. Waiting for my door to open so that I'd be pulled back into the fold of my family. Waiting for one of them to come tell me that everything was going to be okay. I was young enough back then to believe that was possible.

At some point I must have drifted off to sleep. When I woke, the cottage was silent, and I foolishly took comfort from that fact. I got up out of bed, planning on going into May's room to wake her up and demand that she tell me all she'd heard. When I tried to open my bedroom door, it was locked. I thought about banging and calling out for someone. Then the thought crossed my mind that whatever drama had been happening downstairs between my parents had been put to bed. I certainly didn't want to be the one to bring it to life again. So I crawled back into my own bed and once again waited, convincing myself that everything was fine, that the rest of my family had gone to bed and would rescue me in the morning.

When I woke up, I tried the door, and it was unlocked. I stood in the hallway, confused and listening for some understanding of where everybody was, when May suddenly stepped out of her room. She was pale, and her eyes were red and puffy. I was opening my mouth to ask what was wrong with her when my mother called from downstairs.

May rushed to my mother's summoning, and I quickly followed. The locked door, the yelling the night before, my father's arrival, and May's appearance all fell away into unanswered oblivion when my mother told us that my father had left and was not coming back. That we must pack up our things and leave Avril Island.

*   *   *

My phone buzzes with a text, returning me to the present. It's from Ezra. He's going to be back earlier than expected and asks if I want to have our date tonight. The thought of seeing him again so soon and not having another night alone makes me nearly giddy. I wait a few seconds before replying, not wanting to look as desperate and excited as I am, then send a simple reply: *Sure. Sounds good.* He writes back that he'll pick me up at eight PM and I send him a thumbs-up emoji, then curse myself for it.

No longer wanting to sit here with my past and my confusion over the locked door, I decide to get up and move. I'll give my trail a test run and hopefully burn off the nervous energy that tonight's date is already causing. I push up off the glider, leaving it swinging, and go inside to put on my running things.

*   *   *

I have to keep my eyes on the ground, as there are still rocks to avoid, but I'm able to look up every so often and appreciate the view of the water on one side, the forest on the other. I go at a slow pace, since it's been a while since I've done a full run. Not so slow that I don't get a good sweat going, though.

I make it to the end of the island and stop to splash some water on my face. Since I'm there, I decide I might as well take a look at the tree, make sure that it still hasn't been disturbed by anybody. As soon as I reach the clearing, I wish I hadn't come.

The wooden cross is once again propped up in the dirt in front of the tree. "What the fuck?" I actually say out loud before bending down, grabbing the cross, and snapping it in two. The sound of the wood breaking echoes too loudly through the trees. Holding a piece in each hand, I look around guiltily, as though someone will appear to reprimand me. Nothing happens, of course, so I fling the pieces in opposite directions.

It's got to be a group of kids fucking with me. Until I arrived, they were using Avril Island as some secret meeting place. My presence has pissed them off, so they're trying to freak me out. It's the only plausible answer.

I make a mental note to put up NO TRESPASSING signs, maybe some fake security-camera signs as well. Feeling only slightly better at the thought, I return to the main trail. Wanting to rid my mind of locked doors and reappearing crosses, I push myself hard on the run back, arriving at the cottage dripping with sweat, my legs burning, and my brain, fortunately, empty.

*   *   *

I choose the dress with red flowers for my date with Ezra. I aired it out on the line earlier today, along with all the other dresses. It was quite a sight, a dozen versions of my mother blowing in the wind. May would have taken a photo for sure. I couldn't bring myself to.

I'm standing naked in my room, going through my underwear, trying to decide which pieces look the least worn. I brought only comfortable underthings with me on this trip, not imagining there'd be a reason for anything else.

Thinking of the expensive collection of lingerie just sitting in my mother's drawer down the hall, I wander down to her room, all the while wondering how weird it would be if I wore my mother's underwear. Pulling out a black lace bra, I easily find a pair of underwear that matches. I'll just try it on, I think.

The underwear fits perfectly; the bra is a bit tight, but in being so, it gives me some very attractive cleavage. Surveying myself in the mirror I'm able to forget that they belong to my dead mother. Who will ever know, anyway?

I get the dress zipped up, slide into the matching shoes, and then lean over the bathroom sink to apply some makeup. I find a tube of red lipstick on my mother's dresser, and after cleaning the tip with some makeup remover, I'm able to spread some on my lips.

By the time Ezra arrives, I'm already on the dock waiting. He's brought a different boat this time. It's much bigger, with a flatter hull and a covered area where the steering wheel is. He eases it up to the dock and hops out. He's wearing khaki shorts and a black T-shirt and no shoes, of course. I feel absolutely ridiculous in my dress, heels, and red lipstick.

"My god," he says. "You look stunning, June. And I hope you don't mind me saying, but from a few feet out I would have sworn I was looking at your mother's ghost. And that's meant as a compliment," he's quick to add.

"Well, I'm feeling slightly overdressed. I'm not sure what I was thinking."

He holds a hand out to me. "It's perfect. I mean it." I take his hand, and he pulls me in. "Don't change a thing," he says into my ear, his voice low and gruff.

Butterflies kick up a storm in my stomach. "Not even the high heels?" I ask.

He takes a step back to look at my shoes. "I'd say ditch the heels. Or ditch the dress and keep the heels. One works, but not both." I swat him on the arm and he laughs, then pulls me in for a hug. "Is it weird to say I missed you?" he says, holding me close.

If it were anyone else, it would be weird and it would scare me, but Ezra has always been like this, open, loving, and intense. I wouldn't know him any other way.

"No," I say softly, before stepping out of his embrace. "So, seriously. Are shoes needed where we're going?"

He shakes his head. "No. I try to avoid those places at all costs. Just leave them on the dock, and let's go." I kick the shoes off, and he guides me toward the boat and takes my hand to help me in.

"This is a pretty serious boat," I say, glancing around at the shovels and rakes hanging inside the covered steering-wheel area.

"It's my work boat," he explains as he starts the engine. "Not the fanciest mode of first-date transportation, I know. I mean, it's no limousine." He eases the boat away from the dock.

"Well, a limo wouldn't do us much good out here on an island. And anyway, despite what you may think, I'm not a fancy-transportation kind of girl. A utility boat will do just fine."

He smiles and pushes down on the throttle. The boat planes immediately and plows through the water steadily. I move out of the cab area and stand in the wind, my skirt blowing back behind me, the lake air filling my lungs. I've missed this place, this lake, this life, so badly that the pain of it still reverberates through my bones. We drive straight across the bay in the direction of Windset. Ezra slows the boat down as we get closer, and it's clear that the old resort is our destination. Turning, I shoot him a look of confusion, but he just sends back a mischievous smile.

It's even sadder to see the details of the decay up close. Boards are missing from the docks, the stone retaining wall has crumbled in places, the grass is high, the once immaculate white paint of the buildings is peeling or has fallen away in chunks.

Ezra passes right by the docks, raising the motor up and bringing the boat in to the sandy beach area. He cuts the engine, hops out, and ties the boat up to a light pole on the shore.

"I don't trust that dock," he says, coming back for me.

"Are we even allowed to be here?" I whisper.

"They're a client of mine," he mockingly whispers back. "They hired me years ago to keep an eye on the place. I come once a week to make sure there's no vandalism or animals living in the buildings." He holds out his hand and helps me step from the boat into the shallow water of the beach. "So technically I'm just doing my job."

"No shoes was a good idea," I say, holding my dress bunched up in one hand so it doesn't get wet.

I make my way onto the shore, and he goes back to the boat to grab a cooler and a shopping bag. "I brought supplies," he says, holding it up.

"I would have brought something," I'm quick to say. "If I'd known."

He shakes his head. "Don't worry. You keep your minimal groceries and wine for yourself." He puts the cooler and bag down. "How about a tour before dinner?"

"I'd love one."

Reaching into the cooler, he pulls out two beers. "We'll take these along." He twists the cap off one and passes it to me, then takes my hand and leads me away from the beach.

It feels normal somehow, holding hands with Ezra and walking the grounds of an abandoned resort, drinking beer in a fancy dress and no shoes. That's what's always been so wonderful about him—his world is interesting and quirky, and when you're in it with him, it feels like exactly the right way to be.

We follow the flagstone paths that lead around the resort. They're all still intact, walled in by tall grasses that whip against our legs as we move. We go first to one of the private cabins with a lake view that sits on the shore. Pulling out a heavy set of keys, he searches for a few seconds, finds the right one, and then opens the door.

There's still furniture inside—a bed, dresser, desk, love seat, art on the walls. It smells of stale, closed-up-cottage air. Back in the day, this would have been one of the most expensive lodging options. There were a handful of private cabins and then hotel-type rooms in the main lodge.

"What a waste," I say, wandering around the space.

"It is. Apparently it's being kept now for tax purposes. They apply each year for permits to reopen, then let them expire. Definitely some shady stuff involved."

"And these are your employers?"

He shrugs. "I take what I can get."

"Is it a coincidence that the first place you brought me has a bed in it?" I narrow my eyes and flash him a half smile, loaded and very suggestive.

He laughs nervously and actually seems to blush. "No. I mean yes, it's a coincidence. I wouldn't just presume that because—"

"Ezra!" I loudly interrupt him. "I was just joking."

"Well, the fact that you thought of it makes it pretty obvious what you have on your mind," he says with mock indignation.

I take a step closer to him. "And what if I do?"

He moves in. "I'm fine with that."

I grab hold of his T-shirt and pull him to me, then move my hand up and stroke the stubble on his face. "Not a fan of shaving?" I say softly. I can feel his growing excitement against me. I like a slow buildup.

"Not particularly." His voice is a strained whisper.

I move my hand up into his thick, dark hair while studying his face up close. It's still hard for me to reconcile the boy I once knew with who he is now. "You grew up into a very handsome man, Ezra Keen," I say, before brushing my lips across his.

He leans in to prolong the kiss, but I pull back.

"And you've grown into an incredibly beautiful woman, June Bennett," he says.

And there we are—the secret password. I push into him so that our lips crash together in a kiss. Unlike the last time, we go right into frenzied passion. I walk him backward toward the bed, not even thinking about how old or dirty it might be. Our mouths stay locked together, our tongues working fast, until I drop down on the bed and lie back—physically granting him permission to have me however he wants.

He shoves the fabric of my dress up around my waist and kneels on the floor in front of me. I lift my hips as he pulls to free me of my black lace underwear. Then he slows right down, running his hands up my calves to grip the backs of my knees. He leans into me, his breath hot against my skin. I sigh with pleasure as he begins to slowly kiss his way up my leg.

I try to lose myself in the sensation of him, but the dress is suddenly too tight, and the underwire of the bra digs into my left rib. Readjusting my position only intensifies the discomfort. I close my eyes and I see her. My mother, in the exact same position I'm in now, same dress, same everything, with West kneeling between her legs.

I sit up fast. "Stop."

The word seems to physically throw him backward, away from my body. "What's wrong?" His eyes are full of confusion and fear. "Are you okay?"

As I look into his face, the image of my mother and his father slowly fades away. "It's nothing." I laugh in an attempt to rid myself of the horrible feeling inside. "I'm sorry. I just thought I saw a mouse or something." He glances around the room and then, seeing nothing, starts to move toward me again.

I shove the skirt of my dress down and stand up. "Can we go somewhere else?"

He pushes himself off the floor. "Ah, sure. Like another cabin?"

"Um." I struggle to find the words, not knowing what it is that just happened to me or what I now want. It's never happened before. Being with a man has always been a guaranteed escape, my mind becoming an empty vessel that fills only with him and with the physical. "Let's just finish the tour and have dinner and then see how we feel."

He nods, but the confusion lingers in his expression. "Sure. That's fine. Whatever makes you comfortable. We don't have to do anything, June, if you don't want to. I just like spending time with you."

A frustrated sigh escapes. "Ezra, save the sensitive-guy crap. I just saw something and it distracted me, okay? I want to fuck you. I do. But maybe not in this rodent-infested cabin."

His eyes go wide in shock. "All right then." He goes over to the desk, grabs his beer, and takes a sip. "I forgot how delicate you are, June." His voice drips with sarcasm, and I can't tell if he's mad or not. He goes to the door and pulls it open. "Ladies first." I grab my beer and move to leave, but he quickly steps in front of me. "I said ladies first." He steps through the door, and I burst out laughing.

*   *   *

There's something quite beautiful about the decomposing resort. The way nature has grown up around it, the sense of being suspended in time between the past and present, the silence and solitude of a place that used to buzz with activity.

Ezra shows me to the main lodge. There are still rocking chairs lined up on the verandah. The white paint of the building peels off in long, dripping curls, and piles of leaves have collected up against the main door.

We go to the boathouse, where boats still sit above the water in their lifts, their insides nesting grounds for animals and birds. A shadow moves from one boat slip to the next—a beaver that's built its dam in the corner of the long building. Ezra says he's been there for years.

We check on the golf clubhouse, which is still stocked with golf clubs and golf balls even though the greens are grown over. A lineup of golf carts sit at the side of the building, their batteries dead from years without a charge.

"It's all such a waste," I say, as we make our way toward the dance hall. "Why didn't they at least sell things off or give them away?"

"Who knows," Ezra says flatly, taking a swig of his beer.

I throw one hand up. "It just doesn't make any sense."

"People with money are weird."

It's hard not to feel as though my family is being lumped into the group. "You mean, like having a family cottage but telling everyone it's been sold and then nobody goes to it for almost thirty years?"

He gives a quick nod. "Yes. Exactly like that." I can't help but laugh. "As weird as it may be," he says, his tone serious, "I'm glad that your mother didn't end up selling it and you came back."

"Me too," I answer, emotion making my voice low and gruff. I clear it away. I consider telling him about my visit with Leslie Swann, about the $50,000 and my mother refusing to sell Avril Island, about her visit back after my father disappeared, but something stops me. Maybe the hardwired sense to protect my mother, maybe shame.

"I thought we could eat in here," Ezra says as we approach the dance hall. "It's my favorite building." He unlocks the door and pulls it open for me. "I'll go grab the food and meet you inside."

The dance hall is a tall, round building with windows running the entire length of it looking out at the lake. I've never been in it before. It was used for grown-up events, and I was never grown-up enough to go. Stepping inside is actually exhilarating. I imagined my mother and father in here dancing on so many occasions that it's quite exciting to finally be inside.

A set of wide, red-carpeted stairs leads up to the main level. I could so easily visualize the men and women, all dressed in their best, making their way up these stairs for a night of drinking and dancing.

At the top of the stairs is a long hallway with doors leading off it. Two are marked WASHROOM, one is marked OFFICE, and one is marked DRESSING ROOM. At the end of the hallway is a collection of framed photos. They're of guests in the dance hall—some individual shots, some groups shots—as well as the live bands that came to play here.

I find one of my mother, which surprises me—although it shouldn't, considering what a regular she was here. She's sitting at a table, holding a drink up to the camera, smiling wide, her teeth white against the bright red of her lips, her cheeks flushed, her tanned shoulders revealed in a strapless sundress. Suzanne Swann is sitting beside her, giving the camera a reserved smile, looking almost dowdy next to my beautiful mother. Mr. Swann sits on the other side of my mother, not beside his own wife. He smiles up at the camera as well, his hand on the back of my mother's chair.

I take my phone out of my purse and snap a picture of the photo, then move along to study some more. There's another one featuring my very photogenic mother. She's in the arms of a man—who's not my father—on the dance hall. She has one hand on the man's shoulder and is using the other to blow a kiss at the camera, her lips puckered, her eyes bright.

"Whatcha looking at?" Ezra calls out as he makes his way toward me.

"Nothing," I call back. Moving away from the photos, I trail my hand along the wood-paneled wall, enjoying the way the thump of my fingers against the grooves echoes through the quiet emptiness.

I feel ashamed of the mother in those photos and don't want Ezra to see them. It's bad enough that she destroyed his family with an affair; he doesn't need to see her spreading her flirtatious ways everywhere else as well. And if I'm truly honest with myself, right now her sins feel a little too close to my own. Too much of a "the apple doesn't fall far from the tree" kind of thing, and I don't want to share that with Ezra.

The hallway opens up into a large, airy room. The view from the wall of windows actually takes my breath away. "This is amazing," I say, looking up at the high domed ceiling and then turning a full 360 degrees to take it all in.

Ezra is already spreading a blanket out in the middle of the floor. He starts removing items from the shopping bag—a block of cheese, a baguette, some olives, a salami that looks like it's been cured in a Mennonite barn for years.

I walk over to the blanket. "My god, Ezra, two times in a row."

"I just picked up a few things at this great deli in the town where I got my client's new boat," he explains.

I have the irresistible urge to move around the large, open space. I slide away from Ezra while he finishes setting up our picnic and begin to twirl around the perimeter of the room. My bare feet slide easily across the well-worn floor, making a soft shushing sound. The skirt of my dress rises up into a full circle around my thighs as though my legs have wings.

Within seconds I'm light-headed and dizzy, but I can't stop. The lake view whizzes past with each turn, as does Ezra, still crouched on the blanket, the inside and outside view blurring into one. I imagine what a fool I must look, and laughter comes. Ezra gets up off the blanket and moves toward me.

I spin away from him, making it a game, but he's quick and reaches out and grabs me with one arm, like catching a butterfly in a net. Pulling me in close, he kisses me gently on the neck. His soft lips move up to my jawline and over my cheek. By the time he reaches my lips, there's a buzzing all through the lower half of my body. Then the photo of my mother in the arms of another man, on this very dance floor, flashes through my mind.

I abruptly pull out of the kiss. "I'm starving. How about you?" Ignoring his look of surprise, I maneuver out of his arms and over to the blanket to sit down.

He doesn't say anything, just walks back over slowly to join me. He pours me a glass of white wine, and I dig right into the food. We're quiet for a little while, eating and drinking. Sitting there in the middle of the dance floor, I appreciate the novelty of the situation. Ezra was always creative in life, and I'm happy it stayed with him into adulthood.

"Just so you know." I pause to swallow down a bite of bread. "I think this might be the best date I've ever been on. You get an A plus for originality." Leaning over, I clink his beer with my wineglass.

He tilts his head and gives me a scrutinizing look. "Are you sure?"

"I wouldn't say it if I wasn't."

"Okay. Just seems like you're a bit off, that's all."

"Off?"

"Well, maybe not off." He rubs the side of his face while trying to find the wording. "Less enthusiastic."

I take a long sip of my wine before answering. "It's not you, Ezra." He stares back at me, and I can tell he won't be happy with my simple declaration. "It's all of it. Being back here. Finding out about the affair. Being reminded of my father leaving, my childhood summers, which now seem like a lie."

"I can understand that," he says, but there's still some skepticism in his voice.

"It's like my mother has been split into two people." I make a cutting motion with my hand, and he nods to show he understands. "The version I had in my head before I found out she'd had a decades-long affair, before I found out she lied about Avril Island, about so many things, and the version I have now." I drink some more wine. "She was always difficult," I continue. "Emotional, selfish, and sometimes even downright mean." I shrug. "But I could reconcile those things, because she could also be loving and generous and fun, and she was beautiful and elegant. It was just my mother and the way she was. Now she feels like . . ." I trail off, not sure how to finish the sentence.

Ezra slides down onto the blanket to lie on his side, propping himself up on one elbow. "People can be lots of things, June, both good and bad. You don't have to write them off just because of the bad. You shouldn't think of your mother as a stranger just because she had an affair." He takes a long sip of his beer, and I watch as his Adam's apple moves up and down his throat.

"The thing is, my mother doesn't feel like a stranger to me. In fact, I feel like I've never known her better."

He looks up at me with confusion. "How is that the problem, then?"

"Because I think that I became her."

He gives his head a little shake. "You're not your mother, June. Just because you look like her and are from her doesn't mean you are her."

"What if I look like her, am from her, and have committed the same crimes as her?"

He pushes himself back up into a sitting position. "I'm really not following."

I look at Ezra, right into his wide, open, trusting eyes, and suddenly all I want to do is confess. To unburden myself of it all. "I had an affair." The words almost get stuck, and I have to clear my throat. "Affairs, actually. I'm the reason my marriage ended. Just like my mother is the reason that her marriage ended." I have to look away from the surprise in his eyes, because I'm pretty sure it will be replaced with loathing in a matter of seconds.

"Okay," he says slowly, and I can almost hear the wheels turning as he processes what I've just told him. "It still doesn't make you your mother," he finally says.

I look down at the dress I'm wearing and think of the black bra and underwear and have never felt more like my mother. "Do you think I'm a horrible person?"

He shakes his head, then reaches out and gives my knee a squeeze. "Of course not. We all do things in life we regret. Mistakes we wish we could take back" His eyes shift away, and for a split second I get the sense that a secret is sitting somewhere in there. "My philosophy is that if you learn from the mistake, then it's not really a mistake anymore." His eyes meet mine again. "And you learned from it, right?"

The hopefulness in his voice makes me cringe. "Oh, I learned from it all right. Self-sabotage and fear of commitment are just a couple of my issues." Ezra pulls his hand away in mock disgust. And once again manages to make me laugh when I feel anything but happy on the inside.

"Well, then we're good," he says. "Forty-year-old virgin living with his mom and forty-year-old divorcée afraid of commitment living alone on an island. Wasn't that how you described us?" I wince at the memory of my bluntness the first night we saw each other.

He gets up off the blanket and holds out his hand. "Come here." I take it, and he pulls me up beside him and then leads me to the wall of windows. Outside the sun has started to set and the sky is tinted with thick bands of color—red, orange, and purple. We stand there in silence for a while, holding hands, staring out at the calm lake and kaleidoscope sky.

"You've experienced a lot of loss in your life, June." His words catch me off guard, sending a lump of emotion up into my throat. "Maybe it's time to cut yourself some slack and just *be* for a while. Stop taking inventory of your supposed failures and fuck-ups and just appreciate who you've grown to be from it all."

"Ezra Keen, are you turning into a life coach on me?" It's good advice he's giving me, but instead of saying that, I go to my default and use sarcasm.

He bumps me with his hip. "Seriously, June!"

I bump him back. "Okay!" I yell, and it echoes through the massive space. "I'll do my best."

He gives my hand a squeeze. "Good."

We take our time packing up the picnic, and I do one more twirl around the dance floor before we leave. It's dark outside now, but the moon casts the whole deserted island in an eerie white light.

Ezra takes his time driving back to Avril Island. The moon is full in the sky and reflects off the water, which is now inky black in the darkness. We pass cottages lit up from within, the light glowing warm, reflected off wooden walls, the dark silhouettes of their occupants moving around inside. This was always my favorite time to go for a boat ride—sliding through the night, being a voyeur, catching glimpses into other people's cottage lives.

Nearing the dock, Ezra tells me he arranged to stay over if I want him to. I do. The thought of having company through the night is very appealing, and I'm relieved that my confession didn't scare him away.

We're in no rush, since we have all night, so we sit on the end of the dock with our legs in the water and drink some more wine. We hurry to fill each other in on all the years we missed. His are stories I'm hungry to hear, and he leans into mine with the same interest. When we were kids and we saw each other for the first time at the beginning of summer, we didn't run off to play. We found some quiet place to sit and caught each other up on everything that had happened over the winter, and it's the same now, only this time we have thirty years to cover.

*   *   *

The wine has long been finished and I'm suddenly desperate to get out of my mother's dress and into something more comfortable, so I suggest heading up to the cottage.

It's dark and quiet inside, but I don't rush to turn on any lights or music. The stillness wraps us up in it and makes the rest of the world suddenly disappear. Without saying anything, I take Ezra's hand and lead him upstairs to my room.

We move up against each other, and lips brush lips. He unzips the back of my dress, and as soon as it hits the floor, I kick it away. He slides the underwear free of my hips, and I reach around and release myself from the black bra, pulling him toward the bed as he divests himself of his own clothing, I don't think of my mother or the things she did. I think of nothing but Ezra.

No words and no light make everything slow right down, infuse every detail with intention and meaning. The creak of the bed as we lower ourselves onto it, the exhale of breath, the soft whisper of skin against skin, the wind through the trees just outside the window. Our years of friendship and separation suddenly culminate into something so much more.

MAY

When I materialize, it's in the upstairs hallway. I'm alone, but I know June is on the other side of her bedroom door. It's the first time I've arrived apart from her. The cottage is quiet, but there's a sense that it's the stillness after an event. The air still pulses with the electricity of action. Not details I would have noticed when I was alive, but dead you feel it all.

I remember a time just like this one, standing on the other side of June's door in the middle of the night. I turned the key and locked her inside her room. The details around it are hazy. There was a fight between my parents, and I know I had left June so I could go hide at the bottom of the stairs and listen in.

I can't remember what the fight was about or how long I stayed down there. All that's surfacing is the moment I locked June in her room. Why would I have done that? The question causes another shift in the deep, dark place where the memory lies. As though it's preparing to rise up, as though it's only a matter of time before I will remember.

I realize, in this moment, that it was me who buried the memory deep down. Deeper than any of my other memories, which is why it's taking so long to surface. That's because it's not just a memory—it's a secret. A secret so dark that I had to bury it deep down, deep enough that even June wouldn't know about it.

JUNE

"May." I call out her name, and it wakes me from my horrible dream. She was here, in the cottage, standing outside my door, and she was scared. I tried to get to her but could only move in slow motion, as though I'd been drugged with tranquilizers. When I finally made it to my door, it was locked. I tried to kick it in, but I was so weak and slow that I barely even made contact.

I'm sobbing, the stress and fear of the dream locking into my grief and overwhelming me. "May," I say, as some kind of explanation.

Ezra holds me from behind and makes gentle shushing sounds. "It's okay. It was a just dream." His grip is tight, and it slowly brings me back to reality.

My crying stops as the embarrassment at my open display of raw grief sets in. Our first night together, and he ends up holding me as I sob after crying out from a bad dream.

I gently move his arm off me and sit up. "I'm okay."

"Are you sure? It sounded like a horrible dream." He eyes me doubtfully.

I give him a weak smile. "It was bad, but it's over and I'm fine," I lie. The feeling of the dream lingers strong. I can't get rid of the sense that May was right here and I couldn't reach her.

I lie back down beside him, and he wraps his arms around me. I think about rolling around to face him, initiating more sex to distract myself from this feeling. But the grief is too heavy. I can't even muster the strength to turn over. So I choose sleep instead, another trusty escape, falling fast and deep with Ezra wrapped around me.

*   *   *

The next time I wake up, Ezra is no longer beside me. I hear noises downstairs and the light is bright in the room, so I must have slept in, but I feel exhausted. The feeling of the dream and my sorrow still sit along my bones, weighing me down. I want to close my eyes and try to find sleep again, just like I did for so many weeks after May died. The reprieve from those feelings is over and they've clearly circled back.

If it weren't for Ezra, I'd give in. Instead, I'm going to use him as a distraction. I push the covers off me and slowly sit up. *Just one step at a time*, I tell myself. If I got free from it before, I can do it again—especially here. I put a hand to my chest; it aches as though the virtual hole my sister left is real and is now pulsing with pain. I inhale deeply and try to breathe it away. All because of one goddamn dream, I think to myself.

I get dressed, each movement slow and deliberate, the choice of clothing laborious. I even put some makeup on to cover the dark circles under my eyes and even out my skin tone. When I'm done, I look much better on the outside than I feel on the inside.

The smell of bacon reaches me as I head down the stairs, which is a surprise, considering I didn't have any in the fridge as of last night. A plate of bacon sits on the table along with some toast and two mugs of coffee. Ezra stands at the stove and is just sliding some eggs out of the frying pan when I arrive.

"Good morning," he says in his typically cheery way. "Come sit down and have some breakfast." He brings the eggs to the table and pulls out a chair.

I plop down in it. "I'm confused." I point at the eggs and bacon.

He sits down across from me. "I packed them along with the dinner food."

A laugh of surprise escapes me. "Well, that was a bit presumptuous, wasn't it?"

"Can you really say that, considering I'm sitting at your table the next morning?" I roll my eyes at him. "I think the packing of bacon and eggs could be called more optimistic than presumptuous."

I can't help but smile. "Fine, we'll call them optimistic bacon and eggs, then."

He pushes one of the mugs of coffee toward me. "I don't know how you take it, so I just left it black. I haven't learned your adult ways since we left off in childhood."

I gratefully wrap my hand around the mug. "I like it black."

"Aw, just like your personality," he jokes, and once again I can't help but laugh. He's literally clearing away the heaviness just by being here.

I hold up the mug in a small salute. "Touché, my friend."

I wouldn't have thought I could eat a full breakfast feeling the way I do, but as soon as I get one taste of that bacon, I become ravenous, eating five pieces, two fried eggs, and three slices of toast.

"June, we really need to take care of your food situation," he says, once my plate has been pretty much licked clean. "Can I take you into town to do some shopping? I mean, every time I put food in front of you, you're like a homeless woman who hasn't eaten in days."

"And you don't get off on that?"

"Surprisingly, no," he says, his beautiful eyes twinkling, making everything in me suddenly feel buoyant.

We pour ourselves another cup of coffee and go out onto the verandah to sit on the glider. As we move it back and forth in unison as we used to, staring out at the crisp blue sky, bright sunlight, and green trees, I feel the grief start to recede once again and I'm confident that I'll get another reprieve, faster this time. Maybe that's what happens with this kind of grief. You get pockets of time without it and then it returns, knocks you on the floor, but you get up again and find your way back. I've heard the term *cycle of grief*, but I didn't understand the *cycle* part until now.

"Your grass needs to be cut," Ezra says out of the blue. "I'll bring my mower next time and do it for you."

"Can I pay you?"

He shakes his head. "No. Just make me dinner or something."

"Fair enough," I reply, thinking how everything is so easy with him. "Also, I think I do need to put up some 'no trespassing' signs. Remember that clearing I was telling you about, with the tree and the cross?" I look over, and he nods. "Well, the cross has been put back for the second time. I'm sure it's just some kids trying to freak me out. It's just a little homemade cross, nothing serious."

"It's strange, though," he says, his cup in midair. "In all my years coming here, I've never noticed any sign of trespassers. And I thought kids were scared to step foot on this island. Rumor has it that it's haunted and if you come here you'll disappear."

"Seriously?" He gives me an affirmative nod. "That's ridiculous. There's no such thing as haunted islands, or houses or cottages or anything."

"Ahhh." He draws the sound out. "So you're a skeptic, then?"

I lean away from him. "Don't tell me you believe in ghosts."

"I like the idea that people can contact us from the beyond. It's comforting, in a way. What's the harm in believing?"

I think about telling him my suspicion that May is visiting me from time to time, but something stops me. It's too private, and if she is, I don't want anyone else to know about it.

"I saw Leslie Swann the other day, and she said the island was haunted," I choose to divulge instead.

He scrunches his face up with disdain. "Leslie Swann? She's a total crackpot."

"Ezra, don't be mean. And how does her believing in ghosts make her a crackpot but you believing in them is fine?"

"It's not the ghost thing. She's always coming to the city council meetings stirring up trouble. Reporting people for stupid things. Giving premonitions about the end of the world. I think she spends too much time alone with her cat and it's gotten to her."

I can't help but laugh. "Sure, she seemed strange," I concede. "But not downright crazy. Or at least not in the time it took to have a cup of tea."

Ezra pulls back from me with an expression of confusion. "Wait a minute. You had tea with Leslie Swann? At her cottage?"

"I stopped in on my way home from the marina yesterday. My mother used to be friends with her mother. I just thought it would be nice to say hello. She invited me in for tea, we talked a bit, and that's all." Again I'm hesitant to tell Ezra the full details of our conversation but not totally sure why.

"Do me a favor, June," Ezra says, more serious than I've seen him yet. "Stay away from Leslie Swann. She'll just find some reason to start a campaign against you."

"Okay," I'm quick to answer. "It's not like I want to be her best friend or anything."

"Good," Ezra says, before getting up from the glider and going into the cottage, putting an abrupt end to the conversation.

His dislike of Leslie is uncharacteristic. Ezra is the kind of guy who likes everyone and never has a bad word to say. I can't help but wonder what on earth she did to make him dislike her so much.

Ezra wants to check in on his mom before going shopping, so we head to his place first. I've never been to his house before, and it makes me realize how tied to Avril Island we were during the summers, and the places that were frequented mostly by cottagers. Very rarely did we mix with local people.

It's right on the lake and has a brand-new looking boathouse with a double boat slip and apartment up top. Ezra tells me he built it when his business started to take off and he needed to have a place to dock both boats and store his tools. He added the apartment for himself so that he didn't have to live in the house anymore but still be close enough to keep an eye on Willa.

The little stone cottage that sits beyond the large boathouse is a stark contrast. Ezra takes me up to his apartment first. He wants to shower and change clothes.

It's open concept, with big windows looking out at the water. I'm impressed. He's made it feel spacious but cozy at the same time, not too crowded but with enough stuff to make it feel homey. Looking around, I note the obvious influence that working in million-dollar cottages has had on his taste.

The floors are new hardwood but look like perfectly aged barn board. The kitchen has all new chef-quality appliances, a long island covered in a pricey slab of marble, and custom cabinetry. The living room is anchored by a massive gray sectional and a heavy antique wooden coffee table, both sitting on a large area rug. Custom bookshelves line the walls and are filled with books.

Ezra tells me to make myself at home and disappears down a hallway to shower and change. I move around the living room, soaking up the domestic details of him. On the wall are some black-and-white photographs that have been blown up and framed. One is of a pair of feet dangling over the lake; you can see right down to the rocks on the bottom. The tanned, dirty feet belong to a child, and I'm pretty sure they're Ezra's. The next photo is of a clothesline lined with white sheets, which are billowing up in such a way that the forest is revealed just beyond them, and if you look very closely you can see the forms of two people standing far away among the trees. The last photo was taken looking up into a tree. The bark is in focus, but the higher up you look the more out of focus the tree becomes, so that you're barely able to make out that someone is actually sitting high up in the branches.

Moving in closer, I get the strange sense that it's me up there in that tree. I take a step back and look at all the photos together and know it right away—they're May's. The breath is sucked out of me. Stumbling on her work without warning is like seeing her ghost face-to-face.

"June," Ezra calls out for me from somewhere in the apartment. I turn away from the photos and follow the sound of his voice.

He's standing in the middle of his bedroom, still damp from the shower, wearing only a towel around his waist. Seeing all that skin, his muscles, the hair on his chest, wipes my brain clean and makes my body start buzzing.

He motions for me to come closer, and I step into his embrace. My hands go to his back, still slick with water, and my mouth lands on his. I can taste the body wash he used in the shower and smell the deodorant he must have just applied. My senses are overloaded with pine, citrus, and sandalwood, and I love it.

The wet from his stubble brushes my own cheeks as he puts a hand on the back of my head and pulls me in as close as he can. I am just about to rip that towel from his body when his cell phone starts ringing on the bedside table.

He pulls free from me. "Shit. That's my mom." Adjusting the towel around his waist, he goes over and answers it. From the one-sided conversation, I gather that she saw him arrive with me and is asking who he's with and why he didn't bring me into the cottage. He tells her my name and reminds her who I am and then says we'll be in to see her in a minute. He's about to hang up but stops and listens to whatever she's saying. "Yes," he says patiently. "Avril Island Bennett. The youngest daughter."

He hangs up the phone and shoots me an apologetic look. "I told her four days ago that you were back, and she seemed so lucid about it." He looks pained. "It's just hard to know which version of her you're going to get from day to day."

"I can imagine," I say with sympathy. "Why don't we just put a pin in that." I point to his bed. "And I'll let you get dressed."

When he comes out of the bedroom, he finds me standing in front of the photos on the wall. "These are May's, aren't they?" It comes out sounding accusatory, even though I didn't mean it to.

"My god," he says, stopping short. "I should have warned you."

I wave my hand in an exaggerated way. "It's fine, really. I'm fine." My voice sounds too high, and I wonder if he knows how I really feel underneath it. "But I'm just wondering where you got them. And the feet—are they yours? And am I the one in the tree?"

He comes to stand beside me. "Those are my feet, and yes, that's you in the tree, and that's us in the forest beyond the clothesline." He looks at the pictures fondly. "Your sister gave them to me. After that time in town when we saw each other but didn't talk. She sent them home the next day with my dad in an envelope and a note saying what each one was and that she thought I might like them. It was like she knew our friendship was pretty much finished and that I might want some memento of it."

I swallow down a thick lump of tears. That was exactly like May. Going around after me to try to make up for the damage I'd done. She was as much a support to Leo through our divorce as she was to me.

"I loved them so much, I had them blown up and framed," he continues. "I hope that's okay with you?"

"They'd be worth a lot, you know," I say proudly. "She was pretty famous before she died."

"I know," he says, matter-of-fact. "But they're worth far more to me hanging on that wall than selling them to the high-est bidder."

Another wave of tears threatens to erupt. I feel like I'm on a roller coaster today; going up I feel happy, coming down I'm sad, and it just keeps running along that track. Ezra seems to sense that, and we don't say another thing about the photos.

"These gardens are amazing," I point out as we walk toward the stone cottage where his mother lives. The whole yard is packed with all kinds of flowers—pink, white, yellow, orange—along with bushy, electric-green ferns.

"Yeah. She still remembers how to do that, which is good. She spends a lot of time out here."

We enter right into the kitchen, and it's like we've been thrown back in time. I can see why Ezra wanted his own space.

There are Formica counters, a mustard-colored fridge and stove to match, and linoleum on the floor that's supposed to look like red bricks. All of it perfectly preserved and spotless.

"My god, your mom is clean," I say under my breath.

"She forgets she's cleaned so ends up doing it almost every day," he whispers back. "It keeps her busy, though, so that's good."

Leaving the kitchen, we go through the dining room and into the living room. It's a small room, with rose-colored plush carpeting and a chintz couch with two matching armchairs. There are shelves with knickknacks, but not so many that the place feels cluttered.

Willa sits in a rocking chair at the big bay window that looks out onto the lake. She turns away from the view when we walk in. "Hello," she says, her voice cracking slightly.

I go stand in front of her. "Mrs. Keen, it's wonderful to see you." I feel like a shy child again.

She stares up at me with an expression I can't quite read. Is it fear, confusion, distaste?

"Mom," Ezra chimes in. "You remember June?"

She gives her head a shake and smiles slowly, still staring up at me. "Yes. Of course. I'm sorry. I thought I saw a ghost for a second there. You look so much like your mother."

My skin bristles slightly. In this house, that can't be a compliment. "I've heard that before, Mrs. Keen." Is all I can think to say.

She waves a wrinkled hand at me. "Call me Willa. Please." Her hair is still long, worn in a thick braid now and almost completely white. The years have clearly taken a toll, the tanned skin of her face a system of deep grooves and wrinkles, each one representing some hardship or tragedy. Her body doesn't seem meant for this world much longer; her frame is so thin that it seems she could flap her arms and take flight at any moment. Her green eyes, though, are still piercing and alert, giving you the feeling that she can look right inside you.

I perch on one of the armchairs, my hands folded in my lap. I'm uncomfortable. There's so much in the past that connects our two families, so much that I feel ashamed about, that I know she suffered because of—but it isn't mine to apologize for. My hope is that there's some kindness in dementia and that she's forgotten all the horrible stuff of life.

Willa looks deep into my eyes. "You got your dad's eyes," she says with a smile.

I just nod in response. My father's eyes were brown and mine are blue, but I don't correct her.

I point out the window. "Your garden is lovely."

She smiles proudly, then begins pointing out each type of flower, what kinds of insects they attract, how long they stay in bloom, and other gardening knowledge that goes right over my head.

I'm able to keep the conversation light by asking her how long she's lived in the cottage, what the winters are like. A few times she stops midsentence and stares at me with deep scrutiny, but I just pick up the thread of conversation and get her back on track.

After half an hour or so, Ezra says we should get going. He goes to his mom and kisses her gently on the cheek. She takes hold of his hand and strokes it for a few seconds before releasing it. The affectionate gesture touches that soft place in me, and I well up with emotion once again.

When I stand up to go, she motions for me to come closer. I bend down and she grasps my shoulders, her grip much stronger than you'd imagine possible. She pulls me in so that she can whisper into my ear.

"You should not have come back here." Her grip tightens. "You promised, April." She leans in even closer. "You promised never to come back."

My stomach clenches with awkwardness. I gently pull myself free and say, "It was lovely to see you too, Willa."

Ezra doesn't seem to have heard what his mother said to me. He tells me to go to the boathouse and he'll meet me there in a minute, that he just has to get his mom some medication. I agree without question—happy to get out of that house.

Stepping out into the backyard, still distracted by Willa's words, I barely have time to duck as a bird swoops down in front of me, a wing just missing the side of my head. I stay crouched on the ground, my heart racing. "What the hell?" I say, quietly to myself.

Pushing myself back into a standing position, I glance over at the stone cottage. Willa's still sitting at the window, watching me. I force a smile and wave, but she sits as still as a stone statue, her gaze seeming to look right through me, her expression dark. I turn away and walk down to the water to wait for Ezra, trying to get the feel of her bony hands and whispered words out of my head. The whole thing gave me the creeps.

"Good morning," someone from the yard next door calls out. A large woman in a loose blue sundress is pruning a bush of white roses that sits right on the property line of her place and Ezra's. She has short, gray hair that's already damp with sweat and a wheezy sound to her breathing. "I'm Judy Bishop. Lived next to the Keens for fifty years."

Not at all in the mood for small talk, I give a polite nod. "I'm June, a friend of Ezra's."

A spark of curiosity lights up her watery, gray eyes. "June Bennett? Is that really you, all grown up?"

My stomach drops, already afraid of what that recognition might bring.

"That's right. From Avril Island."

She takes a few steps closer, openly scrutinizing me. "I used to clean that place for your mom every couple of weeks. Do you remember me?"

There's a vaguely familiar feeling to her, now that she says it, but I'd never have seen it on my own. She was thinner back then, and her hair was brown, not gray. "Yes, of course," I say with fake enthusiasm. "How are you?"

"Oh, can't complain," she says, but I get the distinct feeling that she is the type to complain. "A few more gray hairs and aches and pains than the last time I saw you, but that's just life, isn't it? You sure have grown up," she continues. "The spitting image of your mom, you are." She tuts a couple of times. "Lucky girl."

"Morning, Judy," Ezra says, coming up behind me. I'm grateful for the interruption. "Your roses are looking great," he tells her, causing her to beam with pride. He then turns to look at me. "We'd better get going." I nod, feeling even more gratitude for the escape plan.

"Good to see you again, Judy," I lie with a friendly wave.

"Will you be out long, Ezra?" Judy asks. "If you are, I'll check in on Willa for you."

"Thanks, Judy, but I'll be back later today."

She gives a nod and goes back to her rose pruning.

While untying the boat, Ezra explains that Judy helps him a lot with Willa. Whenever he has to go away, she goes in to make sure his mom eats something and gets to bed.

"She's a bit of a busybody and total gossip, but she's got a good heart," he explains. "You know she used to clean your cottage?"

"She said that, but to be honest, I don't really remember her."

He gives a casual shrug. "Well sure, you were probably too busy enjoying the cottage to take much notice of your cleaning lady." The comment feels like a dig, and I can't help but wonder if the wealth of my family is a sore spot for him.

"Well, I took notice of your dad."

Ezra nods in acknowledgment of that fact. "He actually got Judy that job."

"So your family is close with Judy, then?" I ask.

"She and my mom have been best friends since grade school," he explains. "Except now Judy's more of a caretaker than a friend, really."

"That must be tough," I say.

"Yup" is his short reply before he turns the key in the ignition of the boat and the engine fires up, making further discussion difficult. Pulling away from the dock, he gives Judy one last wave as she stands on shore. The pruning shears dangle at her side as she watches the boat pull away.

*   *   *

The trip to town has made me appreciate my arrival back at Avril Island. It felt as though all eyes were on me and Ezra. He didn't seem to be bothered at all, waving to everyone or calling out a friendly hello. He certainly seems to be popular around here. I, on the other hand, got only curious looks and what might be considered a few glares.

I take my time putting the groceries away, snacking as I do it. Ezra had to leave, saying he probably wouldn't be back until tomorrow afternoon because of work and having to spend time with his mom. I was disappointed to see him go but am now forcing myself to enjoy the solitude, which I've never been very good at.

I go down to the shed by the lake and pull out the hammock that I noticed was in there when I was getting the dock chairs out the other day. There are hooks drilled into two trees not far from the shore where the hammock always went. It was May's favorite spot; she could stay hidden in the folds of fabric but still observe people as they passed by on their way to the dock.

I give it a good shake and then string it up. The gentle swing of it makes my eyes heavy. I stare out at the soft ripples in the lake, sun bouncing off its surface, and try to resist, but it's futile. The late night with Ezra, the dream about May, the trip into town—they all work like a sedative, and before I know it I'm in a deep sleep.

*   *   *

A loud boom wakes me with a start. The hammock is swinging as though someone has given it a push. Both hands clinging to the side, I lift my head, sure I'll see a person there, but instead my view is dark-gray clouds rolling swiftly through the sky. Another crack of thunder splits through the quiet, followed by a powerful gust of wind. A storm is coming.

I tip out of the hammock and go to the dock, where I clumsily put the cover on the boat and then make sure it's tied up tightly. As I'm walking up the path to the cottage, fat drops of rain begin to fall. Breaking into a run, I make it to the verandah right before the drops turn to sheets of driving rain.

It's a typical cottage storm—my first one of the season. I watch as lightning flashes in the distance, connecting the sky to the lake with a bolt of electricity. The rain is so hard that in no time the path becomes a shallow river running down the gentle slope to the dock.

May and I used to come out to the verandah for every big storm—safely tucked under the overhanging roof but able to feel the mist of the rain on our skin. Our mother would often join us, stopping whatever she was doing to marvel at the magnitude of nature. She'd get a look in her eyes as she stared out at the storm. As though she wanted to run right out into it, to abandon everything and let its strong winds carry her away. She would seem disappointed when it cleared up or just turned to soft rain.

The sound of my phone ringing pulls my attention away and sends me inside in search of it. I find it just in time. It's Bea, and right away she scolds me for missing her earlier calls. I pull the phone away from my ear and see that she called four times while I was in the hammock napping. She won the athletic award at school and wanted to tell me herself before it was posted on the school's Instagram account.

I want to tell her that there was no danger of me seeing it on social media; I haven't looked at any social media since coming to the cottage, though I didn't even realize it until now. Instead I let her prattle on about the end of school, the pool party she and Madeline are going to this afternoon.

Only when she's run out of news does she stop and ask me what I was doing when I missed her calls. I don't want to admit that I was napping in a hammock, so I tell her I was doing some gardening and had forgotten my phone inside.

I start to tell her about the storm, but she cuts me off to say that Leo wants to talk to me. He gets on, politely asks how I'm doing, and then scolds me for not answering Bea's calls. "She was worried, you know?" he says, as though missing my daughter's phone calls makes me the worst mother in the world.

"You know, there was a time when we weren't reachable twenty-four hours a day, and somehow we all survived it."

He sighs loudly into the phone. "Point taken, June, but you're across the country missing important things, so the least you can do is try to be accessible."

I want to tell him and his high horse to fuck off, but instead I concede and say I'll try not to forget my phone again. I ask to speak to Madeline, but she's out, so Leo and I hang up and I'm left with that familiar feeling of failure that always seems to linger after talking to him.

By the time I've finished dinner, the storm has mellowed slightly and I hear only a few low rumbles of thunder in the distance. I put on some music and make myself a fire to keep the damp away.

Opening one of Ezra's beers, I plop down on the couch to stare at the fire. It's cozy inside with the rain still coming down, but all I feel is lonely and depressed. Not to mention pathetic. I actually miss Ezra, and it's only been a matter of hours. What is wrong with me? I've never been this foolish about a man before.

I imagine asking May that exact question and I can almost see her standing in front of me, ticking off the possible reasons on her fingers: *You're far away from your home and the girls, you're still grieving about my death, you've just learned about Mom and her affair, he's the most familiar thing around you right now, and he makes you feel safe.*

I hold up my beer, pretending to "cheers" someone who isn't there. "Right as always, May," I say to the empty room.

Did my mother feel the same way about West? The question forces itself into my mind, and I no longer try to keep my thoughts around their affair at bay. I have to face them sometime. Ironically, sitting here as an adult, I can even understand why my mother fell in love with West.

He was handsome in a rugged, outdoorsy kind of way, with blond hair highlighted by the sun and blue eyes as clear as the lake. He was also everything my father was not. Calm, good with his hands, slow-moving, and kind, caring more about nature than money or material things.

My father couldn't even change a lightbulb without hiring someone to do it. He was wound up too tight, always stressing about appearances, and money mattered to him. He'd grown up with it. His hands and middle were soft because of it. And he treated May and me like we were just extensions of my mother, things for her to take care of and for him to discipline and question now and again.

West was one of the kindest men I knew. He always let me help him with his work when I asked, and he never scolded me for interrupting him if Ezra and I needed help building a fort or getting a Frisbee out of a tree or the canoe up on shore. He'd stop me as I passed by and point out different types of birds on the island, often placing one large, heavy hand on the top of my head, grounding me to the earth and to him. The light that dances in Ezra's eyes, just like his easy and genuine nature, was most definitely influenced by West.

I suddenly have an overwhelming need to write things down. I've learned so much since returning to Avril Island; writing will help me make sense of it all. It used to be the only way I processed things. Writing gave me a way to interpret the world, my life, but I lost the motivation to do that somewhere along the way. I'm surprised and excited to finally have it back.

Going up to my room, I find an old notebook in the desk drawer. It has a few story ideas scratched across the front page in my childish penmanship, but otherwise it's empty.

There's no real rhyme or reason to what I'm writing, just descriptions of people, things, and events. I have a feeling that if I can write enough, I'll be able to string it all together into something more tangible, but for now I just want to get it down. It feels good, like something in me has been curled up and hidden away and is finally unfurling.

*   *   *

I've completely lost track of time when a sudden crack of thunder and then a flash of lightning jolt me out of my writing trance. Another storm is rolling in. Late-night storms are not as much fun as daytime ones. Even as a full-grown adult, they creep me out.

My hand aches from all the writing, so I decide to stop there and go up to bed and read until I fall asleep. I close the notebook and tuck it under my arm with a sense of accomplishment. I haven't written that much in years, and it feels good.

I've just turned all the lights out downstairs and am feeling my way to the stairs when another roll of thunder booms through the sky, causing each pane of glass in the old windows to quiver. A bolt of lightning follows right after, illuminating the whole living room. In that split second of light, I'm sure I see the outline of another person standing by the couch. I rush to a light switch, throw it on, but nobody's there.

That doesn't mean my heart isn't racing. It was obviously just a shadow, the storm igniting my imagination. I take a few deep breaths, scan the room once more, and then head upstairs, leaving a light on just in case. Counting the seconds between the thunder and lightning, just like West taught me to do.

*   *   *

Something woke me. A sound from somewhere else in the cottage, and I'm pretty sure it wasn't part of my dream. A heavy stillness sits over everything, as though the whole cottage is holding its breath, and it's dark—abnormally dark, no light coming in from the hall or the moon. I hear another sound, closer this time, and I'm fully awake now, so I know it wasn't part of a dream. Sitting up, I reach out to turn the bedside light on, but when I pull the chord, nothing happens. The power must have gone out because of the storm. I grab my phone and curse under my breath when I see that it's dead.

I'm almost positive I hear the sound of footsteps on the stairs, but I can't tell if I'm imagining it or not. Is it just the place settling after the storm? Then there's a creak in the hallway just outside my door. There's no way I imagined that. I lower both legs onto the floor and reach for the base of the bedside lamp, the only thing in this room that could be used as a weapon. My door slowly swings open to reveal a dark figure. I try to raise the lamp up over my head, but it's still plugged in and is yanked out of my hand and comes crashing down on the floor.

"June?"

"Ezra!" I yell.

"June," he says again.

"What the hell are you doing?"

"The power's out," he says, as though that's an adequate explanation.

"And I would have slept right through it if you hadn't been creeping around."

He moves toward the bed. "I'm sorry. I just thought I should check on you, since you're out here all alone and it's your first power outage."

"For fuck's sake, Ezra, I'm a full-grown woman. I can take care of myself." As soon as it's out of my mouth, I regret it. "Sorry. I appreciate your concern. You just scared me, that's all."

"No, you're right," he says, sounding nothing but apologetic. "I should have realized I'd do more harm than good, sneaking in here. I really am sorry. My intentions were good, though, right?"

I give his arm a swat and end up releasing drops of wet from his raincoat. "Yes, your intentions were good. Aren't they always?"

He cocks his head to the side. "I wouldn't say always. For instance. I intend to convince you to come outside with me right now and smoke a joint. So that's not the most honorable temptation to put in front of you."

"What time is it?" I ask, absent-mindedly reaching for my phone, then remembering it's dead.

"One thirty," he answers. "It's pretty amazing out there," he coaxes. "The calm after the storm. You wouldn't want to miss it."

"Yeah, sure, why not?" How easily corrupted I am.

Ezra shines the flashlight on his phone while I feel around for a sweat shirt to throw on and put the lamp back on the bedside table. Downstairs we light the candles on the mantel and find some to bring outside with us.

The storm has retreated. The remainder of the clouds have broken apart to reveal patches of clear sky and glimpses of the moon as they roll through the darkness. Thin tree branches litter the lawn in front of the cottage, and puddles of water nestle in the grass. The lake is eerily still, recovered from the wind and rain that churned it up for hours. A thin veil of fog rises from its surface.

"It certainly is beautiful out," I whisper, as though my voice might disturb it all. The spark of Ezra's lighter is his only response. He inhales, releasing a sweet, earthy scent into the air.

He holds it out to me. "I love summer storms. Especially right after."

I take the joint from him, and we both stand in silence for a few seconds, appreciating the quiet stillness.

"Why do you dislike Leslie Swann so much?" The question comes out of nowhere, and Ezra looks surprised by it.

"I never said I didn't like her," he's quick to answer, his voice laced with defensiveness.

"No, you didn't say that, but I could tell."

He sighs, pulls the joint from between my fingers, and takes a long inhale. "I feel like if I tell you why I don't like her, it will cause problems and make things weird."

"Well, now you have to tell me."

"Can I go get a beer first?" I nod, and he flees into the cottage.

As I wait for him to return, my mind runs through every kind of scenario involving Leslie Swann. Did he work for her, get a bad tarot card reading, sleep with her? The last consideration makes me shudder.

Ezra appears, saving me from my thoughts. He holds a beer out to me and I take it, happy to wash away the dry earthiness that weed always leaves in my mouth.

"Go on, then," I encourage, although at this point I'm nervous about hearing the truth.

He clears his throat, and my hand tightens around my beer. "Well, ever since Leslie came to live up here for good, she petitioned to have Avril Island declared abandoned and the cottage torn down."

"What? Torn down? On what grounds?"

"She claimed the building was derelict. A danger to wildlife and any kids who might trespass here." He pauses, giving me a chance to speak, but I'm actually speechless. "I fought her on it. Gave proof that I was keeping an eye on the place, maintaining it as best I could, but she just didn't let up."

"Funny," I say, finding my voice. "She didn't mention a thing about that when I saw her."

"That's not all," Ezra says, with another deep sigh. "A couple of years before your mom passed away, she stopped paying the property tax on this place."

My stomach drops. It seems every road up here leads back to my mother and her bad behavior.

"So we almost lost the place for real?"

"Leslie tried her hardest. Somehow she found out about the arrears and started to put pressure on the municipality to sell the place. And apparently she wanted first rights to it. I, of course, got involved, begged them to hold off."

"But why? She has her own goddamn cottage." My anger is escalating with each bit of the story, along with my disbelief at how she was able to sit there having tea with me as though she hadn't tried to steal Avril Island. "And how did she even find out about the status of my family's property taxes?"

"It's a small community, June. All you need is one guy from the tax office telling his friend over a beer, and the whole town knows." Ezra sighs deeply. "I saw her out one night at the Bridgeside Tavern. She has a group of friends from around here who enjoy the odd big night out. Anyway, she was pretty wasted and came up to me spitting and hissing about trying to keep Avril Island from her. I asked why the hell she cared so much, and she said she wanted to burn the place to the ground in memory of her dead mother. Said that April Bennett was a menace to society and should pay for what she'd done and a string of other bullshit that didn't make much sense."

"She wanted to buy it just to burn it down? That's absolutely ridiculous."

"It's the Swann way, June. That family has always had more money than they know what to do with. Suzanne Swann inherited a trust worth millions, and then so did Leslie."

"And yet she had a revenge plot over fifty thousand," I mumble to myself.

"A what?" Ezra asks.

I end up telling him everything Leslie told me the other day at her cottage—about my mother wanting her mother to lie to the police and borrowing money that she never paid back.

"Seems like small infractions in comparison with wanting to burn down your cottage," Ezra says, making me feel better about the whole thing. "But like I said before, Leslie is a crackpot, and her mother probably was too. You need to stay away from her, June."

"I know." I give him the answer he wants, but in truth I want to drive over to her cottage right now and tell her what I think of her.

"Seriously, June, she knows a lot of people in this area, and she's unpredictable."

"I understand, Ezra. I certainly don't want any trouble. No more than I've already brought on myself by coming back here."

"Good," he says sternly. "Do you regret coming back?" His voice has softened.

"No, not at all. I would never regret coming back here. Coming back to you. It's just brought a lot of stuff up, that's all. But it's worth it, I promise."

Ezra pulls me to him, wrapping his arms around me, making all the bad stuff disappear. Even if it's just for a few seconds, I'll take it. I'll take any reprieve I can get at the moment.

MAY

He's here again. Ezra. They're on the verandah in the middle of the night, hugging. June steps out of the embrace when I arrive and looks over her shoulder in my direction, a flash of confusion running through her expression.

June? I call out, but she turns back to face Ezra.

Ezra holds up his empty beer bottle. "I think I'd better go. I have to get up in a couple of hours for work. I have a dock repair that's going to take all day. Maybe more." He rubs June's arm. "You're okay?"

"Of course," June says with a forced smile. "Thanks for coming to check on me. Even though you scared the shit out of me and I almost knocked you out with a lamp." He laughs and pulls her in for another hug.

She stands on the verandah and watches him go. The moon has come out from behind the clouds, illuminating his departure. Watching his tall, thin frame recede brings forward a random sliver of memory that doesn't seem to be attached to any specific event, but it's right there, so clear.

It's of West coming up the path in the middle of the night, the moon lighting his way because my mother hadn't turned on any lights. We both stood there watching him come—there was a sense of relief at his arrival for both of us, but I don't know why. It's out of place and strange to have him arrive under the cover of night. There's a sense to the memory, that it's tied to something bigger—the secret that I've buried down deep and which thankfully has yet to surface.

If that's the case, then it means that my mother and West were involved in the secret as well. This fact makes it all even more unsettling. What was West coming here to do in the middle of the night? And why was it me along with my mother standing there waiting for him, relieved at his arrival?

June goes into the cottage once Ezra's boat has driven away from the dock, and I follow. She wanders into the kitchen, gets a glass of water, and sits down with it at the kitchen table. I should be sitting across from her. We'd open a bottle of wine or make some tea and eat our way through a bag of cookies while we talked. We'd solve all the problems or at the very least find a way to laugh about them through the tears.

And now she sits alone. I circle around her, hoping my motion will make waves of something that she'll pick up on. Passing by the kitchen window, through a beam of moonlight, I feel that tug again, the sense of solidity I got the first night I was here. I pause, soaking up whatever power the moon is giving off.

June looks right at me. She squints her eyes and leans forward. "May?"

Yes, I scream. *Yes*. I make the mistake of moving forward, out of the moonlight, and the solid feeling disappears. I shift back, but by then June has put her head in her hands and is gently shaking it back and forth.

"Don't be ridiculous," she says out loud to herself. "She's gone." The last words are a mere whisper. She stays like that for a while, looking as though she's in some kind of sorrowful prayer, her head still bowed.

I move around in the moonlight, hoping something will catch her attention again. She must have seen me or at least a flash of me. *June, June, June, June, June, June, June . . .* I say it over and over again, but she's doing everything to block it out.

June. This time I use every bit of energy I have to scream her name. She pulls her head from her hands and sits up but keeps her eyes averted from me and the moonlight.

"She's gone," she says again, louder this time, and then gets up from the table and leaves the room.

I float there in the moonlight until the sadness, the longing for my sister and the real world, overtakes me and sends me back to where I actually belong.

JUNE

The next morning I don't get out of bed right away. I lie there thinking about my visit with Leslie Swann in the new light of what Ezra told me last night. Did my mother actually do those things, or did crazy Leslie make it all up? Did my father disappear, or did something horrible happen to him? Each time I've gone looking for answers about what happened back then, it has only created more questions.

My mind then drifts to the strange interaction I had with Ezra's mother, Willa. When she called me April. Did she actually think I was my mother? And what did she mean, *you promised*? Could my mother and Willa have had some agreement between them? Seems strange for a woman to collude with the same woman who has had an affair with her husband. Could Willa know things about my mother?

Without even trying, a sneaky plan forms quickly in my mind. It involves tricking a senile old woman and pretending to be someone I'm not, but it may also mean getting some answers.

I head into my parents' room to execute the first part of my plan. As I step into the room, a blinding ray of light catches me in the eye. I move forward and can see that it's the late-morning sun shining off the glass face of a watch. It sits, on its own, in the middle of the bed.

I definitely don't remember it being there before—or anywhere in the room, for that matter. It feels like someone put it there, in plain sight, for me to find. It's my father's watch. I know it immediately. The black leather band, the thick square face of it, and the Roman numerals are as familiar as the man himself was. I turn it over to find the inscription on the back: *To Simon with love.* My mother gave it to him for their first-year wedding anniversary, well before I arrived on the scene. My father wore it every day.

I close my fingers over it. How did it get here? A powerful shiver travels across my shoulders. Maybe it fell out of one of the shoe boxes when I was going through things the other night. Maybe my mother hid it just like she did the ring. My mind works fast, coming up with logical explanations.

I go to the closet and get the wooden jewelry box down. Taking the ring out, I loop it over the watch strap and fasten it, then put it on the dresser. I'd had a lot of wine that night when I was going through the closet. I make another note to self not to drink too much wine. I have to keep my wits about me; there's just too much stuff coming up on Avril Island for me to be fuzzy-headed.

How mature and level-headed of you. Makes me proud. I once again hear May's voice in my head, half-mocking, half-serious, the kind of comment that would have elicited a little slap on the arm from me, and then we both would have laughed. I wonder if I'll do that until the day I die—hear her voice respond to my thoughts and imagine I see her in the middle of the night in patches of moonlight. Part of me hopes so and part of me really hopes not.

Finding the watch has made me even hungrier for answers. I go to my mother's closet and choose one of her plainer dresses and a pair of her shoes. As I survey myself in the mirror, guilt starts to creep in about what I'm about to do, but I push it away. It will just be a quick visit, just a few questions, no harm done.

On the approach to Ezra's dock, the guilt resurfaces, but I don't turn back. I make sure his utility boat isn't there, meaning the coast is clear, and then very carefully dock my own boat.

Willa is sitting in the same spot at the living room window. She watches me approach, her face unreadable, no acknowledgment of my arrival. I knock twice and then push the door open and let myself in.

"Willa?" I call out. There's no answer, so I move deeper into the house. "Can I come in?" Still no answer. Only once I'm in the living room standing in front of her does she look away from the yard to greet me—a curtain seeming to lift from her gaze, bringing her back to the real world.

"Ah, June," she says, and my heart sinks. I really thought she'd think I was my mother, given how I'm dressed and what happened the last time. "What a nice surprise," she says. "So lovely to have visitors."

"Is this a good time?" I ask. She nods with enthusiasm and gestures toward a chair by the window. "How are you doing today, Willa?"

"It's a good day, June. A good day. The peonies are in bloom." She points out to the garden, where several green bushes are heavy with pink-rimmed white blooms as round and large as serving plates.

"They're beautiful."

"Cut some and take them home with you. Spread the wild, I say." Her eyes almost disappear in the creases of her aged skin as she smiles wide. I wonder, do I just continue making small talk, or do I still ask what I came here to ask?

As though sensing my internal debate, she leans toward me and says, "Was there something you came to talk about?"

"Yes." I hesitate, unsure how to broach it. "I guess there is."

"You were gone a long time. Must be a lot of catching up to do." She chuckles to herself.

"I was wondering, actually." I pause and smooth the skirt of my dress down, suddenly feeling ridiculous in my getup. "Do you know anything about my father and what may have happened the night he disappeared from Avril Island. Anything at all?"

Her whole body tenses, but her expression gives nothing away. "Your father? What was his name?"

"Simon Bennett."

"Ah yes. That's right." She shakes her head, making the wisps of white hair around her face sway. "I didn't know him so well. Just to recognize him on the street."

"Did you ever speak to him personally?" I push, not buying her story of not knowing him.

She shakes her head again. "There wasn't much mixing between summer folk and locals," she explains.

"But you knew my mother, April?"

She gives a little shrug. "Not very well."

"West worked for us. At Avril Island. If I remember correctly, you came out now and again to help with gardening." I'm not going to let her get away with pretending she didn't know my family. That we were just summer residents who might have passed her on the street. That we don't have a family drama sitting between us like some two-headed elephant in the room.

She cocks her head to the side, as though trying to conjure something up. "I don't really remember. It was a long time ago."

I decide to try another angle. "I read in one of those newspaper articles about my father's disappearance that they thought West might have had something to do with it. Do you know anything about that?"

A pained look flits across her face, and I can tell I've struck a nerve. "It was so long ago," she says. "I don't remember too many details. The police came one day, and West, he . . ." She trails off, a dazed look coming into her green eyes.

She glances around the room as though looking for something and then focuses back on me, sitting across from her. "Oh dear," she says. "How rude. I haven't even put on the kettle." She starts to struggle out of her chair.

"That's fine, Willa. I don't need any tea." I lean forward to stop her, but she moves quickly and is up and disappearing into the kitchen before I can say another word. I fall back into my chair with a huff of frustration.

There's a stretch of silence. It goes on long enough that I wonder if she's forgotten all about the tea and gone out the back door. Then the sound of cupboards being opened and closed and dishes being arranged reaches me out in the living room. Willa starts talking quietly to herself, one long string of conversation, as though someone else is in the room.

I stare out the window at the cloud-like blossoms blowing gently in the wind and the birds fighting one another for room at the feeder. I'm just trying to figure out a way to make a quick escape, to end this failed charade, when Willa reappears, empty-handed. She looks shocked when she sees me sitting there. "How did you get in here?" she asks, fury in her eyes.

"I came through the back door," I answer, gesturing toward the kitchen.

She moves right into the room to stand in front of me. "How dare you show up here again." The shine of tears appears. "We had a deal," she says, the whisper of it full of emotion.

It's what I came for, getting Willa to think I was my mother, but I didn't realize how upset she'd be. Still, I can't turn back now. I need answers.

I slowly get up from my chair. "Can you remind me of that deal, Willa? I seem to have forgotten."

She points a finger at me, and I notice her hands are shaking. "You *know* what deal," she hisses. "You promised never to come back, and I promised to never tell."

"Never tell what, Willa?"

"About Simon or the girl. Or the affair." She sinks down into a chair, tears now streaming down her cheeks. "My West."

"What about Simon and the girl, Willa? Who's the girl?" There's a frantic edge to my voice.

"Stop it," she says, turning away and holding a hand up to keep me at bay.

"Please, Willa, just tell me about Simon. What happened to Simon?"

Her head suddenly whips back in my direction. "Get out of my house," she screams, startling me.

"June?" I jump again at the sound of my name. Turning, I find Ezra in the doorway of the living room, his expression a mix of fear and confusion. "What's going on?"

I glance down at Willa and then back at him. "I just came for a visit. I thought it would be nice for her, since she's alone so much. I didn't mean any harm, Ezra." I shake my head. "Really I didn't."

He looks me up and down. "Can you please go wait for me outside?"

I turn back to Willa to apologize once again, but her hands cover her face while she cries. "I'm sorry," I say to Ezra instead, as I leave the room. He doesn't say anything or meet my eyes as I pass by.

Walking down to the boathouse, I look back and see Ezra on his knees, trying to comfort her. I take my shoes off and toss them in the boat, then sit down on the edge of the dock with my feet in the water. I feel like a complete asshole.

I'm carefully going over everything Willa said when Ezra arrives on the dock. "I know why you're here, June." His voice is stern and, for the first time since I've been back, unfriendly. "It's wrong, what you did."

I get to my feet. Looking at his face, I realize there's no point in trying to play innocent here. He can see right through me. He always has. "I'm sorry, Ezra. I didn't realize how bad it was. That I'd upset her so much."

"How could you not? You brought up the most painful time in her life."

"But I think she might have some answers about what happened to my father. I think it was more sinister than we thought it was."

"Because you think my dad killed him?"

"I just wanted to know if she knew anything."

He puts a hand up to stop me. "I think you should go, June."

"She said that she and my mother had a deal. She would keep the secrets if my mother stayed away. Which means she knows something, Ezra."

"She's a senile old woman, June," he yells, interrupting me once again. "She doesn't even know what she ate for breakfast."

I've never seen him this angry before. "Ezra, give her more credit than that."

He crosses his arms and looks down at the ground. "Just please go. I don't want to be around you right now."

"But what if she does know something?"

He looks up at me, his eyes cold. "That's my mother, June. Not just another person to use for your own benefit."

What he says stings, but only because there's truth to it. "I'm sorry. I don't know what else to say. If I'd known how much it would upset her, I never would have come here." He doesn't say anything or look at me. "You of all people should understand the need for answers."

He lifts his head and glares at me. "That I do, June, but I certainly wouldn't risk someone's well-being to get them." His words are like a punch in the gut. He turns toward the stone cottage, crosses the backyard, and disappears inside—back to his mother.

While hastily untying the boat, I notice movement out of the corner of my eye. Glancing up at the neighbor's yard, I spot somebody sitting in the shadows of the screened-in porch. I put a hand over my eyes to shade them so I can get a better look. I can tell from the size and shape of the person that it's Judy. She's close enough to have heard everything that was said between me and Ezra.

"Out causing trouble, are you, June?" she calls to me. "Just like your good old mom." The coldness in her voice is unmistakable, and it sends a chill through me. I give a curt wave and get into the boat, never feeling more unwanted somewhere than in that moment.

MAY

Something is wrong with June. She's lying on my parents' bed, dressed in one of my mother's dresses, with an arm thrown over her eyes to block out the afternoon light.

The sheer white curtains move with a soft breeze coming into the room, but it does nothing to cut through the stillness. Sweat glistens across June's chest. Why is she wearing that dress? And why is she in here? It was always the hottest room in the cottage on sunny days like this.

It could be June or it could be my mother lying on the bed. That's how similar they look—the body, the hair, the facial features, the dress. My mother would be proud. She loved pointing out how we were similar to her. The strength of genetics and influence pleased her.

As we got older, my similarities to my mother lessened. She often commented on how like my father I was, and from her pursed expression, you could tell it wasn't a compliment. And so she put more focus on June, who was just naturally more like her.

She used to call her *June bug*. She only ever called me May. Some mornings I would go into my parents' room and find June in the bed beside my mother, the two of them stilled from sleep, looking like twin china dolls, a child version and an adult one. I could have felt left out—resentful that June was favored. I didn't. I was relieved that it wasn't me and worried for June.

She never learned that my mother's attention came at a cost. You were expected to be her enthusiastic playmate, her confidante, her emotional support. Essentially, you were expected to fill the bottomless well that was my mother.

But no one could ever actually fulfill that responsibility, especially not a child. And so the fallout would always come. June would say something wrong, not show enough gratitude or enthusiasm, show too much devotion to me or a friend, and my mother would turn.

You're a taker, June. You're selfish and inconsiderate. You don't appreciate all that I do for you, how much I love you. You're deceitful, manipulative, always trying to get your own way. My mother whipped those character assessments into June's soft flesh. It's no wonder June grew up to embody them. I just wish she'd learned that essentially my mother was describing herself, not her younger daughter.

After the fallout, June would attach herself to me—literally. Holding on to the end of my T-shirt so that I couldn't walk away, curling up at the foot of my bed, pressing herself against me on the couch, putting one foot on top of mine under the dining room table. She did that until she'd been filled up with my love. The quiet kind that didn't need big words or actions. That didn't have any terms attached to it. That spread easily by osmosis from the skin of my heart to hers.

I didn't escape my mother's cutting character assessments entirely. I was the *aloof daughter, closed off, too serious for my own good, no fun at all.* I accepted her evaluation, used it like a shield; it was what protected me. At least enough to allow me to take care of my sister when she needed me to. My wounds didn't go quite as deep as hers.

June suddenly sits up and lunges forward toward my mother's dresser. With a roar, she wipes everything clean from its surface. Perfume bottles, an old jar of face cream, a hairbrush, and tubes of lipstick fly against the wall and scatter across the floor. She pulls at the zipper of the dress, freeing her upper body from it before sinking down onto the floor, her back against the bed. There are no tears, only frustration and anger in her blazing eyes. It scares me.

I bring myself as close to her as I can, wrapping my essence all around her like a virtual ghost hug. *June. What's wrong?* I ask, knowing I won't get a reply.

She shivers. "My god, May. I wish you were here."

I'm here June. I'm right here. I say the words forcefully, hoping she can at least feel them if she can't hear them.

"It's so fucked up." She sounds like she's on the verge of tears but holding them back. "Mom had an affair." She chuckles. "But I guess you already knew that. What else did you know, May? What didn't you tell me?"

She looks up into the room as though searching for me. "So many fucking lies and secrets, May, and you're not even here to . . ." Her voice catches and she trails off.

She can't hold the tears back any longer. She lets them fall down her cheeks onto the fabric of the dress, the light-blue fabric dotted dark with each drop. It's the kind of crying that has no force behind it because you're too weighed down by grief.

She shakes her head. "How can she still be fucking with us even when she's dead?"

Because she's our mother, I reply. Her blood mixed and running through our veins, her influence blanketing across our consciousness, her twisted version of love a stake right through our hearts. Only bloodletting, lobotomy, and a heart transplant can exorcise them out.

"And now here I am, talking to my dead sister like some kind of nutcase." June roughly wipes the tears away. She pushes herself up off the floor, moving right through me. Once again I feel her as she goes, her warmth, her smell, her feelings—all of them at once.

Pushing the dress all the way off her body, she goes to the closet and hangs it up, then gets down on all fours in her bra and underwear to clean up the mess she's made.

I watch her slowly crawl around half-naked, the bones of her spine rolling up and down as she moves, her face tearstained, her eyes red, painfully vulnerable and alone. My helplessness rips through me, the need to be there with her a choke hold. Can I die a second time from this kind of pain?

JUNE

I get up off the floor and leave the room, which now reeks of my mother's face cream and perfume after the bottles broke when I wiped her dresser out. I actually made it worse in there; now my mother's presence is inescapable.

Displays of temper like that are not my style, nor is dressing up like my mother to fool old ladies or seeing apparitions of my dead sister. I really am losing it. Like Jack Nicholson in *The Shining*, I might be one day away from putting an ax through the door and saying, *Here's Juney.*

I'm just pulling a sundress over my head when I hear a knock at the door. My heart jumps into my throat. It must be Ezra, coming to make up. "Coming," I call out, as I quickly brush some powder across my face to hide the fact that I've been crying.

At the bottom of the stairs, the heart that was in my throat only seconds ago sinks all the way down into my gut—heavy with disappointment. It's not Ezra standing there in the living room but Leslie Swann. She's wearing a wide-brimmed straw sun hat pushed down over her gray curls, a dirty white tank top, and wild- print parachute pants.

"Ah June," she says, with a strange breathlessness. "So sorry to barge in on you. Didn't think you'd mind too much, though, as you did the same to me just the other day." She laughs in an effort to lessen the slight, but I stay straight-faced, refusing to give her anything.

Taking her sun hat off, she fluffs out her curls, sending a whiff of perspiration and lavender my way, her bracelets jangling. "The place certainly is run-down after all of those years on its own, isn't it?" She glances around the room with disdain.

"What do you want, Leslie?" I just can't play nice, not after what Ezra told me about her. Not after the morning I've had.

She looks shocked at my bluntness but smiles through it. "I was hoping we might sit down again, have a cup of tea?"

"I don't think so." My lack of hospitality turns her smile to pursed lips, as though she's eaten something sour. "Why did you come here, Leslie?"

"Well, I guess I'll get right to the point, then, since we're clearly not doing niceties today."

"Please do," I encourage, the anger building in me with each second that she's still here.

"I've reconsidered your offer, June. The one to repay your mother's debt." I stare back at her blankly, not saying anything. The silence is uncomfortable, and she grips the brim of her sun hat so tightly it folds over. "I only want it for healing purposes, June, on both sides. You'd feel better; I would feel better. I'll donate it, of course. To a favorite charity of my mother's. You can pay me in installments. I mean, I—"

I put a hand up to stop her from blabbering on. "I think you need to get the fuck off my property, Leslie."

My words actually cause her to gasp and put a hand to her chest. "My goodness, June. Where on earth is this hostility coming from? Surely we are more civilized than this."

"But you see, I don't consider you civilized, Leslie. I consider you to be vengeful, petty, and a liar. Ezra told me all about your attempts to destroy Avril Island. So I'm sure you can understand why I will feel the need to call the police if you are not off my property in the next three minutes."

Her eyes go wide with shock, and she begins to shuffle her way backward toward the door. "That's just ridiculous, me trying to destroy Avril Island. You should consider the source, June. You really should. Ezra Keen may be all smiles and handsome on the outside, but you don't know what lies underneath that shiny veneer. Don't fall for it, June. I warn you. "

"And you should get off my property." I take a step toward her.

"You are as bad as your mother, June Bennett. A menace, all of you—your sister, your whole family," she spits at me.

"You watch what you say about my sister, Leslie," I say, slowing walking toward her, forcing her to move faster. "She was nothing but wonderful. Not a menace in the slightest. Me, on the other hand, I won't argue that title."

She pushes through the screen door. "I wish my mother had burned this place to the ground back when she had the chance; you would have gotten what you deserve," she yells at me, before turning and scurrying down the stairs.

I stand on the verandah until she's pulled away from the dock and is only a speck on the lake beyond. Then I go into the kitchen and, with shaky hands, open a bottle of wine and pour myself a very full glass.

Leslie's words about Ezra ring loudly through my head—*consider the source, what lies beneath the shiny veneer, don't fall for it, I warn you.* I picture his angry face, his harsh words spoken to me at his house earlier in the day. It was a side of Ezra I'd never seen before. Could there be other sides unknown to me, hidden away, ready to surprise?

I quickly try to wash away the thought with a gulp of wine, thinking briefly of the plan I made only this morning to drink less, to stay clearheaded. That plan is quickly discarded once the wine reaches my lips, travels down my throat, and enters my bloodstream, softening the edges just enough to keep me wanting more.

*　*　*

I wake up groggy, my eyes sticky with sleep and a film of sweat on my body from the stuffy room. I forgot to put the fan on. It's already well into the day; I can tell from how hot it is in here. I drank a lot of wine last night, as planned. I may actually have gone overboard in an attempt to drown every thought in my head and get some silence. I can smell it sweating out of my pores now.

I rub the sleep from my eyes and reach for my phone to see if Ezra has texted me. He hasn't. I could lie in bed and obsess over it, allow Leslie's words to resurface and wreak havoc, but instead I force myself up and into my running clothes. I have to clear the fog somehow. I'll go for a run, come home, and give him a call. Maybe he's waiting for me to make the first move, since I'm the one who fucked up.

Standing against the counter, eating a banana and enjoying a cup of coffee, I commend myself. My mind-set about Ezra is healthy. In the past, if things went sour with a man, I'd just run away, move on to the next one. It was my pattern both before Leo and during. I won't do that with Ezra.

Walking to the front door, I wonder if I might be able to convince him to come for dinner. I'll cook this time, maybe dig a little deeper to get a better sense of him. I bend down to tighten my laces, do a few warm-up stretches, and then pull open the door, ready for my run.

It's the smell that hits me first—rot, the meaty kind. Then the flies, so many I can hear the loud buzzing. My eyes sweep the verandah, and at first I'm not really even sure what I'm looking at. Dozens of small black specks. It takes a few seconds to connect the smell to what is laid out in front of me. When I do, I stumble backward and fall through the open doorway. Dark carcasses, wings folded tight against the body, black glassy eyes still and empty. A crowd of dead birds littered across the verandah floor.

Crab-walking myself back into the cottage, I shut the door with my foot and collapse onto the floor. My heart is pounding. I gag out of reflex, the smell lingering in my nostrils. How did they get here? What kills birds? Flying into a window, but not that many and I would have heard it.

Taking a deep breath, I order myself to get up. I can't stay here all day. I go to a window that overlooks the verandah. Having glass separate me from the horror just beyond allows me to stand there and survey the carnage. There are exactly twelve birds out there, all black in color. Smaller than crows, but I can't tell what kind of bird they are. The longer I stand there and stare at them, the more disturbing it is.

Feeling as though I might be sick, I turn away, pull my phone out of my pocket, and dial Ezra's number. It's the only thing I can think to do. It takes some explaining, but he when he finally understands that I have a verandah full of bird carcasses and that I'm scared, he says he'll be right over. Through the window I snap a few photos. Then I retreat deeper into the cottage.

The sound of Ezra's footsteps on the porch makes me brave enough to open the front door. He's standing in the middle of the mess, his eyes narrowed in confusion, his mouth open in shock.

"What the hell?" he says.

"I came down this morning, and they were all here like this." I take a tentative step outside. "I Googled and there are mass bird deaths, but not on someone's verandah, and they were starlings, which I don't think these are. Somebody must have put them here. Leslie Swann. She did this." I point at the carnage in front of me.

"Okay, slow down, June. Let's take this one step at a time."

"You don't believe me?" I accuse him. "You're the one who called her a crackpot. Wouldn't this classify as crackpot behavior?" I don't give him a chance to answer. "She was here yesterday, Ezra, and I told her to get the fuck off my property."

He puts a hand to his head and closes his eyes for a second as though it's all just too much to deal with. "I believe you. I do. We'll figure it all out, but right now I think you need to go inside and call animal control to make a report." He gestures to the birds. "And I'll clean this up."

"Are you sure?"

He waves me away. "It's nothing. I've dealt with this kind of thing before. Racoons, mice, moles, pheasants. If it's wild and up in these parts, I've seen it dead and had to remove it from someone's cottage." I gratefully go inside and leave Ezra to clean up the dead birds.

Animal control takes my report but tells me I'll need to call the police if I think someone did it deliberately. They say I could save one of the birds to bring in for an examination to determine the actual cause of death but I wouldn't get the results for up to a month.

Frustrated and still shaky, I do the only thing I can think to do—go into the kitchen to make a pot of coffee. Hopefully Ezra will stay and have some. Only as I'm pouring water into the machine do I realize how badly my hands are trembling. The door swings open with a bang and I jump, splashing some over the sides.

Ezra arrives in the kitchen. "I'm not sure coffee is what you should be having right now."

"I know. I'm pretty jumpy after coming down to that." I thumb in the direction of the verandah.

"I don't blame you," he says, going to the sink to wash his hands. "That would be an awful thing to come down to this morning."

"You didn't pick them up with your bare hands, did you?"

He laughs, drying them on a tea towel. "No, of course not. I used a pair of work gloves. And the birds are in a garbage bag in my boat now. I'll get rid of them for you, but I'm gonna take one by animal control to get it tested. And you should probably wash the verandah down with a few buckets of soapy water."

"Animal control said it could take up to a month to get any results." I throw a hand up in exasperation.

He shakes his head. "Don't worry about that. I know someone that works there, and he owes me a favor. I'll make sure we get the results faster than that."

Affection for him swells in me, almost muffling the anxiety. Even mad at me he comes here and takes care of everything. What Leslie implied about him yesterday is literally blown apart. Ezra Keen is a good man, I'm sure of it.

"I'm really sorry about yesterday," I say. "It was totally selfish and out of line. And I don't think your dad killed mine. I was just asking questions, trying to get her to talk."

He shakes his head again. "I shouldn't have reacted so strongly. I know you're dealing with a lot of new stuff up here and want answers. Just like I did. Still do."

I sit down across from him. "So we're okay then?"

He reaches out and takes my hand and gives it a squeeze. "We're good."

I'm about to launch into a recount of my encounter with Leslie when his phone buzzes. He looks down at it and frowns. "I'm really sorry, but I have to go. I was right in the middle of a landscaping job when you called me, and I left a guy there on his own. Apparently, he's knocked down the corner of a stone wall."

"You have guys?"

"Yes, I have guys," he says, with a deep chuckle that moves my insides. "Just three who I bring on for the bigger jobs." He gets up from the table, so I do too. "Are you going to be okay here on your own?"

"I'll be fine. It takes more than some dead birds to scare me away. I'll just spend the day thinking up my revenge for Leslie Swann."

Ezra laughs and shakes his head. "Come on, June, you can't be sure it was Leslie unless you caught her in the act."

I give Ezra a quick synopsis of what happened yesterday when Leslie came over. "So you see? She's the only one with a motive."

He huffs out a laugh. "I wouldn't say the only one."

"What? There are other people you could see putting dead birds all over my verandah? Seriously?"

He runs a hand through his hair and looks as though he regrets making the comment. "It's just . . ." He pauses, trying to find the right words. "Your dad's disappearance and my dad being accused of having something to do with it caused a lot of conflict around here, and division. Local people, especially the ones who knew my dad well, saw it as a class thing. Rich cottagers relying on locals and then turning on them. The police were criticized for bringing my dad in, but then cottagers complained not enough was being done to solve the mystery of your dad's disappearance. Tensions ran high after you guys left. Locals even turned on each other. The ones who thought my dad was guilty and that he'd caused bad press for the community, and then the ones who thought he was innocent and resented that not everyone backed him up."

I have to give my head a shake. "It's still amazing to me—confounding, actually—that all of this was going on and we had no idea."

Ezra frowns. "Your mom knew. She knew about it all."

"The entire extent of it?"

He's quick to nod. "I'm sorry to say, June, but she did things that made it worse."

I take a deep breath, not sure I'm ready to hear it but not sure I have much choice either. "What kind of things?"

"Do you remember how your parents donated a bunch of money to fix the roof of the local church? The one that held a Sunday service just for cottagers?"

"I don't really remember the donating-money part. My parents were always donating money to things; I never really paid attention. I do remember my mother dragging us there on Sundays."

"Well, in return for donating the money, they dedicated an entire pew to your family with a plaque on it. After everything happened, some people demanded to have the pew removed and get rid of all recognition of your family's contribution. Your mother heard about it, and she said if they did that, then the church would have to pay back the entire donation. She threatened them with lawyers, and so the minister of the church felt he didn't have much choice but to leave it there. And then he was transferred to a different church. There was also the investigating officer of your dad's disappearance. When they didn't arrest West for it, your mother tried to get him fired."

I bring both hands to my head and give my temples a massage. I can feel a massive headache coming on. "Okay," I say. "I get it. My family is not popular in these parts. I wish I'd known that before coming."

His phone buzzes, and his attention goes right to it. "It's all in the past, though, and people know you're not your mother," he says distractedly. He takes a few seconds to type something into his phone, then gives me his focus again. "It probably was Leslie who put those birds there, but let's not jump to conclusions just yet. It does seem right up her alley, but if you go on some revenge mission, she'll have you arrested; I guarantee it. She's practically best friends with the police chief's wife." His phone buzzes yet again, and he outwardly winces. "I'm sorry, but I've really got to go. Things are falling apart over there."

"Yeah, yeah, of course. Go. We'll talk later."

He reaches out and strokes my cheek with the back of his hand. "Do you want me to come back as soon as I'm done working?"

I lean up to kiss him as an answer, and he returns it. There's a tenderness to it, our movements slow, our lips soft, our tongues tentative—the physical equivalent of an apology from both of us.

I walk him to the front door, and when he pulls it open, the lingering stench of dead birds wafts into the cottage. I put a hand over my mouth. "I'd better take care of that right away." He shoots me a look of sympathy and then slides through the door, shutting it fast behind him.

*   *   *

What I want to do as soon as Ezra leaves is start scavenging the island for dead animals to leave on Leslie Swann's cottage porch, but I think it's best to heed Ezra's warning about her having me arrested. I also can't help but wonder, after everything Ezra just told me, if there might be somebody else who was motivated to defile the front verandah with dead birds. After learning all that I have about my mother since coming back to Avril Island, I wouldn't be surprised if she has a lineup of enemies waiting for the chance to get their revenge.

I decide to call the police. They take down an account of the event and all my information and explain that they can't really do anything until they speak to animal control. They promise to get back to me once they know the cause of death. The officer I speak to sounds only mildly interested in what I'm saying, and I have to correct him twice when he calls me Jane instead of June. I get off the phone feeling frustrated and annoyed.

In an attempt to take my mind off the birds and Leslie and the phone call to the police, I call my girls and gratefully listen to them ramble on about every little detail of their innocent lives. It's a good conversation, but it empties me out with longing for them. Makes me feel hollow and scraped out on the inside. You don't know before having children how much they fill you up, become the matter under your skin that makes you feel like a whole person.

After we hang up, I flood the verandah with hot soapy water, hoping it gets rid of the smell, then finally head out for my run. Instead of it clearing my head as it normally does, I feel myself getting angrier about the dead birds. About someone trespassing on my island to do something like that—the violation, the malice behind it. All I wanted was to come back here for some peace and quiet, time to grieve my sister. Instead I'm left to suffer from the mess my mother made and deal with outdated bids for revenge.

I stop at the opening of the path into the clearing, deciding to go check on the tree, hoping to catch someone there who I can unleash my fury on. When I arrive at the tree, that fury is quickly extinguished by the chill that runs through me. It's not the same as before; it's even bigger this time, the branches thicker, more string used to hold it all together. A new cross leaning up against the tree, one that would be impossible for me to break in two.

I slowly back away from the tree, not even daring to touch it. The new, bigger cross feels like a very clear message—whoever put it there doesn't care that this is my island; they are not going to back down. Somebody wants me off this island. I just have to find out who and why, because I'm not going anywhere.

*   *   *

I've told Ezra that I have to mail a letter and suggested that we meet at the Bridgeside Tavern, the only bar in town. I head there an hour before our scheduled meeting time. I want to sit at the bar on my own for a little while, see if I can attract some locals over and get them talking. I have a feeling that Ezra is careful with what he tells me, worried that he'll upset me. But I need to know the uncensored truth. I need to know how many people in this town have it out for my family and why.

*   *   *

Summer is in full swing at the lake now. A steady stream of cars rolls down the main road, and cottagers weave their way along the sidewalk, ducking in and out of the shops. The beach is crowded with families—kids in their bathing suits, skin already tanned deep by the sun, running around screaming, kicking sand up and then splashing into the water. Teenagers strut around, reveling in the opportunity to show off newly developed bits of their bodies—muscles they didn't have last year, breasts that now amply fill bikini tops.

I pass the government dock with a group of old men fishing off it and then reach the bridge that connects the downtown area with the more residential part of town. A group of boys in bathing suits climb over the side of the bridge like a cluster of spiders. They perch on the metal beams on the outside of the bridge, waiting for a boat to pass underneath before dropping down into the water below and quickly swimming out of the way of more boat traffic.

Sitting on the other side of the bridge is the Bridgeside Tavern. It looks as worn and weathered as it did thirty years ago. Inside is dark and cool. It takes my eyes a few seconds to adjust to the change. I go sit at the bar, since I'm alone. The woman serving drinks gives me a good up-and-down. She pours me a beer and sets it down in front of me on a worn, warped coaster.

"You lost?" she says, with a sly but friendly smile.

She's a middle-aged woman with one of those generic not-long-but-not-short bob haircuts, blond, with the hint of gray roots coming in. The red T-shirt she wears has the name of the tavern stretched across her ample chest and reveals a slight paunch that I'm betting is the result of a few kids. She's heavy on the makeup, but it doesn't do a very good job at covering up the dark circles under her eyes or the evidence of the rough life she's clearly lived.

"Lost?" I pull my beer toward me.

"We don't get many seasonal folk in here." She nods to the crowd behind me. I turn and survey the rest of the bar. It's mostly older men who look as though they've worn trenches into their seats over time.

"I'm not lost," I say, after turning back to face her.

She wipes down the counter in front of me, even though it's spotless. "What part of the lake you from?" I can tell I've piqued her curiosity, which is a good start.

"Avril Island," I say, before taking a sip of my beer, watching her over the rim of my glass.

Her eyebrows rise in surprise; then she gives me a knowing nod. "Well I'll be," she says. "I heard a Bennett was back but thought it might just be rumor. Which one are you?"

"June. The youngest one."

She actually gets more comfortable, leaning into the counter and crossing her arms. "What brings you back now?"

"My mother told me and my sister that she sold Avril Island years ago. She died, and we found out that she had in fact lied and it was still in the family." I'm aware that the *we* I'm referring to is me and my dead sister, but I like talking about her as though she's still alive. It feels more right than talking about her like she's dead.

The woman's eyes go wide again. "Get out," she says, clearly relishing the gossip. "That woulda been a doozy to find out."

"Yup." I take a long drink of my beer, enjoying how it cuts across my throat before making its way down. Leaning in a bit closer, I say, "You know another thing my mother lied about?" My best approach is to look like I'm a victim of my mother's, not an ally, if I'm going to get anyone to talk to me. It feels strange, betraying her after years spent protecting her, but it's also incredibly liberating. "She told me and my sister that my dad ran off on us. Not a thing about the disappearance or the police investigation." I slice my hand through the air for dramatic effect. "We had no idea about any of it."

Her mouth drops open in shock, and she shakes her head. "You don't say?"

"I have no idea to this day whether my dad is out there somewhere, still alive, or dead."

A customer approaches the bar, and the woman signals a young man washing glasses to take care of him so she can keep talking to me. I didn't realize how easy it would be.

"I hate to be the bearer of bad news," she says, although I think she likes to be the bearer of any news, "but my uncle was on the police force back then. I overheard him telling my mom some details of the case, and from all that they had, it sure sounded like somebody had been murdered."

The breath catches in my throat in a moment of uneasy excitement. I was finally getting somewhere. I take another sip of beer to steady myself. "Are you sure?"

She gives me a pitying smile and nods to show she's on my side. "They found your dad's boat, washed up on an island. Apparently there was blood on the steering wheel that matched his, and"—she takes a quick look around to make sure nobody is listening, then leans in even closer, bringing with her the smell of hard alcohol and stale body odor—"they found West Keen's fingerprints all over the steering wheel. That's what made them bring him in for questioning. They searched West's house, didn't find a thing. Then searched his boat, and your dad's watch turned up in the glove box." She taps her own wrist, even though there's no watch there, a satisfied look on her face from the valuable inside information she's just dropped in my lap.

The clench in my jaw and the shock that's locked itself in my bones keep me from responding as these new facts sink in. The woman doesn't seem to notice and takes a deep breath before launching into more explanation.

"My uncle, he was a real fan of West's. Thought the whole thing was a setup. Said it looked like the clues had been placed there on purpose. But with the affair and all, even the best of men can go savage over love, don't you think?"

Her eyes suddenly flit over to the door, and whatever she sees there causes her to push off the bar, stand straight, pick up her cloth, and go back to wiping down the already shining wood. "Well, speak of the devil's offspring," she mumbles under her breath.

A hand on my back causes me to jump. "June?" I look up into Ezra's face. "You okay?" he asks. I just nod. Looking at the woman behind the bar, he says, "Martha," an unmistakable edge to his voice.

"Hey, Ezra. It's been a while. What can I get you?" she asks, the friendly-bartender act suddenly seeming forced.

He takes a look at the drink in my hand. "Whatever she's having," he says, putting a five-dollar bill on the bar. Martha sidles away to pour the beer. "Let's go sit in a booth," Ezra says, pointing to an empty one by the door.

I move off my stool as Martha passes Ezra his drink. I wait until he's on his way to the booth before thanking Martha for the information.

She gives my hand a pat. "My pleasure," she says. "And be careful with that one." She nods in Ezra's direction. "He's too damn good-looking for anyone's good." She lets out a laugh, but it's an empty one.

Twice now I've been warned about Ezra, I think to myself, walking over to the table he's chosen. Am I missing something? Is there actually reason to be wary of him, or is it just small-town bullshit with nothing behind it?

"What the hell were you two talking about?" Ezra asks as soon as I slide into the booth.

"Just passing the time while I waited for you." He has a strange scowl on his face that confuses me. "Why, do you not like her or something?"

He gives a little shrug. "She likes spreading rumors. Told people we slept together years ago when we didn't."

"You didn't sleep with her?" I ask, just to confirm.

He takes a sip of beer and then licks the foam away. "Never, but I did turn down her many offers and dodge her messy advances whenever I came in here for drinks. She likes to sample what she's selling through her shifts." I think of the strong scent of alcohol she emitted. "I just stopped coming here, and the rumor eventually died down. Water under the bridge now. I'm just not a fan, that's all."

"That makes sense," I say, silently wondering what other bits of history I don't know about Ezra. His explanation does give a reason for why she dislikes him and why she'd warn me against him. *A woman scorned*–type thing.

He reaches out and rubs my hand. "Anyway, how are you doing? Feeling any better after those birds?"

I shrug. "I'm okay. Like I said before, I think it was the handiwork of Leslie Swann. Her weird form of revenge after our heated exchange yesterday. And I can take her, so I'm not that worried."

I was hoping to make Ezra laugh, but there's only concern in his eyes. "The thing is, June," he says, "I did a bit of asking around, and Leslie went to Boston around six PM yesterday for a Reiki conference. Won't be back until tomorrow morning."

The information sits like a hard lump in my gut. If she didn't do it, then who did? Without her as my culprit, it could mean anyone, anywhere in this town is responsible. I look away from Ezra and glance around the room, suddenly feeling wary of the whole damn town.

"Don't worry," Ezra says, giving my hand a squeeze. "We'll get those results back from animal control and get the police looking into it. We'll figure out who did it. I promise." I nod, appreciating Ezra's attempt to comfort me but not able to shake the feeling of exposure that hangs over me.

"I was wondering," Ezra says, letting my hand go. "My mother, yesterday, thought you were April, didn't she?"

So much has happened since I went to see Willa yesterday that it takes me a few seconds to change gears and focus on what he's asking. "Um, not at first," I answer, thinking of when I arrived. "She knew it was me when I got there, but then when she went into the kitchen to make tea, she came out and I could tell she was different. That's when she started talking to me like I was my mom."

"Yeah, even after you left, she kept on about how April broke into the house, told me I should call the police."

"Did she say anything else about me, or I guess I should say, my mother?"

He shakes his head and laughs, the uncomfortable kind. "You don't want to know."

"I do. Tell me."

He rubs his face with both hands and groans. "It's not very nice about your mother."

"Tell me."

"She called you, as in your mother, a slut."

"And? Tell me exactly what she said."

A pained expression crosses his face. "What's the point? She wasn't making any sense anyway."

"Just please tell me," I plead.

"Fine. Her exact words were, 'That slut ruined everything. She may not have done it, but she's the one with blood on her hands.' Then she told me to call the police because she was going to tell them everything." He takes a sip of his beer while surveying my reaction.

It takes a few seconds to digest what he's said. I try to piece it together with everything else so that it makes some kind of picture. "What does she mean, blood on her hands? It makes it sound like murder."

Ezra sits up straighter, defensiveness already in his eyes. "You mean, a murder committed by my father?"

"I'm not saying that, Ezra. I'm just wondering why your mother would use the words *blood on her hands.*"

"Your mother and my father had an affair. Your father found out and left without a trace. My father was somehow implicated in it all and he left too, probably to escape jail time. It seems pretty straightforward to me, June."

"Why didn't you tell me about my father's boat being found with blood and your father's fingerprints on the steering wheel? Or the watch found in the glove box of your father's boat?"

I can tell my questions have caught him off guard. "Where did you hear about those things?" I inadvertently glance over at Martha, who's still tending bar. He nods, and a bitter smile spreads across his face. "Wow, it didn't take her long to divulge the one bit of gossip she has about your dad's disappearance."

"So you knew about those details?"

"Everybody knew about those details eventually," he replies, the chip that he's had on his shoulder about them all this time becoming visible. "Even the police can't keep secrets in this town. No matter what, they were not enough to convict my father of anything. And there are still ways to explain them. Your father's blood in the boat could have been from a harmless cut at any point. My father's fingerprints on the steering wheel could have been from some time that he needed to drive it while out there for work."

"And the watch?"

Ezra narrows his eyes, and I suddenly feel like we're no longer on the same side of things. "To be honest, June, I think your mother planted that watch in there to make him look guilty. I'm not sure why, maybe so she could get your dad's money faster, maybe the shame of having her husband leave her so she wanted to make it look like something else. I really don't know. All that I do know for sure, one hundred percent, is that my father did not do anything to hurt your father."

"Okay," I say.

He looks surprised, as though he expected more of a fight from me. "Okay?"

"Ezra, I can't dispute what you're accusing my mother of. After everything I've learned about her in my return to Avril Island, she may very well have planted that watch in your dad's boat to make him look guilty. I honestly wouldn't put it past her at this point. I'm not out to prove your dad's guilt in anything. I'm just trying to piece together what happened."

His whole body relaxes, his expression softening. He reaches for my hand again and holds it tightly. He's about to say something when his phone rings. He looks at the screen as though he might ignore it, but when he sees who's calling, there's a flash of panic on his face and he quickly answers it. It sounds like a woman on the other end, and she does most of the talking. He replies with *uh-huh* a few times, then asks *what time* and *where is she now*, then says he'll be right there and hangs up. I know from his furrowed brow and dark eyes that whatever it is, it isn't good.

"What's wrong?" I ask.

"It's my mom. Judy found her in the road in her nightgown. She said she's really upset, not making any sense. She has her back at the house, but she won't go inside and keeps asking for me." He sighs and runs a hand through my hair. "And my dad."

"Your dad?"

"She hasn't done that for a long time. Or had an episode like this."

I wonder if my visit brought it on, but I don't say it. I don't have to. It sits between us like dead weight. "Can I come and help with anything?"

He's quick to shake his head. "No. It's better if it's just me."

"I understand," I say, selfishly feeling relieved. "Will you come out to the cottage later?"

He winces, sucking air through his teeth. "I'm not sure. Depends how she is." He quickly slides out of the booth. "I'll text you if I can, but if you don't hear from me, then just go to bed and I'll get in touch tomorrow." He leans down and gives me a quick kiss, then glances over at Martha to see if she saw or not, but she's no longer at the bar. "Make sure you lock all the doors June. Just to be safe," he says, before rushing away from the table and out the door. His words send a shudder through me.

* * *

Arriving back to an empty cottage with a million questions swimming around in my head, I feel nothing but lonely and agitated. I flip through the records, trying to find something uplifting to listen to, and come across *The Sound of Music*. May and I used to listen to it on repeat, dancing around the living room, acting out each different part.

I put it on and go into the kitchen to find something I can call dinner. Leaning against the counter, I robotically shovel some leftover spaghetti into my mouth and sip carefully at a glass of wine. The soundtrack is doing the opposite of lifting me up; it's making me sad and nostalgic.

I want my sister. I want her here listening to this cheesy album with me, laughing, talking, helping me figure out what the hell happened back then. Giving me advice on Ezra, sharing the bottles of wine that I keep drinking on my own. *Open your heart and you will feel your sister all around you.* I hear Leslie Swann's words in my head, despite my efforts not to.

I'm not even sure what that means. I pour the rest of my wine down the sink, wondering if I would have heard or noticed anything last night if I'd been sober. Being clearheaded seems like the right plan, no matter how lonely or sad I may be feeling.

Things seem more serious with the knowledge that Leslie could not have been the one to put the dead birds on the verandah. Standing there in the kitchen, I go over everything Ezra has said and what Martha told me today, trying to imagine who else it could be, but there's almost too much to process and Julie Andrews's voice certainly isn't helping.

Going into the living room, I put on a quieter record, Joni Mitchell's *Blue* album, which was one of my sister's favorites, and then get my notebook to write things down, help me keep my thoughts organized. I make a list of people who have reason to hate my family, from the police chief who almost got fired because of my mother to Judy the next-door neighbor who is such good friends with Willa.

Something troubling dawns on me as I'm creating this catalog of revenge seekers—Ezra should be at the top of the list. My mother had an affair with his father; my mother created suspicion that his father had something to do with my father's disappearance; all of it made his father leave. I don't write his name down. Instead I turn the page and begin writing down all the things I do know about when my father disappeared. What the newspaper articles said, what Ezra and his mother have revealed, Leslie Swann's version of things, and last, everything I learned from Martha today.

It all boils down to only a few tangible points. My mother had many secrets and told many lies. Willa knows at least one of those secrets but is afraid to tell. West was involved in whatever actually happened, whether he wanted to be or not. And last, my mother was capable of pretty much anything, maybe even murder.

At ten o'clock I give myself permission to go to bed. I've written several pages and feel as though I've definitely exorcised some demons. I take the needle off the record, putting an end to Joni Mitchell's beautiful lamenting, and turn the player off. Then I make sure the front and back doors are locked, turn off the lights, and head upstairs.

* * *

Sounds from beyond my sleeping world pull me free of a fitful sleep full of dreams about black birds and my mother. I open my eyes into darkness. It takes me a few seconds to understand what actually woke me—music. The clock reads 1:17 AM.

I slowly push back the covers and slide out of bed. Phone in hand, I tiptoe to my bedroom door and open it a crack. It's coming from downstairs.

At the top of the stairs I'm greeted by a tunnel of darkness below me. Using the light of my phone, I quietly make my way down. As I get closer to the bottom, I recognize that the song playing is "Blackbird" by the Beatles. Not the Joni Mitchell album I was listening to before going to bed. I've not given in fully to fear just yet. I mostly expect to find Ezra on the couch rolling a joint. It's only when I step out of the cover of the stairway and flip on the light switch at the bottom of the stairs that a heavy dread floods me.

Ezra is not sitting on the couch. Nobody is. The room is completely empty. I rush to the record player and bat the needle off, creating a static-filled screech before deafening silence. Fear runs its cold fingers up and down my spine. Who or what turned that record player on?

I go to the front door and check that it's locked. I'm heading into the kitchen to make sure the back door is still locked when a flash of something out the window catches my eye. Peering into the side yard of the cottage, I see a shape, distinctly human, disappear into the woods along the path that I've been using for running. I open my phone, ready to call 911, but the futility of that quickly dawns on me. They'll never get here in time to catch whoever is out there, but I'm here now and I can.

Fueled by anger and urgency, I grab a poker from the fireplace, slip on my running shoes, and rush out the front door, phone in hand to light my way. I move swiftly but not so swiftly that I'll actually overtake the person. I only want to get a glimpse of them, maybe snap some photos to show the police.

The night is dark, the moon at only half its glory and slipping behind clouds every few seconds, but I know the path well and move along it easily. A soft wind pushes through the trees around me, causing some branches to creak and leaves to whisper against one another, but otherwise the night is quiet. I don't see or hear any evidence of movement ahead of me, so I quicken my pace.

I'm thinking they may have headed off into the woods in another direction when the sound of an engine rumbles through the quiet. It doesn't have much power behind it, but I can tell it's coming from the far side of the island.

I break into a run, the fire poker held out in front of me, the light from my phone bobbing up and down with each stride. I'm no longer worrying about staying out of sight, focused only on catching up to the shadowy figure before they make their escape.

Reaching the other side of the island, right where the path makes a detour to the clearing in the forest, I see a boat pulling away from the island. Breaking through the thin brush that's grown up along the shore, I make it out onto the rocks to get a better look.

A small tin boat with an outboard motor is about a hundred yards from shore. Driving the boat is a hooded figure, definitely the same one I saw disappearing into the woods. I lift my phone higher to snap a few photos. The person looks back over their shoulder as they go, but it's too dark to see any distinguishing features and the hood provides too much cover. Still, I stand there watching until they've vanished into the darkness.

It seems like no coincidence at all that the boat took off right where the other path is on the island. Maybe whoever put the cross at the tree is the same one who was in that boat. Maybe it started with a cross to freak me out and now the pranks are escalating.

* * *

Rushing back to the cottage, I call the police. Breathlessly I tell them about the record player starting on its own, about the person I saw running into the woods, about the boat and the tree with the cross. Saying it out loud makes it sound paranoid and made-up even to me.

They advise me to either get off the island and go somewhere safe or go into the cottage and make sure all the windows and doors are locked. They said they'll send a boat out there as soon as possible to do a perimeter scan of the island.

I arrive back at the cottage feeling only mildly better. Inside I turn on as many lights as I can, but it does nothing to dispel the sense of violation that comes after a break-in.

Exhaustion presses in on me from all sides. The courage and adrenaline I felt when chasing that person into the woods have suddenly vanished, leaving me drained, emptying my reserves completely. All I want now is a soft bed, but the thought of heading upstairs to mine makes me shudder. I know that every sound will make me jump, every creak will be a footstep on the stairs. So, before I can second-guess the impulse, I grab my purse, walk out the front door, and head down to the dock to escape Avril Island.

It's a bit of a risk, fleeing to his place. Hoping his door is unlocked, hoping he won't mind me crawling into bed with him. Hoping somebody else isn't already in there. The thought dawns on me only as I finish tying the boat up at his dock.

We've never actually called it a relationship or discussed exclusivity. I just assumed it because it's Ezra—my Ezra. What will I do if he does have someone there? Do I get mad or politely apologize and then let myself out?

I shove these thoughts from my mind and climb the stairs to Ezra's apartment as quietly as possible. The door is unlocked, which doesn't really surprise me. Slipping inside, I shed my shoes and soundlessly make my way across the smooth hardwood. He's left the oven hood light on, which guides me down the hall and to his bedroom. The door is wide open. I don't even realize I've been holding my breath until the exhale of relief comes. There is only one sleeping form in his bed.

Standing over him, I study his face, the slight part of his lips, the deep-purple shade of his closed eyelids—the vulnerability making him even more handsome. Listening to the rhythmic sound of his deep breathing calms me. I planned on waking him up immediately to tell him about the intruder and my chase across the island, but he's so deeply asleep, so peaceful, I don't feel right disturbing him.

Instead I slip my pants off and pull my sweat shirt over my head before easing my way into his bed. He groans and rolls away, allowing me to settle in beside him. Then he rolls back, his arm coming down to pin me in place. I expect him to say something, but his breathing is deep and he's silent.

I work hard to settle into the safe closeness that Ezra offers, to relax into sleep. I manage to shed most of the anxiety I brought with me from Avril Island, but one question keeps surfacing that creates a new kind of unease. Why did a woman slipping into his bed unexpectedly, in the dead of night, not wake him in alarm?

*   *   *

When I open my eyes, I'm not sure where I am. A familiar panic rises in me; it's not the first time I've woken up in a strange bed. Then I remember. I'm not that person anymore, and I came to Ezra's last night. He materializes with the thought of him.

"Good morning, gorgeous." He holds a cup of coffee out to me.

I push myself into a sitting position to take it. "You're a very accommodating host. I show up announced, get into bed with you, and then you bring me coffee in the morning."

"You can get into bed with me unannounced any night, my dear." He sits down on the edge of the bed. "But in all seriousness, what the hell brought you across the lake in the middle of the night?" He takes a sip and studies me over the rim of his mug.

I run a hand through my bed head. "You won't believe what happened last night," I say, still not quite believing it myself. "I was dead asleep, and the sound of music woke me up. I went downstairs and the record player was playing." I pause for dramatic effect. "On its own."

He looks nonplussed, like I knew he would. "Old record players can be funny sometimes. Isn't it possible that it wasn't fully turned off and just somehow reset to start playing?"

"That's a stretch, but regardless, it was playing a different record than the one I was listening to before bed."

"So you hadn't been listening to the Beatles before turning it off?"

I go to shake my head, then stop. "Wait a minute. How do you know what record was playing when I came down?" I suddenly have this gross feeling that I may have been the butt of a very mean practical joke.

"You kept talking about the Beatles in your sleep this morning, so I just assumed." He looks away from me to put his mug on the bedside table. Then he pushes the covers off my legs and starts very gently running his hand up and down my thigh. "Did you have some drinks before bed? Is it possible that you forgot what album you put on last?"

I swat his hand away. "No, I actually didn't. I went to bed early, sober, and was totally aware of what was going on."

He puts his hand back on my leg. "Okay. I'm sorry. I'm just trying to think of all angles here."

I lean forward. "And do you know what song it was playing?" He shakes his head. " 'Blackbird.' "

He winces. "That's a bit creepy, isn't it?"

I slap his hand. "Yes!"

"Could the album have been under the one you were playing and you put it away, not even realizing you left the Beatles one on the record player?"

I have to actually stop and think about that possibility. "I don't think so. I played a couple of records last night, and I would have noticed if that one was still on the player."

"Probably."

"Anyway," I say, in an attempt to get to the main part of the story, "after the record player woke me, I was checking to see if the doors were locked, and I saw a person out the window running into the woods. So I followed them—"

"Hold on," he says loudly. "You saw some stranger on the island and you went after them? That's incredibly stupid, June. And dangerous."

"I took a fire poker with me," I explain.

"June," he practically yells. "A fire poker does not make you safe. Staying inside with the doors locked makes you safe. Calling the police makes you safe."

I motion for him to calm down. "I did call the police. After." He rolls his eyes and releases an exasperated sigh. "The person had a boat, one of those tin tippy kinds. They left it on the other side of the island, and that's how they got away. I didn't get to them in time, but—"

"In time for what, June? To beat them with a fire poker?"

"To see what they looked like. I wasn't actually planning on accosting them."

He throws his hands up. "Well, that's good, at least."

I glare at him. "Anyway. The police said it might just be some kid who thought that nobody was on the island and were looking for somewhere to drink or smoke up."

That explanation seems to calm Ezra down but only a little bit. "I guess," he says, but he sounds unconvinced.

"But then how do you explain the record player? And what about the dead birds? It seems a bit coincidental, don't you think?"

"It does seem like a coincidence, those two things happening back to back like that. And you seeing someone on the island lurking around at night. But both the birds and the record player can be chalked up to cottage things. There are a lot of birds in the area, so dead birds are not so unexplainable. Old funny wiring in a cottage, also normal up here."

"And there was this one night when I got locked in my bedroom and had to climb out on the roof to escape."

"What? Why haven't you told me about that before?"

"I don't know. It's kind of embarrassing but also really weird. I climbed out on the roof and over to the fire escape, and when I got back into the cottage, I found the key in my bedroom door, like someone had locked me in there."

"Old fussy locks. Another cottage thing."

I shake my head. "I know what you're saying, and if anyone likes a no-drama, practical explanation for things, it's me. It's just . . ."

"What?"

"I feel like someone must have done all of those things. It's just too random to blame them all on cottage things." I make air quotes.

"Unfortunately, I agree. I want to tell you that it's nothing, but it sure sounds like something. Either kids fucking around with you due to the whole haunted-island thing or maybe Leslie Swann, although her being in Boston doesn't explain the dead birds." He bends down to kiss my knee. "I'm thinking you should just move in here. Problem solved."

I shove my hand deep into his thick hair. "I've already lost too much time at Avril Island. I'm not going to lose more."

He nods. "I understand."

I move my hand down to his neck and gently massage it. "How about you come and stay with me instead?"

"I would, but there's the issue of my very senile, prone-to-outbursts, elderly mother to consider."

"Was it really bad last night?"

"It took me a while to get her back in the house. She kept insisting that she had to go see my father."

"How did you calm her down?"

"I just told her that he was going to be home soon. That we needed to go inside and wait for him."

"And that worked?"

He shrugs one shoulder. "She agreed to go into the house, but then she just sat in the living room, staring out at the lake, rocking back and forth. I left her alone and eventually she just fell asleep in the chair, so I covered her with a blanket, put a footstool under her, and left her there for the night." He thumbs in the direction of the house. "I went in early this morning, and she'd made her way to her bed and was still sleeping, so I guess whatever she was going through has passed for now."

I reach out and rub his back. "That sounds awful."

"Yeah. She's gotten a lot worse lately. I think I may have to find a care facility for her. And that's something I never wanted to do."

"Yes, but you also can't be expected to run a company and take care of your senile mother."

He nods, true sorrow suddenly flooding his face. "She's had such a hard life with my dad and everything, I just never wanted to, you know, abandon her."

"It's not abandoning her," I'm quick to say.

He holds up a hand. "Can we talk about something else? I don't have much time before I have to go to work, and I don't want to waste it on such a depressing subject."

It's unlike Ezra to shut down like that, and I can't help but feel a bit hurt by it. I wanted to make him feel better, not more alone, but I smile and nod. "Sure, of course. Just know I'm here for you and we can talk about it again if you need to."

He gives me a tight smile. "Thanks."

An awkward silence falls between us, which I can't help but feel is full of bad history, the one created by my mother and his father. I may be imagining it, but I can almost feel the blame radiating from his body: if it weren't for my mother, his would not be the way she is now.

"Maybe we could take turns," I say, in an attempt to move away from the topic of his mom. "You stay with me at Avril Island tonight and then I stay here kind of thing." He frowns. "Or vice versa. I mean, whatever you want."

"It's shitty timing, but I'm away tonight. For work. It's a big job and has been planned for months, so it's not like I can even get out of it."

It's childish, but I groan out loud. "Are you sure you can't get out of it?" I whine, not caring how selfish I'm being.

He grabs my hand and gives it a gentle pull. "Just stay here tonight?"

"On my own?"

"I don't want you staying on your own at Avril Island. Not until the police know for sure who was roaming around last night. Even if it is just some stupid kids, I'd feel better knowing you were here and not there alone while I'm away."

For a split second I think about being brave and asserting my right to stay wherever I please, but I also like having Ezra's excuse to not be brave and stay here for a night with Wi-Fi, a TV, a shower, and some human population around.

"Okay," I say, working hard to make my compliance sound reluctant. "If it will make you feel better, I'll stay."

He leans over and kisses me. "Good. I'm glad that's settled. Now, how would my beautiful guest enjoy breakfast in bed?"

"She'd love it." He turns to go, but I reach out and grab the bottom of his T-shirt to keep him there. "Since you brought up the topic of guests."

"Yes?" he says, eyeing me suspiciously.

"Why was it that me slipping into bed beside you last night didn't seem to surprise you? Do you often get middle-of-the-night female guests?"

He throws his head back and laughs. "I'd like to say I do, but no, you're my first one."

"But you weren't surprised?"

"June, I was exhausted. I'd worked all day in the sun; then I spent hours getting my mom settled down after the neighbor found her out on the street. I was fast asleep when you arrived. I knew it was you and figured you'd just decided that you didn't want to be alone after the dead birds so came here. I didn't feel the need to wake up and have a full conversation with you about it." He waits for an answer, but I just stare back at him, assessing the believability of his reasoning. "Okay?" he says firmly.

"Okay," I say back.

I'm not sure why I'm so suspicious when it comes to him. Especially when there isn't even an ex-girlfriend I know of or any sign of another woman. In fact, there doesn't even seem to be much of a dating history. Maybe that's the problem. I know Ezra so well and so little at the same time. There's a thirty-year gap in our history, and other than what he voluntarily tells me, I don't know much.

What I do know is that he's gorgeous, kind, considerate, successful, funny, and smart but has never been married and has never spoken of a long-term relationship. He bends down and kisses me gently on the lips before leaving the room to make me breakfast. I slide back down under the duvet, wondering why such a catch of a man has, as far as I can tell, remained uncaught.

* * *

After Ezra leaves for work, I head to Avril Island. The police called while I was eating breakfast and said they'd be by around noon. As I arrive back in the light of day, the night before just feels like a bad dream.

The morning couldn't be more perfect. The lake is like glass, the only movement a duck cutting through its silky surface. The sky is a clear blue, not one cloud in sight. Dragonflies zip above me, catching early-morning bugs. Nothing could be scary in this setting.

I sit with my feet hanging off the end of the dock. The water is so still I can see right down to the round rocks and old logs that cover the bottom. The odd fish swims lazily through the underwater obstacle course.

It's mornings like these that I remember from childhood. Looking back, it feels like every single one was like this. May and I would bring our cereal or toast down here, still groggy from sleep. We would have woken up, put on our bathing suits and maybe a pair of shorts. Grabbed some breakfast and a towel and headed down here. We'd eat in silence, both of us taking from the morning what we needed. Then we might go swimming if we'd woken up enough. Or lie on our towels on the dock in the sun—the boards already warmed with its heat.

My mother would come down at some point with her coffee and Baileys—a veritable force, upsetting the gentle morning balance of May and me. Wearing one of her bright, flowing bathing suit cover-ups, a bikini on underneath. She'd drop her tote bag beside a lounge chair and spread her towel out before shedding the cover-up.

Pulling out a tube of Bain De Soleil, she'd spread the orange tanning cream all over her already dark skin. The tropical-smelling substance enhanced one's tan; it didn't protect against it. Skin cancer was not a thing back then.

May often slipped off the dock at that point into the cover of the water, staying under as long as she could in the suspended, green quiet of submersion. I usually picked up my towel and moved it onto the lounge chair beside my mother's and asked to use some of her tanning cream so that I could smell her on me all day.

So many mornings bloomed from this dock into days full of swimming, tanning, friends, sailing, cliff jumping, water skiing, and lazy afternoons in the hammock. So many mornings identical to this one but now so far out of my reach.

*   *   *

The day is already hot, and just sitting there in the sun, I've broken a sweat. I wish I had my bathing suit on so I could dive in and cool off. Then it dawns on me that this is my island and I can do whatever I want. Who cares if some stupid kid is trespassing and catches sight of me? Maybe it will scare them off. I stand up and peel off my stale clothes from last night.

The breeze brushes against my liberated skin, and I wonder if anything feels better than this. Moving to the edge of the dock, I plant my feet and make a graceful dive into the cool, clear water. All the bits of myself that are usually covered by a bathing suit celebrate the sensation. It feels like swimming through silk as I pump my arms and legs through the deep water.

How have I not done this yet? I think to myself as I rise to the surface. And why not with Ezra? The thought brings on a fluttering of butterflies. I hang out in the water for a little while, then pull myself up onto the dock. I didn't bring a towel, so I hurry up the path and into the cottage.

Running across the living room to get to the linen closet, I reflexively cringe, expecting the scolding that always came if we walked through the cottage without drying off first. The silence reminds me once again that I'm alone and I'm in charge. When my girls come, I won't say a word if they decide to traipse though the place soaking wet. It doesn't hurt anything; the footprints dry right into the age-old wooden floor. Not having the same rules that my parents did is a liberating feeling.

Being back here is changing me. I can feel it. I'm slowly shedding the doubts and insecurities that grow like warts on your insides as you get older, rising from a breeding ground of multiple failures, controlling husbands, character assessments made by your parents that you never seem to fully escape, and other countless shards of life that get buried in your subconscious.

Avril Island has given me back some part of myself—the twelve-year-old girl I was when I left here so long ago. She didn't know enough about the world yet to be afraid, she didn't know enough about people yet to shut them out, and she didn't know that failure was even a possibility. That girl's been here waiting all this time for me to show up and reclaim her.

MAY

There are police here. Two of them—a man and a woman. They're standing over by the record player with June. The male police officer is holding the cord in his hand and examining it closely.

I understand why after I hear June explain how it turned on by itself in the middle of the night. June walks them over to a window and points outside to where she apparently saw someone run off into the woods.

The police ask her some standard questions about the doors being locked, and apparently she'd checked them before bed and they were. They seem to think the record player and stranger are an unrelated coincidence.

The male police officer speaks the most. He's about ten years older than June and maybe twenty years older than the female police officer. He has that condescending tone that older men in positions of power so often have, mostly directed at women, as though he's talking to imbecilic children. You can tell he used to be quite good-looking, which never helps in the attitude department. He wears a wedding ring, the skin puffy around it, so you can imagine him taking it off at night and massaging the blood flow back to the area.

Taking in all of these details, I realize I haven't seen anyone other than June and Ezra since I died. I'm a recluse even in death. Just for fun I move right up close to the female police officer. She shivers and glances over her shoulder, then puts a hand on her utility belt. She's pretty in a plain kind of way, her blond hair pulled back into a tight bun, no makeup, her body a well-worked-out machine.

The longing to feel the softness of skin, the press of lips, the cushion of breasts suddenly floods my space. How is a dead person supposed to deal with the longing for love? It makes me wish I'd spent more time on it while alive, gotten over the shame and just lived in my truth.

I had several girlfriends over the years, but my inability to go public with them always eroded away at the relationship, leaving me single in the end. The one-night stands I collected were brief encounters and left me feeling only shame. June always encouraged me to come out, to force my mother to accept it, but I just couldn't. I couldn't bear to give her more ammunition.

June is saying something about chasing the person into the woods and them getting away in a boat. The female police officer asks June to take them there, then glances over at the male police officer to make sure she's made the right request. I move up close to her again and say right into her ear, *Don't let the asshole intimidate you. He doesn't know any more than you do.* She turns her head in my direction and frowns before lifting a hand to her ear to brush my words away.

I don't follow them. Instead I watch from inside the cottage as June leads them both down the path into the woods, the sight of which brings a chunk of memory floating up to the surface. It's definitely part of the one I had the last time I was here, of West coming up the path toward me and my mother in the middle of the night.

In this bit of the memory, I'm standing at the very same window I am now, watching my mother and West disappear together into the forest with only the light of the moon to guide them. My mother is carrying a shovel; West is carrying something in his arms. I can't see what it is, because he's facing away from me, but I can tell by his pace and posture that it's something heavy.

The memory has a distinct feeling to it, one that surges in me now. I stood here watching something that caused me terror. I don't want to know what he's carrying or where they're going. I don't want to know why. The resistance brings the fading on. My visits are getting shorter, the bits of memory clearer and more ominous. I wonder how much time I have before the entire memory rises up to show itself. Will it break me apart completely, send me back to the quiet for good? Whatever is going to happen, I know it won't be long now . . .

JUNE

The police say that nothing was seen last night by the police boat but that they'll have a boat go by again a few times tonight to check on things. I take them to the place on the island where I saw the tin boat leave from, and I show them the tree with the cross. The male police officer just stands there looking bored, while the female police officer asks me some questions and takes a couple of photos of the tree.

They think it's a good idea to stay at a friend's for the night and wait for me to pack a bag before we all leave the island at the same time. I can't help but feel that I'm abandoning her all over again.

* * *

The day is hot, scorching to be exact; we've definitely entered a heat wave. Just tying my boat up to Ezra's dock in the sun causes sweat to roll down my back. Coming around the boathouse to make my way up to Ezra's apartment, I notice Willa digging in the garden. She's not wearing a hat, and her face is bright red and shiny with sweat. She really shouldn't be out in the sun on a hot day like this. She'll get heatstroke for sure, if she hasn't already.

Ezra told me to just steer clear of his mother while I'm here, that Judy will take care of everything, but Judy is nowhere to be seen. I can't just leave her out here if she doesn't know enough to go inside on her own.

I put my bag down and start a slow approach across the lawn. "Willa?" I say, as cheerfully as possible. "It's me, June." This time I definitely do not want her to think I'm my mother. She looks up, confusion on her face, which doesn't clear even when I'm standing right in front of her. "I think you should go inside. Get out of the sun. It's very hot out here."

She gives a weak nod and lets me take her by the arm and help her up. She's unsteady on her feet and leans against me as we make our way into the stone cottage. It's cool in the kitchen, and she breathes a soft sigh of relief.

"Why don't you go sit down in the living room, and I'll bring you a glass of water?" I offer.

She turns and shuffles off. I go in search of a glass and then, when I find one, fill it to the brim with cold water. Not sure if she's eaten anything all day, I make her a plate with some grapes and crackers, just in case.

She's sitting in her chair by the window, staring out at the yard, her hands folded in her lap. I place the plate and glass down on a small side table so that it's within reach.

She looks up at me, and I can't tell if she's still in the present or has disappeared again.

"I could have forgiven him if it weren't for the girl," she says quietly.

"Could have forgiven who?" I ask.

"West. I could have forgiven him." She shakes her head. "But it's all because of her. The girl. If it hadn't been for the girl."

"I'm sorry, Willa, but I don't know what girl you're talking about."

She laughs while at the same time tears appear in her eyes. "Why are you doing this to me?" The tears being to fall now. "What do you want from me? I already gave you everything." She points at me. "You took everything. All I have left is my son, and you can't take him too. Do you understand?" She clenches her hands into fists. "I will not let you take him."

I hear the kitchen door open, and seconds later the neighbor, Judy, appears in the living room, same blue sundress. "Well, what do we have here?" she says, even though it's quite obvious. "June. Didn't Ezra tell you to stay away from Willa while you were here?" She sounds like a kindergarten teacher who's just arrived to break up a fight.

The fact that Ezra told Judy to keep me away from his mother stings. "Willa was out in the sun when I arrived," I explain calmly, "without a hat and looking on the verge of sunstroke, so I just wanted to get her inside. I did look around for you, but you were nowhere to be seen, so I took it upon myself to get her out of the sun." I can't help but get that little dig in.

Willa suddenly stands up, her eyes locked on me and wild. "You stay away from my boy," she says loudly, white spit collecting at the sides of her mouth. "You stay away from him, do you hear me?"

Judy swoops in and takes Willa's arm. "Don't you worry, dear," she says to Willa. "June's not going to go near your boy. Ezra's fine. Just fine."

"It's the girl," Willa says, calmer now. "It's all because of her."

Judy gives me a quizzical look, and I just shrug in response. "What girl is that, Willa?" she asks, turning back to face her friend.

Willa lifts her arm and points at me. "That girl. She's the one."

Judy motions for me to go into the kitchen and goes back to talking to Willa in a soft, soothing voice, ignoring the talk about *the girl*. She leads her out of the living room and toward what I assume is Willa's bedroom. I hear a door close and then only low murmuring.

Not sure what else to do, I flop down at the kitchen table and try to sort through Willa's wild ramblings to see if anything rings true. She clearly wants me to stay away from Ezra, but what mother wouldn't want their son to stay away from the daughter of the woman who had an affair with her husband? *The girl*, though—I can't figure out why she said I was *the girl* or what that even means.

"I gave her a sedative," Judy says, coming into the kitchen, interrupting my thoughts. "She's out for the count for hours."

"I really was only trying to help," I say, a little too defensively. "She could have gotten heatstroke out there."

"Yeah, well, you don't tell Ezra that she was out on her own in the sun and I won't tell him that you got her all worked up again. Deal?"

I really can't decide if I like this woman or not, but I nod in agreement anyway.

She thumbs toward the door. "Come on over to my place and have a beer."

I don't love the idea of spending time with her, but she might know some things, and the offer of a drink is more than appealing right now.

*   *   *

We leave through the kitchen. She locks the back door with a key but then also slides a bolt that's fastened on the outside of it. "Ezra put this on a little while ago to keep Willa inside. The front door too," she explains. "For her own safety, you know?

So, you don't have to worry about her getting out in the night while you're here". She laughs warmly. "She does like to wander."

"That's good. It's a lot of pressure on Ezra to be the only one taking care of her." I follow Judy up onto her front porch.

She points to a set of worn wooden Adirondack chairs. "Have a seat, and I'll go get us that beer."

I do as she says but wonder why we don't sit on the lake side of the house, which in my opinion would be much nicer. She's back minutes later and hands me a bottle of cold beer. Easing herself down into the other chair with a deep sigh, she pulls a pack of cigarettes from inside the chest of her sundress.

"I like to watch the street traffic go by," she explains, before lighting a cigarette and inhaling deeply. "Good to know your neighbors' business, if you know what I mean." I actually don't. I'm the keep-to-yourself kind of neighbor, but I nod anyway.

Even sitting still, out of the sun, a layer of sweat collects along my top lip. It's almost six o'clock and the heat shows no sign of letting up. I take a long, grateful sip of beer. "It's certainly a hot one today," I offer up as conversation.

"So you and Ezra are close?" she asks, squinting as she takes another inhale, detouring from the small talk entirely.

"Yes," I answer easily. "We were good friends as children and have just sort of picked up where we left off as adults." *But now we have sex*, I think to myself, but of course I don't include that fact.

She takes a quick swig of her beer. "Funny," she says.

"What's funny?" I take the bait.

"Just that, after everything that happened between your family and Ezra's you can still be friends, he was mighty angry. I know he blamed your mom for his dad leaving." She takes another sip of beer. "And for his mom losing her marbles and all. Hell, I blame her too." She looks over at me, a challenge in her cold eyes.

"I can see why," I reply.

She gives a curt nod of approval. "I don't give two shits about West, if I'm honest. The minute he stepped out on Willa with your mom, I lost all respect and fondness for the man. It's Willa I care about, been friends with her all my life. She's a good woman, should never have been put through what she was put through. First not being able to have kids and having to adopt Ezra, then her marriage falling apart, her husband accused of who knows what, murder maybe. Then he up and leaves. It's enough to drive any woman mad."

I'm deeply regretting coming for the beer. It feels as though I've been brought over to sit in penance for my mother's sins. "Nobody should have to go through those things," I say, hoping my obvious sympathy for Willa will end the discussion.

"You know, I saw him that night." She takes a long inhale of her cigarette.

"Who?"

"West." His name comes out on a plume of smoke. "It was a hot one, just like today. I couldn't sleep." She pauses to take another sip of beer. "It was before I had the air con installed," she adds as an aside. "I went out back to sit by the lake and cool down a bit; was around one AM. Saw West come out through the back door and get in his boat and drive off in the direction of your cottage." She points at me.

It's a piece of information I didn't have before. Was West at our cottage the night of my parents' argument? And if he was, why? "You don't know for a fact that he went to Avril Island, and even if he did, it doesn't prove anything."

She cocks her head to one side with a smug look on her face. "The police sure thought it did." She drops her finished cigarette on the porch floor and crushes it under her sandaled foot, then with great effort bends down to pick it up and put it in an old coffee can. "Besides," she continues. "If he wasn't guilty, why the hell did he run?"

"I don't know" is all that I come up with. I'm suddenly overwhelmed with exhaustion about the whole thing. I've convinced myself that West had nothing to do with my father's disappearance, but now I learn he may have actually been there that night and cracks appear in the case for his innocence.

"Two men just vanish into thin air?" She snaps her fingers. "Two men in love with the same woman? It's no small coincidence." She chuckles to herself. "My friends accuse me of reading too many crime novels. Say it's gone to my head, but in my opinion the police gave up too easily."

"So you think West may have had something to do with my dad's disappearance?"

She holds both hands up in an exaggerated shrug. "What do I know? I'm just the neighbor. Just telling you what I saw is all. Don't have any more to go on than that."

"Does Ezra know that you saw his dad leave that night?"

She nods. "It was a sore spot for a long time between us. Me going to the police with it. He got over it though, eventually. Was a right angry kid for a long time and made sure everybody knew it." She gives her head a shake and chuckles. "He even went out to your place after you all left and spray-painted some nastiness across the side of the cottage, chucked a couple rocks through some windows. Police caught him, though, made him paint over the graffiti, and Willa paid to have the windows replaced."

More details about back then that Ezra neglected to tell me. I'm starting to wonder how truthful he's actually been with me. Is there nobody in this town I can really trust? Is there anyone who doesn't have some reason to hate my family?

"So you see," Judy unfortunately continues, "why I find it surprising that Ezra has become such good friends with you?

Or you with him, for that matter, if you're suspecting his dad might have caused your dad harm."

"I guess we both just decided to leave the past in the past," I say, before draining the last of my beer. I hold up the empty bottle. "Thanks for this, Judy. I certainly needed it."

"My pleasure. Come on back for more later if you want. I'll be here." She starts the process of lighting another cigarette.

"Thanks, Judy, that's kind of you," I say, getting up out of my chair.

"Kindness is all you have these days," she says. "Some people round here weren't happy to hear that a Bennett had returned, but you didn't have nothing to do with what happened back then, so I say give you a chance." She leans back in her chair and narrows her eyes at me. "Now, if it was your mother turning up, well, that would be a different story. I'd certainly have some comeuppance to bestow on that woman."

"Understandable," I say, thinking she'd have to get in line. I give a last wave and head toward Ezra's yard.

* * *

Halfway to the boathouse, my phone rings. It's a local number that I don't recognize, but I answer it anyway, thinking it might be Ezra from a landline. Before leaving, he told me that reception would be spotty where he was going.

It's not Ezra; it's animal control. Apparently, he gave them my name and number when he took one of the dead birds in for examination.

"The bird was poisoned," the woman on the other end of the line says, wasting no time. "Probably rat poison, but it's hard to say if that's the thing that killed it," she goes on to explain. "Due to the fact that it had also been frozen at some point, which may have been the cause of death."

It takes my mind a few seconds to compute what she's saying. I stop in the shade of a tall oak so I can concentrate better. "So, it definitely wasn't natural causes?" The question sounds stupid as soon as it comes out and hangs there between us.

She chuckles a bit. "Only if the bird ate a pile of rat poison and then flew itself into a freezer."

"There were twelve of them," I say, ignoring her poor attempt at a joke. "Twelve birds dead on my doorstep." I appreciate the stunned silence I get in return.

I hear her readjust the phone and then clear her throat. "Well then, miss, it sounds like a case for the police rather than animal control." I tell her I've told the police and that they're looking into it. She says she'll give them a call to provide more details on the situation. She wishes me luck, which I suddenly feel I'll need, and then hangs up. It takes a lot of maliciousness on someone's part to poison birds and then freeze them so they can be placed on a verandah. I'm not sure even Leslie Swann would have been up to that task, even if she had been in town the night it happened.

It's cool inside Ezra's place. It smells like him too—woodsy and clean, which would normally be comforting, but right now it's not. Learning that someone put those birds on the verandah on purpose, systematically killing them first, combined with all the negative talk from the neighbor, has truly fucked with my head. I don't feel safe at Avril Island, and now, thanks to Judy, I'm finding it hard to feel safe here at Ezra's. I really don't know who to trust anymore.

Deciding I have no choice but to make myself at home, I plug my phone into Ezra's stereo to play some music. There are too many voices and questions in the silence. I find some burgers in the freezer and a lone beer, a perfect dinner for one, so I busy myself preparing that, taking it out to the deck to eat when it's ready.

As I sit outside with the sun slowly beginning its descent, it feels like nothing could be wrong in this world. Could I actually do what I told Judy I've done, leave the past in the past? Could Ezra and I just focus on each other and the future we could have together? It's not such an easy question to answer after hearing about so many things that he neglected to tell me. Withholding the truth is as good as lying, Leo used to tell the girls whenever they wouldn't admit to a wrongdoing. I always disagreed, thinking it wasn't quite as bad as a lie—until now.

*   *   *

It's only nine thirty, and I've run out of things to do. I hung out on the deck until the bugs arrived, then cleaned up the kitchen, called the girls, and watched some crappy TV. As I sit now in stillness on the couch, the question I've been avoiding all evening refuses to be ignored—*How well do you know Ezra, really?*

It's just light snooping to begin with, pulling open some drawers to see what they hold, going through the pile of bills on his counter, looking at what's in the medicine cabinet. As I go, I convince myself that I'm just getting to know him better. That if he'd had anything to hide, he certainly wouldn't have invited me to stay over for the night without him here.

I wander down the hallway and into his office. It's meticulous, just like the rest of the place. Going through the filing cabinet, I find nothing other than well-kept records on work he's done at local cottages and tax documents. The desk doesn't hold anything of interest either. Could the man literally have nothing to hide?

There's an antique wooden trunk sitting in the corner of the room. I try to open it, but it's locked. I look around the office for the key but don't find one, so I decide to move on to the bedroom.

Nothing but clothes and shoes occupy the closet; pens, half-finished crosswords, and a broken Fitbit rest on the bedside table. It's a disappointing search, and I'm not ready to give up just yet. I return to the trunk in the office. It's the only thing that's locked in this whole place. Why?

I go to the key rack in the front hall, but there's nothing there that would fit such an old lock. So, I head into the kitchen to find something I can use to jimmy the lock open. Determination to get inside that trunk has eclipsed any guilt I might have had over snooping.

With metal skewer in hand, I head back into the office. It takes a little finagling to find that sweet spot that releases the lock, but eventually I hear a pop and am able to lift the lid and reveal what's inside. A pile of yearbooks, some baby clothes, an old Boy Scout uniform, a collection of wood carvings that I'm sure he made with his dad, and an old cigar box. No body parts or drugs or guns, just life stuff collected over the years.

I flip through a few of the yearbooks and find Ezra's class photos. It's exactly the boy I remember, only a little bit older. He played football, was on the debate team, made the honor roll, won medals in track. A pretty upstanding high school career, considering his dad had taken off when he was twelve. I certainly got into more trouble than he seemed to.

Putting the yearbooks back, I reach for the cigar box next. The scent of stale tobacco wafts free when I flip open the lid. The box holds a mess of photos. As I lift the top one out for a closer look, confusion and surprise knot together in the pit of my stomach. The photo is of me when I was little. I remember the dress made of thin red corduroy with yellow flowers on it. I'm holding a pink balloon in one hand and a half-eaten banana in the other. Flipping the photo around, I see my mother's familiar handwriting: *June 3 years old at cottage.*

There's another photo, a close-up of my mother holding a baby that I'm pretty sure is me as well. I flip the photo over, and sure enough, in my mother's handwriting, it says *June 6 months*. There's also a photo of May and me in matching bathing suits on the dock at Avril Island. The back reads *May 10 and June 7 at Avril Island*. There's a photo of Ezra and me fishing off the end of the dock. The last one is a close-up of me at around age eleven, just my face while I look off into the distance. I remember May taking a bunch of these photos, telling me to ignore the camera and look deep in thought.

Sitting among the photos is a poem about summertime. I don't remember writing it, but it's signed at the bottom by me and looks like it was ripped right from one of my notebooks. There's also one of my old rope bracelets and a thick lock of dark-brown hair tied with a ribbon. I have a pretty strong suspicion that it's my hair and drop it back in the box with a shudder.

Ezra must have stolen the photos from my cottage, and the poem and bracelet, and god knows how he got a chunk of my hair. I pile it all back in the box and place it in the trunk before slamming the lid down. Pushing myself up off the floor, I return to the living room, where I come face-to-face with May's photos of Ezra and me at Avril Island. Did she actually send those to him, or did he steal them like the other items in the cigar box?

I wrap my arms around myself and sink down onto the couch. I don't even know what to feel—anger, flattery, fear. Why would he want those photos of me and the poem and bracelet and hair? Judy said he was angry at my family after everything that happened, so why keep souvenirs of one of us?

No matter how I frame it, the whole thing feels insidious. Not wanting to be here, not wanting to be at Avril Island, not wanting any of this, I pull a blanket off the back of the couch, slide a pillow under my head, and curl up right there, wishing it would all go away. But with every breath, I breathe in the scent of the man I've accidentally fallen in love with. The man who in an instant has become unknown to me, who has an unhealthy obsession and an agenda that I just can't figure out.

MAY

The cottage is dark and quiet when I arrive. I can tell without looking that nobody is here. It's the first time I've arrived in the living realm without anybody being there. Am I no longer attached to June? Has she left Avril Island, leaving me in the process?

I float up to the second floor and am flooded with relief when I see her belongings still scattered about the room. Why, then, am I here? Floating from room to room, I search for the point of my presence here, in the shadows and in the light that comes in from the moon.

I glide through the tunnel-like darkness of the stairwell, but something stops me at the bottom, as though I'm here in the flesh and my dress has gotten snagged on a nail, holding me in place. It's not a nail, though, that I'm caught on; it's another bit of memory dislodging from deep down and floating to the surface, tethering me to the spot where it happened.

It was the night that I left June upstairs so I could secretly listen in on my parents' fight. My father's arrival on a Wednesday was too unusual, too disruptive to not investigate. So I ordered June back to her room, promising I'd be back soon with an update, then went downstairs and tucked myself into the shadows on the second-to-last stair to listen.

The memory is fuzzy; I can't remember what my parents were even arguing about. All I do know is that my plan had been to go unnoticed, to simply collect information and then return it to June. But what I heard caused me to rise up out of hiding and charge out into the bright light of the living room.

My appearance brought shock to the faces of both my parents. "I heard you," I yelled at them. "I heard you." I don't remember what happened next. The memory refuses to reveal itself entirely, stopping there in the midst of the anger and tension.

It leaves me frustrated but relieved at the same time. Inserting myself into the middle of my parents' argument might have only brought on a scolding. Maybe I was just sent back to bed, only to wake up the next morning to find my father had left us all.

It doesn't feel that simple, though. I can sense that the rest of the memory hidden down there in the dark is much bigger than that. Why else would I have buried it so deep?

JUNE

The ringing of my phone wakes me. I've spent a restless night on Ezra's couch, going over everything in my mind and getting only a few hours of fitful sleep. Grabbing the phone from the coffee table, I manage to croak out a hello before the caller hangs up.

It's the female police officer who came to the island yesterday. She says they circled the island several times last night but didn't see any activity at all. I ask if she's spoken to the woman from animal control about the birds, but she says she hasn't. I tell her exactly what the animal control woman told me, and the police officer says she'll follow up with them right away.

Before hanging up, she asks me if the cross in the clearing could be a grave for a family pet or animal we buried as kids. I tell her we didn't have any pets growing up. I also remind her that I got rid of the cross twice and it reappeared.

"Ah, right," she says. "That's quite the mystery, then, isn't it?" She goes on to apologize for not having any substantial information for me and promises to get in touch as soon as they have anything else.

I'm only half listening, my mind already back at Avril Island doing my own detective work. She didn't have anything specific

247

for me, but she made me realize that there may have been a crucial piece of the puzzle sitting right there in front of me this whole time and I didn't even realize it.

*   *   *

By the time I arrive back at Avril Island, Ezra has called me three times, but I just let it go to voice mail. I'm not sure what to say to him. Do I admit to snooping, or do I pretend I didn't find a small creepy shrine dedicated to me in his office? I need more time to come up with a plan, so for now I'll ignore him.

The day is hot again, and I don't relish the idea of spending it shoveling, but I have a very strong feeling that the tree that keeps sprouting crosses is the place to start in my search for answers. I grab a pair of work gloves and go in search of a shovel. There's only one in the tool shed. It's rusted, and the wooden handle is splintered in places, but it will have to do.

The quiet of the forest is penetrated by the sound of my shovel hitting the dirt, over and over again. I start away from the tree to avoid the roots, but breaking through the green ground cover to get to the damp soil below is hard. Only twenty minutes in, I'm dripping with sweat. It's even hotter today than it was yesterday.

Every few minutes a voice in my head tells me to give up, that I'm crazy and won't find anything, but something in me will not let my body stop putting the shovel in the soil and tossing it to the side. As the hole gets bigger, adrenaline releases through my veins to keep me going.

The occasional bird lands on a branch close by to mock me with its call. The sweatier I get, the more flies I attract, but other than stopping for water, I just keep digging. And then finally, the swoosh of my shovel sinking into dirt becomes a clunk, the impact traveling up my arms and into my shoulders.

Clearing away some of the loose earth, I see what looks like a wooden board. It takes time to shovel the rest of the dirt away until I've uncovered the entire length of it. Next, I dig down along the sides to loosen it from the ground. It's then that I realize what it is—the long, wooden blanket box that used to sit under a window in the living room of our cottage. It was used as a window seat and to hold the scratchy woolen blankets that we never actually used.

I stumble away from the hole, hands throbbing, my head pounding, sweat burning my eyes. Pulling off the work gloves, I throw the shovel to the side and rush back along the path out to the lake to bend down at the shore and splash water on my face. Holding my hot, throbbing hands under the surface, I imagine falling forward to let the cool water claim me, floating away from what I'm sure I will find in that wooden trunk—the body of my dead father. But I've come too far for that now. I lift my hands from the water and force myself back to the tree.

The forest pulses with silence as I stand beside the hole I've made. Fitting the blade of the shovel under the lip of the trunk, I push down hard on the handle, using the ground for leverage until I hear the gentle pop of wood separating from wood.

Getting down on my knees, I take a deep breath, ignore the roll of nausea in my stomach, and lift the lid of the trunk. No matter what I was expecting to find, the skeletal remains in the trunk still send an electrifying shock through my body and a high-pitched wail from my mouth.

I fall back onto the freshly turned earth with a hand to my chest. The silence suddenly pounds my ears with its force, making me feel more alone than I ever have. It was a mystery in my head to be solved, a challenge, but now that I've actually uncovered a part of its truth, all I want to do is unknow it.

What feels like an eternity passes. I'm frozen on the ground with fear, not knowing what to do or who to turn to. Eventually I work up the courage to inch forward toward the hole. Placing my hands in the dirt, I lean forward over the grave. There is no question that it's an adult who was buried here; the knees are folded up against the body. I'm looking for signs that it's my father, but all of the clothing has disintegrated.

Reaching in, I shift some parts around to get a better look at things—trying not to gag as I do. I lift the left hand, looking for a wedding ring, but the fingers are empty, which makes sense because I found my father's ring in the cottage. I lean in further and lift the right arm, ignoring the unpleasant crunch it makes as I separate it from the rest of the body. I have to look away for a second and take some deep breaths. Manhandling this skeleton is making me feel like I'm going to pass out.

With some deep breaths, the feeling passes, and I'm able to turn back and keep going. There's something wrapped around the right wrist. I give it a good tug and it comes free. It looks like a bracelet made of leather, about an inch wide. I think it used to be brown, but it's black in places as well, so it's hard to tell.

This detail confuses me. I don't remember ever seeing my father wear a bracelet, but something about it is so familiar to me. I can picture it wrapped around a man's tanned wrist, which means my father must have worn it at some point. Why else would I remember it? I tuck it into the pocket of my shorts. It's the only clue I have; there's nothing else left on this body.

Abandoning the open grave, I head back to the cottage. If I can find a photo of my father with this bracelet on, I'll have my proof. Then I'll go to the police. They'll have to reopen the investigation. They can do DNA testing, go back to the evidence they collected years ago, and finally figure out what really happened. It's time for the truth to come out, even if it's a truth that in the end proves that West really did kill my father.

MAY

It's dusk. The sky is streaked with bright orange and pink. There's a stillness to everything, as though the entire island is holding its breath. Heat bugs chirp in the trees, even though the sun is setting and everything green is wilted slightly as though weighed down by the humidity. It must be a heat wave.

June hurries across the backyard, a frantic look in her eyes. Her skin is streaked brown with dirt, her hands are bloody, and her tank top is soaked through with sweat. She looks as though she's fought her way out of a fox's den.

The screen door swings open wide as she rushes through it and then snaps back fast, sounding like a gunshot. She goes right to the liquor cabinet in the dining room, pulls out a bottle of Scotch, and struggles to get the lid off. Taking one of my father's tumblers down from the shelf, she pours at least two shots of the amber liquid into it. Watching her lift the glass to her lips, I see that her hands are shaking. She throws the Scotch right down her throat, coughs, and then pours herself another.

Finishing her drink, she moves into the kitchen, where she runs her hands and arms under the tap, then rubs soap onto her skin, wincing as it soaks into her cut hands. For once I wish

Ezra were here, or anybody, for that matter. I need her to talk—to tell someone what's going on so that I can hear as well.

She dries herself with a tea towel and then heads straight upstairs. She's on a mission; I can feel it buzzing around her and see it sparking in the blue of her eyes. She goes right into my room and gets down on her knees in front of my bed to pull my suitcase of photos out.

Sitting cross-legged on the floor, she flips through them at a rapid pace, mumbling to herself as she goes. She bypasses photos of herself, of me, of my mother and of the cottage. The only time she slows down to actually study a photo is when my father is in it, but even these she tosses back into the suitcase with a huff of frustration. There's black dirt packed under her fingernails and a line of red blisters along the palm of each hand.

Getting up off the floor, she reaches into the pocket of her shorts to pull something out. It looks like a piece of old brown leather. She turns it over in her hands, rubs the surface of it with her thumb, her brow furrowed in concentration.

After staring at it for several seconds, she looks up, and I can almost see the answer dawning in her head. She sinks back down to her knees in front of the suitcase and begins to once again sort through the photos, slowly this time. After a few seconds she finds something, bringing it out of the box to study it closely. It's a photo of June, Ezra, and West. They're looking right at the camera, holding up the wood carvings they've just finished. I remember taking the photo.

June stares at the picture, looking as though she's seen a ghost. She lifts the piece of brown leather up to the photo, her eyes moving between both as if looking for a match.

"It's not him," she whispers into the empty room, her eyes wide with shock, her lips parted. "It's West."

What is West? I ask while passing right through her, hoping she'll say more. All she does is shudder and look with confusion around the empty room.

Her phone starts to ring. Ezra's name sits on the screen as it chimes loudly.

She shoves it away from her. "Oh my god. Ezra," she groans, clutching at her stomach and bending over as though in pain. The ringing eventually stops, but she stays as she is, staring at the phone blankly—grief all over her beautiful face.

Is this my penance for some unknown sin I committed in life? To watch my sister suffer while I hang in the atmosphere beside her, helpless to do anything?

JUNE

The night is thick with the fragrance of the forest and heavy with heat. The sound of a boat engine in the distance skips across the calm lake to reach me as I make my way back along the path to West's grave. I decided to cover it back up. I don't want animals or rain to get in there and disturb it. I'll tell Ezra about it and let him be the one to decide what he wants to do next. I have no idea how West's body came to be buried on Avril Island. All this discovery has done is create yet another mystery.

Using my phone as a flashlight, I carefully make my way through the dark. I'm light-headed from the Scotch and an empty stomach, and there's an unsettling tremor all through my body from adrenaline and the effort of digging up a grave. My island that is supposed to be my refuge has turned into a waking nightmare.

I keep getting flashes of May, her scent, her voice, the feeling that she's in the room with me. It's comforting, so I tell my skeptical side to shut up. I don't want to be alone in all of this, so what harm can come from imagining my sister is right here with me, even if she's dead?

As I turn onto the path that leads to the tree, the light of my phone grows dimmer. It's at only six percent battery. I silently curse myself for not taking the time to charge it.

Stepping into the small clearing, I'm thinking I'll end up filling everything back in by dark, only to find that the hole has vanished. There's still enough light from my phone to see that I'm not imagining it. Only flat earth sits in front of the tree. I move right up to it for a closer look. All the earth has been returned to the grave and carefully packed down. I spin around, looking for whoever completed the task, but there's no sign of anyone. Even the shovel is gone.

It's as though the grave uncovering never even happened. For a split second I wonder if it actually did, but then the pulsing of the blisters on my hands reminds me that I did not imagine it. I'm not crazy. Someone covered that grave up, which means I'm not alone on this island and they could be anywhere. Maybe even in the woods, watching me right now.

Rushing back out to the main path, I scroll through my phone until I find the number for the local police station. Before I can even hit call, my phone dies. This is when real fear sets in. Someone else is on this island with me, and my only tether to the outside world has been cut.

I break into a run back toward the cottage. My mind desperately swings between two plans: get inside, lock the doors, and plug my phone in to call the police, or grab the boat keys, get off the island, and drive to town.

Before leaving the cover of the forest, I stop and scan the lawn for signs of anyone, my gaze skimming across the windows of the cottage as well—sick at the thought that I may see a dark silhouette pass by at any moment. But the cottage remains still and quiet, the lawn empty.

I decide to rush inside, get the boat keys, and get off the island altogether. The back door is closest, so I make a run for it. I grab my purse from the counter in the kitchen and keep moving into the living room, where I grab the boat keys from the key rack.

Without stopping, I go right out the front door and down the steps of the verandah. As soon as my feet hit the path to the dock, I start to feel a bit better. I can see the boat down there, waiting to take me to safety.

Only a few feet away from the lake, I hear a rustling in the bushes just behind me. Before I have a chance to turn and see what it is, an explosion of pain erupts across the back of my skull. White sparks flash behind my eyes, and then everything goes black.

MAY

June lies motionless on the couch, and a strange woman is tying her wrists together with a long piece of rope. June looks dead, but I know she's not. I can feel her life and see the gentle rise of breath in her chest.

The woman is much older than she was the last time I saw her. The hair is now white, the skin wrinkled. It's Willa—Ezra's mother. I'd recognize those piercing green eyes anywhere. She mumbles to herself as she secures June's ankles together. She's wearing a white nightgown, but it's stained brown and makes her look as though she's been sleeping on a bed of dirt.

June, I scream, with as much force as I can muster. Willa looks up, a slash of confusion upsetting the determination on her face, but it passes and she returns to tightening the ropes.

June groans loudly, and Willa jumps back, startled. I push between the old woman and my sister, a wall of spirit separating the two. I don't imagine it will do much, but it makes me feel better. June's eyes flutter and then slowly open. She looks up at Willa, and I can see her struggling to make sense of things.

"Willa?" she says. Moving to sit up, she realizes her hands and feet are tied. "What the fuck?" Anger quickly replaces the confusion. "Willa, untie me." The woman shakes her head. June propels herself up into a sitting position, then winces in pain. There's blood on the back of her head. "Was it you who hit me?" Willa nods. "With what?" June asks, unsuccessfully trying to reach around and assess the damage.

"A shovel," Willa answers matter-of-factly.

"But why?" June asks, sounding like she might cry. "Why would you do that? And why are you even here?"

"You thought I didn't really know anything, didn't you?" she asks with a smug smile.

June leans forward. "Willa, I'm June. Not April. Do you know that?"

"I know damn well who you are," she snaps back. "That day I came here to blackmail you, you thought I was just bluffing. Didn't you?"

June shakes her head. "I don't know what you're talking about, Willa. Just please untie me."

Willa pokes a bony finger at June. "West told me everything." The old woman doesn't even seem to be hearing June. There's definitely something not right about her, something dangerous, I can feel it.

"I believe you," June says calmly. "I believe that West told you everything. So, why don't you untie me and we can talk about it." She lifts her hands up. "This is hurting me, and I think I might need stitches in the back of my head. Please, Willa, I need your help."

Willa flinches and looks away from June, confusion twisting her features. She gives her head a little shake, mumbles something to herself, and then looks back at June with new resolve in her eyes. "If you really believed that West told me everything, then you never would have come back. You would have been too scared to." She pokes herself in the chest. "But I do know everything. I do."

June stares up at Willa in silence, and I can see her trying to figure out which new tactic to take. "That's right," she says, her demeanor suddenly changing from pleading to challenging. "I don't believe you know everything. So, prove it. Start from the very beginning, then."

I'm guessing June's strategy is to play along with Willa in the hopes that in the end she'll be able to convince the woman to untie her. It's a risky plan, but hopefully June knows what she's doing.

Willa rocks side to side, from one foot to another, looking as though she can't stand to be still. "West and I got in a fight, and that's when it all came out," she quickly begins, as though she's been waiting all along for someone to come and release the story. "About the affair, even about the girl," she says, fury building with each word. "He said he was leaving me." She suddenly stops moving and stares straight ahead, looking as though she's been transported back to that very time. "I was mad, so I called Simon and told him everything that West had told me. That's why he came rushing up here." She pauses, the fury surprisingly replaced with a look of remorse. "Because I told him."

"You don't know what happened to Simon, though, do you? After he came here," June pushes, intensifying the tension in the room.

Willa looks down at June. "I do know what happened to him. I do. He was killed that night. Murdered. I swear it."

June pulls back as though she's been slapped. "My father is dead? You know that for sure?"

Willa looks confused. She stares at June for a few seconds as though trying to figure out who she is. Then her gaze slips away, back to the past. "The daughter, she overheard everything," she explains.

"I didn't overhear anything," June says, before it dawns on her that Willa is talking about me. "You mean May overheard everything?"

Willa nods and then points at the staircase. "West said she'd been hiding in the stairwell, listening to her parents fighting about the affair, the girl. Then she came rushing out at him. It all happened so fast." Willa slams her palms together, causing June to jump. "Happened just like that."

"What happened so fast?" June practically yells.

"She killed him. May. She heard it all and killed him."

The color drains from June's face at exactly the same moment that the rest of the memory dislodges. The ancient sea creature has woken, ready to drag me down to the depths of truth.

*　*　*

The things I heard while hiding in the stairwell that night had made me desperate with panic, blind with rage. I rushed into the living room wanting only to make my father stop saying the horrible things he was saying. I didn't have a plan; nothing about it was premeditated.

I rushed at him, pushing against him with all my strength. He was caught off guard, stumbled backward. I smelled his cologne and the pungent scent of alcohol, my forceful shove releasing it from his clothing into the air. It would have been fine if it hadn't been for his briefcase sitting on the floor behind him.

There was nothing for him to grab hold of and it happened so fast, the briefcase knocking his feet right out from under him, sending him crashing to the floor, the back of his head connecting with the edge of the fireplace hearth on his way down—making a fatal-sounding thud of flesh against stone.

My mother moved forward to help him, but I stood fixed to the spot, watching the strange spasms that coursed through his body for a brief few seconds before he went still. A small pool of blood spread out around his head, and his eyes stared blankly at the ceiling above him.

My mother said nothing as she searched for a pulse, listened for breathing, put a hand over his heart. Only when she found no sign of life did she turn to me. "You killed him," she said, in an eerily calm whisper.

I sank down to the floor, my body shaking, my teeth chattering so hard I was sure they would break apart in my mouth. My mother lifted me up and guided me to the couch, wrapped a blanket around me, brought me a tumbler of my father's Scotch, and instructed me to drink it.

She covered my father's body with one of the scratchy wool blankets from the blanket box and then went into the kitchen. I heard the sound of the phone receiver being lifted from its cradle, the hum of the rotating dial, and then her hushed voice. I assumed she was calling the police or an ambulance, but it was West who arrived that night, not emergency services.

The Scotch worked quickly to stop the chattering of my teeth and slow the shaking of my body until it was only a slight tremor. When my mother returned to the room, I was coherent enough to focus on her words.

She knelt down in front of me and took my hands in hers, grasping them too tightly for it to feel like affection. "You need to listen to me closely, May Bennett," she said, sounding firm but not angry. "What happened here tonight must stay a secret. If we tell the police, they will put you away for a very long time. Do you understand?" I nodded. "You will have to stay in a horrible place without me or June. You don't want that, do you?"

My mother's stern face blurred behind the tears that filled my eyes and spilled quietly down my cheeks. "No," I whimpered in response.

She freed one of her hands to wipe away the tears, one of the most affectionate things she'd ever done. "Of course you don't, and I'm not going to let anyone take you away." Her conviction was comforting. "You are my daughter and you belong with me. Always."

I didn't know then that she was essentially signing me up for a life sentence to her, that I would be imprisoned by our bond of secrecy until she died. I would never not be able to do her bidding. I would never be able to disagree or argue or assert myself. When she was sad, I was to be the one to comfort her; when she got sick, I was to be the one to care for her; when she was alone, I was to be the one to keep her company. She held my secret, which meant she held my freedom too.

"I'm going to take care of everything," she continued. "No one will ever know what you did. I will make sure of it." She got up off her knees. "Now, go lock June's bedroom door so that she doesn't come down until we've got everything cleaned up."

I surrendered to the calm, competent direction of my mother. It kept me from thinking about what I'd done, about the reality of the situation. I tiptoed back upstairs. From a hook in the hallway I retrieved the skeleton key that locked and unlocked all the bedroom doors. I went to June's door and, as quietly as I could, inserted the key and turned the lock.

Waiting on the verandah with my mother for West to arrive, I watched her, waiting for some signs of grief, but they never came. She paced, she chewed at her nails, but there were no tears. She was deep in thought, not deep in sorrow, over the loss of her husband. I realized not long afterward that I had in fact done her a favor. Saved her from the wrath of my father and the revenge he had planned for her after finding out about her affair with West. I had saved myself and June at the same time, but it was a price I should never have had to pay.

The first thing West asked when he got there was, "Where's June?" I told him that she was sleeping, that I'd locked her door just to be safe. He said that was for the best, and without a word we all knew that June was never to be told what had happened that night.

The cottage was dark—my mother thought it would look suspicious to have lights on so late if someone drove by in a boat. My mother told me to scrub the blood from the floor and wait for them there. Then they both disappeared into the forest, my mother carrying a shovel, West carrying my father's body. By the light of one candle I got down on my hands and knees and washed away the evidence of the murder I'd committed.

*   *   *

"May did that?" June asks, as soon as Willa finishes describing the fatal push I committed that night.

Willa gives one conclusive nod. "So you see, I do know everything. I know about my West helping you hide the body and how you made him drive your husband's boat to an abandoned island so his fingerprints would be on the steering wheel and how you stashed Simon's watch in his boat, then called the police accusing my West of murder." Willa stops to take a deep breath, tears suddenly shining in her eyes. "You see?" she says again. "I know too much."

I want to fade away, forget what I just learned about myself, not see the hurt and confusion and shock on June's face after learning that her sister is a murderer or hear any more of Willa's ramblings about that horrible night. But the fading won't come. I'm supposed to be here, remembering, suffering, witnessing.

Tears are running down June's cheeks now, too, from all that she's just learned. "Willa, it's me, June." Grief has stripped her of the ability to keep up the charade. "Please untie me. I'm not going to hurt you. I'm not my mother. I'm on your side."

Willa starts shaking her head and wringing her hands. "I can't. I can't untie you. There are too many secrets. My boy, he's going to find out if I don't do something. You never should have come back. You promised."

June sighs deeply and wipes her tears away with the back of her tied hand. "I know you had a deal, Willa. You keep saying that, but it was with my mother, and I'm not my mother." The last four words come out as a yell, and Willa jumps.

Willa's own tears start to fall, and she roughly wipes them away. "I tried other ways, I did, but they didn't work," she explains. "It wasn't supposed to come to this." Willa looks down at the floor. "I'm sorry," she says softly. "I'm so sorry. It's for my boy."

Before June can say anything, Willa disappears from the room, and then there's the sound of the back door slamming shut. I expect June to try to get free from the ropes, to yell out, but all she does is sit there staring straight ahead, looking defeated and sad.

I move right up close to her, wishing I could wipe her memory clean of everything or at the very least be there to explain, to comfort. I flood the space around her with my presence, making myself as big as I can.

"Why didn't you tell me?" Her voice is low and quiet. Tears start to slowly roll down her cheeks. She glances around the space as though looking for something. "I know you're here, May. I can feel you." I push in closer so that I'm almost passing into her body but not quite; it's as close as I can get without coming out on the other side of her. "Whatever made you do it, I would have understood. I would have kept your secret." Her tears are coming faster now. The sound of footsteps arrives on the front verandah, and June quickly tries to wipe the tears away.

Through the glass of the front door, I see Willa appear. She's holding something red, but she disappears from sight before I can tell what it is. When she doesn't come into the cottage, I move to the windows that look out onto the verandah.

The red thing in her hands is a gas can, which she has tipped forward so that a steady stream of gasoline pours across the wooden floor of the verandah. I can see that she's doused the entire length of the front of the house. She walks backward down the steps, coating them as she goes. Only when the gas can runs empty does she set it down. Reaching into the pocket of her nightgown, she pulls out a book of matches.

I swing back to June, who's still sitting on the couch, unaware of Willa's plan for her and the cottage. *June*, I scream, at the very same time that a wall of flames jumps up in front of the windows. As it builds, it makes a loud whooshing sound that causes June to twist around to see what it is.

The bright orange light of the fire is mirrored in June's blue eyes, which are already full of panic. Twisting her wrists, contorting her hands, she frantically tries to free herself from the rope. I can see that it's no use. Willa may not know who's who or what day it is, but she definitely knows how to tie a rope.

An ax sits against the side of the fireplace, tucked away so that it's mostly out of sight. If I can make June see it and she can somehow get over to where it is, she may be able to free herself.

The sound of the fire is growing stronger. The glass in the windows has started to crack, and there's a gentle groaning as the fire eats through the wood of the building. It's only a matter of minutes before those flames find their way inside.

I leave June struggling with the rope and go to the ax. I've never moved anything so big before. I focus all my strength on it, call on every bit of will I have, and then move myself as forcefully as I can right at the inanimate object. I may be imagining it, but I think it slips just slightly. If I can get it to fall over, it should make enough noise for her to notice.

Behind me June starts to cry softly. She's scared, sure that she'll die in this fire all alone. She's thinking about her girls and Leo and how badly she wants to get back to them. I feel all of it.

I push in against the ax again, but nothing happens, so I start a swinging motion, moving back and forth over it as fast as I can. I feel it pass through me each time, the wood, the cold metal. The windows blow out, sending a shower of glass into the living room. The flames quickly find their way through the windows and start to lick up the wooden wall to the ceiling.

June screams and slides down to the floor, cowering awkwardly, her hands and feet still tied. I can feel the draining start to happen. I've used up almost everything I have. I stop swinging; it's not doing anything.

So instead I think of all the things I love about my sister—her throaty laugh, the set of her face when she's trying not to cry, the way she looks at her girls when she thinks nobody is watching, how her body folds into mine each time we hug, her scent, her jokes that people can't always tell are jokes, her pain and her strength. I think of it all and then fling myself at the ax with the power of all those things.

It topples and falls forward onto the floor. Better than I'd hoped for. June looks up and sees it sitting there and starts to shimmy across the floor on her bum. I see her slide it between her knees, blade side up, and start rubbing the rope stretched taut between her wrists.

This is why I'm here. Why I've been here all along. To save her at the very same place where I caused the end of my father's life. The thought floods me with peace and calm. June will be okay. Somehow I know this to be true. The fading comes on slowly; I don't fight it. I finally know that I've done what I was meant to do.

JUNE

The ax is dull and it feels like it's taking forever to slice through the rope, but finally I get through one end and am able to untangle it from my wrists. Thick smoke and salty sweat sting my eyes. I have to close them as I work at the rope around my ankles.

The entire front of the cottage is consumed by flames. Staying low, I crawl toward the back of the cottage, but before I even reach the kitchen, I can feel the heat from more fire in that direction. Willa must have started it at both ends.

The only way out is to go upstairs and use the fire escape. Still on my hands and knees, I make it to the stairs and crawl up as quickly as I can. It's only a matter of time before the building starts to collapse in on itself. Flames haven't reached the second floor but the smoke has, filling the upstairs hall, blocking out the light and sucking up the oxygen.

I reach the fire escape door, roll on my back, and kick it open with all of my force. Tumbling out onto the landing of the metal staircase, I gulp in the fresh air.

I'm light-headed and dizzy, my throat is scalded and my lungs are scorched, but I'm alive. Adrenaline keeps me moving despite my shaking legs and the desire to collapse in a heap. I get down to the bottom of the fire escape and rush to the front of the building.

Flames are devouring the cottage. I want to scream for help, but my voice has been burned away. I turn in circles, looking for an answer. My phone is in the cottage. I see a flash of white across the yard. Willa darts out of the woods. She sees me and stops dead in her tracks. I don't know if she realizes it's me or if she still thinks I'm my mother, but her face falls, her shoulders slump as though she's once again been defeated.

Neither of us moves for several seconds, and then suddenly she breaks into a run across the lawn, disappearing behind the burning cottage. I'm ready to chase after her when I hear someone call my name. Turning toward the lake, I see Ezra running up the path, the bright light of the fire illuminating the fear in his eyes.

"June," he yells again, before yanking me to him and holding me against his body. His skin feels so cool against mine. He has not just walked through fire to be here.

I pull free. "Willa." The name is croaked out, stinging my throat as it exits. I move toward the fire, and Ezra reaches out to grab me. Tugging against him, I say her name again, this time stabbing the air with a finger to show him she's here somewhere.

A veil of confusion falls across his face. "My mom is here?" I nod, and the confusion turns to panic. "Inside?"

I shake my head and take his hand to pull him in the direction that she went. We race to the back of the cottage, but she's not there. We both go in opposite directions to check along the sides and meet back at the front.

"Where is she?" he screams at me as I approach.

"I don't know." My own scream comes out like as whisper. "She came out of the woods and went around back. That's the last time I saw her."

He starts screaming her name at the woods, running in every direction across the front lawn. Movement on the roof pulls my attention away from him, and when I look up, I see Willa standing far above us. She's balanced on one of the peaks like the statue of an angel, her white nightgown billowing in the breeze.

"Ezra," I call out. It's not loud, but somehow he hears me. I point up; he follows the direction of my finger and goes very still.

"Mom," he calls out. "Don't move. I'm coming to get you." She shakes her head. "Mom," his voice pleads. She shakes her head again. Ezra moves toward her, and she backs up toward an open window, making it very clear that if he goes up there to get her, she'll go into the burning cottage.

"What the fuck is she doing?" he says, tears and panic heavy in his voice.

I reach out and take his hand. "She wants it to be over," I explain. He doesn't say anything. We both just stand there, watching Willa, who is watching us.

When it's clear that Ezra is not going to come up after her, she puts her hand to her mouth and blows him a kiss. His body jerks forward, but I hold tight to his hand and keep him in place. She finally turns and walks along the peak to the open window, ducks down, and crawls through it. A sob escapes Ezra, but he stands firm. Something in him knows it's the right thing to do. That by not saving her, he's saving her.

We stand there together, hand in hand, and watch. We both know there's no point in trying to stop it. It's an old wooden cottage on an island; it never stood a chance next to Willa's gas can and match.

Only when the whole island is lit up by the blaze and sparks fly into the night sky to land on the ground in front of us do we call the fire department. Then we stand there and wait. The air is filled with the sound of wood splitting, glass smashing, and flames raging. Every now and again the building lets out a low groan as walls cave in and floors buckle. I am watching the slow, violent death of my cottage. Losing my beloved Avril Island for the second time.

Tears stream down Ezra's face. Somehow, I'm dry-eyed. Maybe I'm just happy to be alive. Maybe after all the truth I've learned since coming back here, I'm finally ready to let the island go. To bury the past in the ashes that she will become.

I don't tell Ezra that his father died on Avril Island as well. I don't tell him anything. We stand in silence until the fire department arrives. I give them a partial truth about taking care of Ezra's mother, who suffered from dementia; about how I left her on her own for a short time and came back to find the fire. How we tried to get her out but were too late.

They examine me and tell me to go to the hospital. I lie and say that I will. Then I lead Ezra away, down to the dock. When we get back to his place, he doesn't come up to the boathouse with me. He goes into the stone cottage, telling me he needs some time alone. I let him go, understanding the need to grieve in private better than I ever wanted to. He's stunned and still in shock. I know the feeling well. I know that it will pass, leaving only deep sorrow behind, which will not pass; it will turn to scar tissue that will throb when it rains and burn with movements that are too quick.

I get myself into the shower. I'm covered in the dirt of Ezra's father's grave and coated with smoke and soot from the fire that killed his mother. The water quickly washes all of this away, but it's a superficial cleansing. I will never really be clean of their deaths; they will haunt me forever. Crouching down in the shower, I put my head between my knees and finally cry.

* * *

Fire dreams and the scent of burning skin jolt me awake. I could only have been sleeping for a couple of hours. Once again I've spent the night on Ezra's couch, falling in and out of a trouble sleep. It's morning now, the sun streaming through the window giving the false impression that it's just any other day.

There's a note on the coffee table from Ezra. Apparently, the fire department called and he had to go deal with some things regarding his mom's death in the fire. He didn't want to wake me.

I get dressed and have just started the coffee-making process when Ezra's home phone rings. I answer, thinking it could be something important. It's Ezra. He's at the fire department and needs his mom's year of birth, which she has never revealed to anybody, for some paperwork. He asks me to go into the stone cottage to find her birth certificate and call him back with the information.

There's an eerie feeling inside Willa's house, as though she could appear at any moment. There are dishes in the drying rack and the soft sound of a fan whirring in another room. I find her purse sitting on a table by the front door and go through it but don't find anything with her birth year on it.

I go into her bedroom and rummage around in a small writing desk but find only old bills and receipts for things. The only place left to look is a bedside table. It looks like a drawer filled entirely with old Kleenexes, but when I put my hand in and dig around, I come up with an old wallet. Inside is her birth certificate.

Shoving the wallet in my back pocket, I think about just closing the drawer as is but figure I should probably get rid of the garbage for Ezra's sake. Gathering up all the Kleenexes into a ball, I catch a glimpse of something else sitting there in the drawer. A key ring with two keys on it, both tarnished with age. I lift it out to get a closer look. There's an old tag tied to the key ring that reads AVRIL ISLAND, and the keys are each labeled with pieces of masking tape—one reads DOCK SHED, the other GARDEN SHED. It's pretty much identical to the set of keys that has always hung on the key hook at the front door of our cottage, except that with this set, the main cottage key is missing. If I had to guess, I'd say it was West's old set, and that most likely Willa was in possession of the missing key. I slip the key ring into my pocket and shut the drawer.

From the kitchen I call Ezra with the information he needs. He thanks me and says he'll be back soon. Before leaving the stone cottage, I do a bit more looking around—pulling drawers open, lifting the lids on things to peer inside, opening closets, taking a look in the medicine cabinet.

My search having turned up nothing substantial, I stand at the living room window, debating whether or not to give up and go back to the boathouse. That's when I notice them, three black birds, the very same kind I found on my verandah, hopping around the base of the feeder, pecking at fallen birdseed.

Moving back to Willa's room, I go right to the window. There's a lock at the top and it looks as though it's secured, but when I give the window a push, it pops open easily, providing a very convenient mode of escape. Was Willa my tormentor?

There's the sound of a boat approaching, so I quickly shut the window and rush out of the stone cottage. I'm there in time to greet Ezra as he pulls up to the dock. He looks pale, all of the life drained right out of him. Other people's deaths will do that to you.

"Everything go okay?" I ask, even though I know nothing is okay for him right now. He gives me a weak smile and a nod, then busies himself tying up the boat.

Upstairs, I pour Ezra a cup of coffee. "You look like you could use this," I say, passing it to him.

"That bad, huh?" He tries a laugh, but it comes out more like a grunt.

"Is there anything I can do for you, Ezra?" I ask, wishing I could make the pain that's sitting in his eyes disappear.

"You could tell me why my mother was really at Avril Island last night." His words catch me off guard. "I remember hearing you tell the firefighters that you were taking care of my mom, but I don't really understand why you'd take her to Avril Island or why you'd be the one taking care of her, since it's Judy's job. And the really strange part is that the fire department told me today that they found my tin boat on the other side of the island." He sighs deeply and runs a hand through his hair. "So you see why I'm confused? I mean, what the hell were my mother and my boat doing at Avril Island last night?"

"That's your boat, the tin tippy?"

He nods, eyeing me with suspicion.

I don't need any more proof than that. Willa was the one sneaking around Avril Island, leaving dead birds in her wake and record players on. She was the one I chased that night, the one who escaped in the tin boat.

"She was the one trying to scare me off the island," I say, as the understanding dawns on me.

"Who was the one?" he asks in frustration.

I think of the many secrets other people have woven through the fabric of my life. Thick, black thread that marred everything, changed the structure of it all, and I know I can't be the one to continue sewing that thread. I will not take up that needle and spread it through Ezra's life as well, even if it does mean incriminating my sister and revealing his mother's part in all of it.

"I will tell you, Ezra. I will tell you everything that I know and the things that I don't, but we need to get comfortable. It won't be easy, and it will take a while."

I tell Ezra how I believe it was Willa coming to the island all this time, doing things to try to scare me away. I tell him everything she told me before setting the cottage on fire, even the part about my sister pushing my father and killing him.

He listens quietly, asking only one or two questions, his face serious, his emotions kept mostly at bay. He shows only a split second of shock when he hears that it was May who killed my father and then sympathy for what that must mean for me. We spend some time speculating on what my sister heard that night that brought her out of the cover of the stairs to confront my father with such rage, then accept that we will probably never know and agree that perhaps it's for the best.

I leave the part about his father's grave for the end. I don't have any answers around it, and I don't want to be the person who delivers such horrific news—two parents lost within twenty-four hours is unbearable. But he has a right to know, which means I have no choice.

"There's one last thing," I say, reaching for his hand. "Do you remember me telling you about the cross at the tree, how it kept reappearing?" He nods. "I thought it was kids messing with me, but then it dawned on me that it was actually a grave." He gives me a funny look, but I just keep going, now that I've got the courage. "I dug it up, all around the tree, and I found a body."

"Your father's?" Ezra says.

I shake my head. "Yours."

He narrows his eyes with skepticism, and I feel his hand tense in mine. I quickly tell him about the leather bracelet on his wrist and the photo with West that matched it. How I figure it must have been Willa putting the crosses there and visiting it regularly. "But I don't know how he died or ended up there. Willa didn't tell me anything about your dad."

Ezra gently pulls his hand from mine. "I do," he says, and the room feels as though somebody has set it spinning.

"You knew your dad was dead all this time, but you told me you had no idea where he was?" He nods his head slowly, remorse clouding his blue eyes. "Why did you lie to me, Ezra?"

"I was protecting my mother, June." Like mother, like son, I think to myself.

I pull my legs up under me and cross my arms over my chest, tucking myself away from him, the betrayal sitting large between us. "Protecting her from what?" He doesn't say anything. "I will walk out of here right now, Ezra Keen, if you don't tell me the truth. I just confessed to you that my own sister was responsible for my father's death. You can't get more vulnerable than that."

He gives a nod of concession, then sits up from the couch, leaning his elbows on his knees and staring out at the lake. "It was one night quite a few years back. She was having one of her episodes. Calling out, saying that she saw angels, that they were coming for her. When I went in to console her, she thought I was a priest." He gives his head a shake, as though he can't even believe he's telling the story. "She asked if she could confess her sins so that she would go to heaven. Of course I told her she could. I just wanted her to calm down and go back to sleep."

He gets up and goes to get a glass of water, bringing one for me as well, even though I'd like something much stronger at this point.

"So, she confessed to you?" I encourage.

He takes a long drink of water, then takes his time setting it down carefully on the coffee table. "I guess you could say that," he says, still looking unsure about what he's about to reveal. "My mother said that she had made a plan to blackmail your mother for money, only because she was worried West would never work again. She and my dad arranged to meet your mother at Avril Island. They told her they were going to go to the police with the truth if she didn't pay them."

"Wait," I interrupt. "So all this time you knew what the truth was and didn't tell me?"

He quickly shakes his head. "No, June. My mother didn't go into any details about what actually happened. Just that they knew the truth, whatever that was. Your mom apparently had a gun and said she'd kill them both before she'd be blackmailed. That it would be for the best anyway, since they knew too much. That she could call it self-defense. My mother was mostly afraid of me being left as an orphan, so she tried to backtrack, apologize, and say they wouldn't do it, they'd keep the secrets, but your mother didn't believe them anymore. She thought West had turned on her. My mother apparently became desperate, sure April was going to kill them both. So she lunged at April and got the gun away somehow. She knew, though, that if she hurt April, then both she and my father would go to jail, and again I'd be left on my own." He pauses to take another drink of water.

"This sounds like some kind of bad movie," I can't help but interject.

"And I'm not even done yet," he says. "That night that my mother thought I was a priest, she told me that *she* shot and killed my father. Thinking it was her only way out alive or free from jail time. She said that she and April buried him on Avril Island."

"My god, Ezra, that's crazy. How did you not tell me this?"

"My mother's thinking was that if both she and April had secrets, then neither of them would betray the other. They made a deal that April would leave and never come back and my mother would protect the secrets of Avril Island. She said she did it all for her boy. So that I wouldn't lose her as my mother. I didn't tell you because I didn't want to believe it. I convinced myself that it was just dementia talking, but you found his body, just like she said."

We both sit in silence as this new truth sinks in. My head is throbbing with the realization that my mother and Willa, two women who were enemies, ended up bound together in their lies and crimes. My mother spent her life running from here and Willa spent hers slowly going mad because of what they'd done. The night it happened must have been when my mother asked Suzanne Swann to lie to the police, just in case West's death came back on her somehow. Unfortunately, it all makes sense now.

Ezra gets up from the couch and goes over to a cabinet. He takes out a bottle of bourbon and pours us both some. I gratefully take the glass when he hands it to me. It's not even noon yet, but the things we're dealing with are beyond the parameters of time.

"I'm sorry I kept it from you, June," he says. "I was protecting my mother. I think a part of me always believed it could be true. And then if it wasn't, what good would it have been to go around telling anybody?"

"It wasn't the only thing you kept from me, Ezra." He gives me a look of surprised confusion. "Vandalizing my cottage?"

He rolls his eyes. "My god, June, where did you manage to dig that up?"

"I didn't have to do any digging. Judy told me."

He throws up a hand. "Yeah, I did a stupid kid thing and committed some light vandalism. I was angry and didn't know what to do about it. I also cleaned it up and have more or less taken care of the place ever since because I felt so badly about it."

"Why didn't you tell me?"

"Because I was ashamed of it."

I take a sip of my drink for courage and then get up off the couch and go into Ezra's office. Opening the trunk, I find the cigar box. I bring it out to him in the living room. "And what about this?" I say, holding it up in front of him.

He looks confused at first and takes the box from me to look at it more closely. I can see recognition slowly dawning. "Ah, this," he says, flipping the lid open. "It was my dad's. Where did you get it?"

"I found it in the trunk in your office."

He narrows his eyes at me. "Why were you looking in the trunk in my office?"

"I was snooping around. I admit it. The night I stayed here alone. I had a beer with Judy and she told me how angry you'd been at my family and about the vandalizing and seeing your dad leave that night in a boat headed toward Avril Island." I sink down on the couch beside him. "I just didn't know who I could trust, and I was feeling suspicious."

In typical Ezra fashion, he reaches out and rubs my arm. "I understand, June. I probably would have done the same. I just wish you'd talked to me about it up front."

I point at the cigar box. "Are you sure that was your dad's?"

"Yeah, I'm sure," he says, studying the box in his hands. "A little while after my dad disappeared, my mom and I were cleaning out his work shed. She pulled this down from a shelf. At the time, I was in this total 'don't throw anything of his out' stage. I still thought he was coming back. Anyway, my mom saw what was inside and started crying. She said something about the girl—'if it hadn't been for the girl,' or something like that—then threw it in the garbage and stormed out, calling my dad a bastard. As soon as she was gone, I took it out of the garbage and hid it away in that trunk." He holds up the photo of the two of us fishing. "I think mostly because of this."

The girl. The words roll around my head like a marble in a metal bucket, loud and loose. I'm the girl; Willa told me so herself. The one in the photos in the cigar box hidden away in West's shed; the one that somehow made West's betrayal unforgivable to Willa. Willa used *the girl* like an exclamation point every time she talked about the secrets kept by my mother and West. Suddenly it becomes so clear. I was the greatest betrayal of all—a daughter born from their affair.

And the photo of me, West, and Ezra holding up our wood carvings—West and I stare out at the camera with the same crystal-blue eyes. That's what Willa meant the first day I saw her when she said I had my dad's eyes.

The cigar box—it's not Ezra's shrine to me. It was his dad's shrine to his daughter. My mother would have given him those photos, that poem, the lock of hair. Items to remember me by when we weren't at Avril Island, to mark my growth through the years, times he missed out on.

"June." Ezra reaches out and takes my arm. "Are you okay?"

I pull away. A wave of thick nausea rises up. I rush from the room, making it to the bathroom just in time to empty my stomach, the bourbon burning on its way back out.

I hear Ezra rushing down the hallway toward the bathroom, so I quickly kick the door shut with one foot. He pounds on it, demanding to know if I'm all right, but all I can do is pull a towel from the towel bar and shove it into my mouth to stop the scream.

*   *   *

Bathroom doors are not impenetrable. Ezra eventually gets in and finds me on the floor, sobbing into the bath towel, vomit in the toilet. I let him pick me up off the floor and guide me to the couch in the living room. He brings me a glass of water and tells me to take deep breaths, but every time I try to explain, new waves of grief and anger roll through me, bringing more tears.

He paces in front of me until I can finally talk. It all comes rushing out as though I were accusing him, not his father and my mother. He shakes his head, refuses to believe it, so I get the cigar box, shake it in his face, and ask him why his father would have these things. I repeat every time that Willa mentioned *the girl*.

He is silent for a long time, just standing there studying my face until he can see it there in me—his father. "That bastard" is the first thing he says, and there is true venom in his words. "My mother couldn't give him his own blood child, so he had one with another woman."

"She definitely saw it, *me*, as the biggest betrayal of all. She said once, 'If it hadn't been for the girl, I could have forgiven him.' " I picture her that day in her living room, driven mad with anger and sadness, jealousy and regret. "I just had no idea that the girl was me, that I was the thing that was so unforgivable."

MAY

The night that I sat tucked in a ball of shadow on the second-to-last step of the cottage staircase, I became a witness to all the betrayal. At first it was just my mother saying it was lies, all lies, that Willa was a jealous, crazy woman out to destroy her. Some French words slipped into her defense at times, which let me know that she was scared.

I assumed it was the affair she was denying, but then, in a strangely calm and composed voice, I heard my father say, "I did often wonder if June was really mine." I thought I'd misheard him, but he went on. "The summer before she was born, you wouldn't let me touch you. We didn't have sex even once. Then you come back to the city, have me undressed before you've even unpacked, and lo and behold you get pregnant. And the baby is a month early. Can you believe it?" He laughed a bitter-sounding laugh. "I must give you credit, though, Avril. Getting pregnant by the caretaker and then making me believe all these years that she was mine. Pretty darn clever."

At that point I wished so badly that I could run back upstairs and unhear what I'd heard. June was West's daughter, my half sister, Ezra's half sister? I wanted to climb back into bed and be none the wiser.

My mother started her loop of denial once again, but my father ended it with a fist coming down hard on whatever table he was closest to. It scared her quiet, along with everything else. Even the hum of the ceiling fan in the living room seemed to lessen.

His next proclamation was simple and to the point: "You are a whore, April Bennett. You probably always were, and I was just too stupid to see it." My mother gasped at his harsh words and I hugged my knees tighter to my body, as though becoming smaller could make me hear less. "I'm leaving you," he continued. "I'm taking May with me, and you won't see either of us ever again. You and June can run off with your maintenance man and live happily ever after, for all I care. And don't think you'll be getting a penny from me. Not a penny."

Flashes of light appeared in front of my eyes, and I felt like I was going to throw up. My mother started sobbing, and tears began to silently fall from my eyes.

"You can't do that," she said. "You can't take May away from her mother and sister. You can't."

"I can and I will, April. I'm a powerful man. I can make a lot of things happen. I'm not going to leave my only daughter with a whore for a mother. I'm going to go wake her up, and then we're leaving. You and June have twenty-four hours to get off this island, but after that, if you're still here, I'll have you arrested."

The flashes of light turned to a pulsing red orb that set my entire body on fire. I had only one thought in that moment, and it was that I would not be separated from my sister. Without a plan or any forethought, only pure rage and fear, I lunged free of my hiding space and ran at him. Throwing my entire weight at his body so that he stumbled backward, fell against the fireplace, and died. Setting in motion a string of events that would change people's lives forever.

JUNE

I wake up slowly. After the discovery that West was my father, I told Ezra I needed some time alone and locked myself in his bedroom. The entire landscape of my life had changed in a split second, and I needed time to process it.

I must have fallen asleep at some point, everything in me just shutting down. It feels as though hours have passed and the day is gone. Deciding that I have to face Ezra and the world sometime, I leave the cocoon of blankets I'm wrapped in and go back out into the main part of the apartment.

I'm surprised to see that the sun is starting to go down. Ezra is moving around the kitchen to a soundtrack of jazz. I slip onto a stool at the island, and he slides me a glass of red wine.

"I'm sure you could use that," he says, pausing in the cutting of an onion to survey my face.

"Thanks," I say, before taking a sip of wine and then another. "What are you making?"

"Just a couple of omelets." He brushes the chopped onion into a frying pan bubbling with butter. "I didn't think you'd be very hungry and neither am I, but we should probably eat something."

"You're right. I'm not." An ache starts in my heart and travels down into my belly and legs, then up my arms and neck until it's taken over my whole body.

I drink down more wine, trying to drown my thoughts and focus on the mundane tasks he's performing in front of me. I watch his hands as he breaks eggs into a metal bowl, then whisks them into a sunny yellow batter. His brow is furrowed in concentration, his mouth open just slightly. I know in this moment that I love him. Truly love him. I also know there's an uncrossable chasm of history, lies, secrets, and betrayal that sits between us.

"So, I guess we're brother and sister," I say, trying to infuse some humor into this messed-up situation.

"Ah, no, we're not," he's quick to say, not even missing a beat in his omelet making. "I was adopted, remember? We don't share a bit of blood. And thank god for that, because otherwise I'd be in love with my sister." He visibly shudders.

His proclamation of love, even though I was only just thinking it myself, catches me off guard, his words breaking through the thick skin of my heart. I start to cry. He moves the frying pan off the heat and rushes to me.

"It's going to be okay, June. We'll get past all of this, I promise." He wipes away my tears and holds me to him.

I reach up and pull his face to mine, kissing him deeply, letting my desire for him push away all other emotions. He returns it equally. We move quickly to the bedroom and waste no time stripping away our clothes, coming together with the desperation of two people who have lost too much and are on the brink of losing each other.

* * *

Waking at dawn, I move slowly off the bed, make sure Ezra is still sleeping, and then soundlessly slip out of the apartment.

The sky is gray and the heat has lifted. The bow of the boat cuts through the light fog that swirls across the surface of the still lake. I'm the only one out here, the sound of my motor a cruel interruption to the peaceful silence of the early morning.

The damage to Avril Island, seen in the light of day, pains me. I walk in a wide circle, taking in the wreckage, which spreads all the way out to the trees sitting on the periphery of the lawn. There is nothing salvageable, only the suggestion of what things once were—a black pile of remains. Standing there, I can hear the screen door open and slam shut, smell the musty pine scent that hits you as soon as you step inside, hear the creak of the floors, feel the metal doorknobs in my hands. No fire can burn those memories away, but the loss of their reality suddenly cuts through me, bringing me to my knees.

I put my head in my hands and cry yet again, wondering if I will ever run dry, the sound rising up in the quiet morning to surround me with the soundtrack of my own pain. I have lost so much but still have so much. It is a balance that both hurts my heart and fills it. I could have died in that fire, but I didn't. I know my sister was there, that she helped me get out, made it possible for me to return to my girls.

The same sister who, Willa claimed, killed her own father. I don't have to believe it. I could convince myself that it was the ramblings of a delusional old woman, but I don't. Deep down I can see the truth in what Willa told me.

My father's leaving us affected May in ways that it did not affect me. She was scarred from that night, and I never fully understood why—I do now. I felt it all along, the secret, like a tiny pebble caught somewhere in the fabric of our closeness. You can't know someone as well as I knew her and not sense a secret.

I don't feel anger, only sadness that protecting me kept her from protecting herself, from sharing the burden so that she wasn't alone in it. For there is nothing I would not have shouldered for my sister, no secret I wouldn't have kept, no pain I wouldn't have shared.

Sucking in my breath to stop the tears, I force myself up off the ground. I didn't come here to fall apart. Skirting around the wreckage, I take the path to the tree. The grave is still covered over. So, it wasn't something I imagined in the darkness. It dawns on me only now that it must have been Willa who filled it back in, while I was at the cottage trying to figure out whose body it was.

Avril Island has become a graveyard for the main players in my mother's game of betrayal. The only one who made it off this island alive was her, which is no surprise at all. I see now that she lived her life in survival mode, always calculating her next move. Using people to fill her up, care for her, make her matter, provide things that she herself couldn't, then discarding them when they turned on her or let her down. Had her childhood made her that way, or had she come to it naturally?

"I'm sorry, West," I say to the ground. "I'm sorry that you loved her as much as you did and that it brought you only pain. I will always remember you. Your kind words, your patience with my questions, the way you taught me about birds and plants and fishing and wood carving. Good-bye. May you have found peace, wherever you are." I bend down, put my fingers to my lips, and touch the freshly turned earth.

I'm sorry for West and for Willa, but mostly I'm sorry for Ezra, May, and myself, victims of the decisions and actions our parents made. As children, you just trust in your life and in your family. You have no choice; it's the only way to survive. You convince yourself that what seems wrong is right, that what feels bad is not so bad at all, that what you are being told must be the truth because it's coming from a parent. When you grow up and are finally able to step behind the curtain of childhood, the truth can be blinding.

I say good-bye to Avril Island. I will not be back. There is nothing left here for me anymore but the past, and I no longer want it. This truth pushes deep sadness into my bones, but at the same time, gratitude settles into my heart for having had Avril Island at all—for the chance to swim her waters, to be in her forest, to lie on her dock and sleep in her beds. This place holds my family history, both good and bad. And I can't help but feel that the only way I would ever have escaped it was by having it burn to the ground.

Making my final walk down the path to the dock, it feels as though the island reaches inside me and rips a chunk of my heart free. I let her, hoping she will plant it in her earth and keep it forever.

I drive my boat to the marina. Knowing it's my last time skimming across this lake, I make sure to take in the landscape, to enjoy how it feels to fly across water. I'm grateful that I got to come back here one more time.

I leave here a different person than the one who came. I was always depending on someone else—my mother, May, Leo—to define me, to point out my next steps, to influence my actions and decisions. I did Avril Island all on my own, brought her back to life, searched out her secrets, and then put them and her to rest.

I have survived solitude, grief, finding love and losing it, a bloody house fire, and discoveries that altered my entire history. Avril Island raised me through the summers of my childhood and now has taught me what I need to know in adulthood to free myself of her, my past, and my own mistakes.

MAY

It would appear that the rules of death are ever changing. I'm not attached to June anymore, I think because she no longer needs me to be. And the coming and going has stopped. Now I'm at Avril Island, in the earth, the trees, the rocks; no one thing holds me. I'm everywhere and everything at all times. It's a peaceful way to be.

If I want to pull myself together, I can, but that's only when I feel like going into the cottage. Buildings can be ghosts too, you know? We make each other appear just by being together. So I get my body back for a little while, and she gets her walls and floors and windows and plumbing. Every now and again I like to walk down the hallways, lie across the beds, rock on the metal glider on the verandah. I never spend much time in there, though, only a few hours, because it gets lonely remembering what was.

I still get to talk to June in her dreams. We're always in my bedroom at the cottage. It seems to be our forever meeting place. It makes sense—growing up, it was always our safe place. We spent so much time in there, just the two of us. A cocoon that not even my mother could rip apart.

Eventually the island will start to claim the burnt-out wreckage of the cottage. Moss will climb up and over it, pulling it down into the soil so that it's a less violent reminder of what happened that night. The land has a way of doing that, absorbing our sins in an attempt to cleanse them and make them good again.

My only visitor is Ezra, but he doesn't come to see me. He comes to remember June and to check on the place. He likes to study the ever-changing remains of the fire, walk the trail June restored, visit West's grave, sit on the end of the dock to stare out at the view.

In the beginning his heart was broken into a million tiny pieces, but over time it's mended. I can feel it each time he sets foot on the island; it's almost whole again. The last time he came, he brought a woman with him. I listened to him tell her the stories of this place, and I felt her receive them with empathy and understanding. She is as good as him—I can feel it all around them.

Ezra is proof of one thing I now know for sure—we all heal eventually. As long as we let go. Shed the anger, the regret, the guilt. Stop letting other people's words scream through our heads, accept that not everything is good or right or fair or the way it's supposed to be.

Mothers are not always good just because they're mothers, and fathers are not always good just because they're fathers. Wives are not always faithful, husbands are not always honest, daughters cannot be perfect, and sisters cannot be saviors. The sooner we accept those variables and forgive people for them, the sooner we heal.

JUNE

I will wake up every day, remember that my sister is gone, and mourn her. I will also get out of bed and continue living life. I will talk to her throughout the day, not sure anymore if she's there to hear me but finding my words to her comforting. The piece of me that she took in death will remain an open wound. I will bandage it regularly, but it will never fully heal. She was my sister and she took part of me when she died. A part that nobody else in the world can replace.

For several years I'll have dreams where I get to speak to May, to hug her, lie with her, laugh with her. The ones that help me miss her not quite so much. We will always meet in her bedroom at Avril Island. Then one day those dreams will stop and I'll have to accept that she's moved on to wherever we move on to.

I will have regular dreams of Avril Island as well. Sometimes I'm a child and my mother and sister are there, frozen in time. Sometimes I'm an adult and Ezra is there and so is the fire. No matter what age I am when I dream of it, Willa is there. Maybe in the garden pulling out weeds, maybe a flash of white nightgown through the trees—always reminding me.

Ezra and I will keep in touch through emails, even the occasional phone call; we share too much to fully let go. I will ask him to keep an eye on Avril Island for me, and eventually I will deed it to him and tell him to do whatever he sees fit with it. We will not see each other in person again. That would be just too painful.

I will dedicate the book I write about Avril Island to him. I will thank him for his friendship and remind him that he is forever in my heart, despite the distance that must be. That truth and the writing will help me come to terms with my parents and what they turned Avril Island into.

Time will cleanse the bad memories my parents created, and eventually I will feel only gratitude when I think of the place. Gratitude for Ezra, for May and our time there, for night swims and dock days, rainy-day card games, roaring fires, diving down deep into cool water, sailboats and cottage friends, late-night boat rides, skies full of stars and mornings full of sun.

As I grow older, it will be the place I go to most in my mind to calm me, to cheer me when I need an escape. Avril Island will always be a refuge, even if it's only the memory of her. Because place can be taken away from you, but the imprint of place is tattooed on the inside of your soul, making it yours forever.

ACKNOWLEDGMENTS

Thank you firstly to my agent Carolyn Forde for believing that a publication would absolutely happen, for convincing me of that, and then working tirelessly until it did. Much gratitude to my editor Jenny Chen for seeing what this book could be and guiding me in all the right directions. And to Melissa Rechter and Madeline Rathle for getting me through the final stages.

To my husband Josh, you gave me a room of my own, the time and support to chase this lofty goal and I will be forever grateful for that. To my children, Luke and Ruby who are daily inspiration to do more, be more and never give up on a dream. To my older sister Rebecca, thank you for always being my biggest fan and my safest place. And to all of my friends and family whose support and encouragement never wavered along this long road of writing.

To my longtime friend Megan Bell, thank you for always being there to read and critique, I swear I would not know if something was good if you weren't there to tell me. To my Tea with Wordsmiths writing group who kept me writing through the many times when I was ready to quit.

To my grandmother, the woman responsible for my childhood summers at the cottage. Thank you for making Tyree my most favorite place in the world and for all of the wonderful things that you were to me.

Lastly, to my mother, no matter where we ended up, nothing will ever overshadow, the support, encouragement, and belief you had in me, when it came to writing.